NEW DIRECTIONS 55

N D

New Directions in Prose and Poetry 55

Edited by J. Laughlin

with Peter Glassgold and Griselda Ohannessian

 A New Directions Book

The first number of the New Directions Annual was published by James
Laughlin in 1936. The Publisher regrets that because of rising production
costs Number 55 must be the last in the series.

ACKNOWLEDGMENTS
Grateful acknowledgment is made to the editors and publishers of magazines
and newspapers in which some of the material in this volume first appeared:
for David Antin, *Tikkun;* for Helena Kaminski, *The Harvard Quarterly* and
Paris Review; for Douglas Messerli, *Temblor;* for Eileen Myles, *Scarlet;* for
Fiona Pitt-Kethley, *London Review of Books;* for Peter Porter, *Ambit* (Lon-
don); for Enid Shomer, *Mainstream.*

Marcel Cohen's "The Peacock Emperor Moth," translated by Cid Corman
from *Le Grand Paon-de-Nuit* (© Editions Gallimard, 1990), is printed by
permission of the author and publisher. George Evans's "Five Poems"
appeared in *Sudden Dreams* (Copyright © 1991 George Evans) are reprinted
by permission of the author. John A. Scott's "The Apology" was included in his
collection *Translation* (Copyright © 1990 by John A. Scott), published by Pan
Books, Syndey, Australia, and is reprinted by permission of the author.

Manufactured in the United States of America
New Directions Books are printed on acid-free paper.
First published clothbound (ISBN: 0–8112–1180–0) and as New Directions
Paperbook 726 (ISBN: 0–8112–1181–9) in 1991
Published simultaneously in Canada by Penguin Books Canada Limited

New Directions Books are published for James Laughlin
by New Directions Publishing Corporation,
80 Eighth Avenue, New York 10011

CONTENTS

IMBROGLIO

MURRAY POMERANCE

Emaciated epicene Imbroglio with a monstrous knife is carving a champignon. He's nipped away the base of the stem and slipped off the filthy prepuce and sly Ardenzio, who's taught him a thing or two about fluting, is watching him attempt to flute. It's far too big a blade—the blade's as big as a goose breast—and, truth is, he didn't learn a thing from that thyroid case Ardenzio so the little mushroom, adorable button, is flying pathetically into slivers in a thousand directions while off in the distance some hag tries her lungs at Giuseppe Veronaldi's "Mi credenza di peltazzo per dolor." What a miserable excuse for a song to begin with, and she's flaying it alive. It hasn't rained in weeks and weeks, the Princess of Zulpetsa's daisy beds have been given up for lost. Imbroglio is now being informed by Docteur Bruneto, very politely and succinctly if presumptuously, that there is no possibility he will graduate and become a maestro in the palatial kitchens of Landino. Morsels of mushroom, pinking, all over the straw-littered floor, with the three regimental piglets creeping around and sucking them up for snacks.

•

Let's get out there across the cheery courtyard (where the flagon wagon has gone almost off-balance upon the doltish curbstone, and

1

two pallid musketeers are vying with tarot cards for the chance to climb the vines outside a young boy's window, and a scraggly wench is separating rotting from healthy golden peppers on an oily board, and a squire is drooling to polish a breastplate) to the dank and rancid chamber, perfumed by smoldering staggerwort, where Eglantine the daughter of Tartaglia (Emissary of the Doge) is throwing her swollen lungs against that hallmark of contemporary culture, Giuseppi Veronaldi's "Mi credenza di peltazzo per dolor." There's her agonized maidservant, Filesia, lacing back the curtains to reveal blisters of vapid moonlight. So nice if for ten minutes it would rain and leave a mist. So nice if the singer could sing, but she couldn't save her life with a C-sharp. Magic if we could be persuaded to listen with all our hearts to an innuendo of lyrics but instead she's giving us heartburn by scrounging half of them from the abysmal love letters of Valerio Stupenzo to the Contessa di Frangipane; documents which have more or less tumbled into her hands (along with frilled panties), stuffed by mistake into a shipment of laundry from the steaming vats of Isabella di Laminafra (: huge oaken vats filled with tepid water in which plump hypersensitive girls with their skirts strapped up by snakeskins and with orchidaceous bandanas cupped over their coily hair step rhythmically and with a delirious rotation of the hips, making bubbles that smell somewhat of lamb). But that song, that abysm: "You, you of my dreams . . . you, you, of my revery . . . whose breasts, whose breasts, are figs and walnuts . . . whose breasts delight my lips, my lips, my scarred tongue . . ." It's queer about Eglantine the daughter of Tartaglia (Emissary of the Doge) seeming a hag, because it's true that all the time she was growing up everybody said of her if only she'd keep her mouth shut her beauty would exceed tangerines. Something about the discoloration of her teeth, from eating pound after pound of that infamous cheese from Abruzzi and chocolate from Torrento and cold pickled eel from Castellammare. Delectation of furtive, slithering moonlight, yet where is a bowl of goat's milk, polluted Ofanto water, anything to wet the tonsils? And speaking of tonsils, that song again, that incalculable "Mi credenza di peltazzo per dolor," a melody which would bring tears of sympathy from the moonlit statue of Giuseppi Veronaldi who wrote it if only the three giddy adolescents, Porenzo, Lorenzo, and Credenzo, weren't busy urinating in unison up and down its legs.

•

The unhappy engagement of Valerio Stupenzo to the Contessa di Frangipane ensues: It has to do with a miserable fig tree. The fig tree in question grows in the Contessa's yard. The keeper of the yard is one-eyed Smagegga, who has been teaching himself over these anxious years to converse with doves. "Oooo, cooo, loooo," yes. And there is much in conversation with doves that you do with fingers. But the Contessa's enormous corpulence, a sign of great worthiness in her large family, is maintained by a diet of figs. And on his side, Valerio Stupenzo's ailing father must have figs to keep him from dying, so proclaims Docteur Bruneto making notes in a garbled script and producing a chain of framboise-flavored hiccups. Young Valerio creeps at night over the rough-rock wall until he is in the silent, fragrant garden with the Contessa di Frangipane's fig tree. And there: Smagegga, picking her nightly portion with a dove upon each shoulder. Whereupon Valerio Stupenzo comes out of the shadows and says, "Estimable Smagegga, keeper of the Contessa's figs, confidant of birds, pray let me have a small basket to take to my ailing father, Don Horacio Stupenzo, who will cause the figs to be slit and roasted almonds to be inserted in their crevices before popping them into his mouth, just as the wise Docteur Bruneto has ordered." But for some reason Smagegga is moved, instead of handing over figs, to play the provocative but distracting game, *Undo!*, as follows: every time Valerio Stupenzo reaches out for a fig from his basket Smagegga leans forward, unties one of the fine little knots that is fastening Valerio's purple silk jerkin, and wails, "Undooo!" The doves, of course, think he's talking to them and start ooooing madly. Tying himself up again, Valerio pleads, "Oh, kind Smagegga, do permit me a fig to give my ailing father, for in months it has not rained and in the heart of the fig is the moisture of the gods, so announces the wise Docteur Bruneto," and again the groundskeeper unfastens the jerkin, "Undoooo!" Then: "Sweet Smagegga, oh conscientious Smagegga, grant me the boon of a pair of figs, as the wise Docteur Bruneto advises," and the jerkin comes undone again, "Undoooooo!" "Permit me a fig!" the jerkin is almost removed, "Undoooooooo!" "Cede me a fig," three knots are undone, "Undoooooooooooooo!" "—because the all-knowing, all-curing Docteur Bruneto—" And the doves are bending over trying to make themselves understood, "Vooo, cooo, loooo, stoooo, chooooooo." And Smagegga, having thoroughly stripped the prince, whispers in a Romagnese dialect, "Come, I'll show you *my* fig for a penny or twooooo!"

•

Valerio decides to abandon this activity and commit himself to the safety of quill and parchment.

> My dearest Contessa di Frangipane, would it
> be possible, would it be conceivable, might it be
> thinkable that you would allow, that you might
> entertain the possibility of, that you might be
> persuaded to countenance the notion that

But who is this importunate beggar! Tearing his note to shreds before with bulbous eyes she can have swallowed its purport she commands that the writer be delivered before her, his elbows handicapped with thin bracelets of leathery sausage, his neck weighted with a trio of upside-down plucked guinea fowl. She is dreaming of delicious punishments, biting out the hairs of his chest one by one . . . But on seeing Valerio Stupenzo she falls passionately in love: he is youth, he is light, he is movement! Make the fig tree over to him in writing she will, she promises, and in front of the great judge Scaramouche to boot, if only he, upon a full moon, will mount her in the wet grass by the swan pond, and thence, not to tarry but to marry, lest she parry . . . Poor innocent Valerio Stupenzo, this woman is so obese a specimen even her eyelashes are daunting—in summer, he has heard, like strands of twine they stiffen when her salty perspiration dries and hordes of weary insects perch upon them to sleep.

•

So the kid sells off his innocence, dropping his pretense, his purple jerkin (and much else) for a plateful of figs, a basketful of succulent figs, to drop upon the bed of his ailing father. Don Horacio eats so ravenously he is soon transformed into a staunch knight radiating color and robustness and good looks, *Prestodigitato!* Exactly the sort of subject most adored by such as the great limner Mezzetinto . . . (Docteur Bruneto, meanwhile, freed from diagnosing him, plays the game of *Frog,* mounting every lady he can find in a punctilious squat and, yes, attempting with his bluish tongue to captivate flies.) Don Horacio Stupenzo, galloping through hill and dale on his trusty steed . . .

•

Mezzetinto is gravely at a loss trying to limn a portrait of that staunch knight radiating color and robustness and good looks, Don Horacio Stupenzo. In what wise? For openers, he is accustomed to the inspiration of the sallow Princess of Zulpetsa darning tapestries by his side as he limns, because she will frequently look up—it is her custom frequently to look up—and exclaim, "Oh, how stimulating!" over his shoulder. A kind of optic aphrodisiac, since staring at his handiwork he is led to imagine the fulness of her suppurations. But this morning woe, the Princess of Zulpetsa's daisy beds having been given up for lost in the continuing drought, she has been condemned to forego her postprandial game of *He Loves My Left Breast, He Loves My Right* (an exercise for the spinal column, conducted with the aid of the petals of one of those gigantic flowers), and has employed the groom Pulcinello instead to assist her manually. The groom possesses enormous, but very delicate, fingers. "I love your left breast. I love your right. I love your left breast. I love your right." So that she cannot bring herself to get recorseted until long after the sun has reached mid-sky, bringing on that hazy torpor which leads all sensible beings to insert themselves between sheets.

•

The painter's difficulty, however, is worsened. There is the problem of perspective, under the best of circumstances a taxing conundrum. Everyone has gathered round to play the game called *Look from Here*. (1) Don Horacio Stupenzo is on a platform, seated upon a barrel of olives covered with red and purple Chinese brocade. He has one fat leg crossed over the other. People are viewing him. (2) Scaramouche has gone off behind a pear tree and is peeping through a knothole: "Mezzetinto, look from here!" (3) Filesia is lying on her back staring up Don Horacio's skirt to see if she can tell whether his hose are fastened with or without a cord: "Mezzetinto, it's wonderful if you look from here!" (4) Imbroglio and Ardenzio are hanging from the boughs of a weeping willow, and, because for months it has not rained, the leaves are dry and shuffle hysterically as the two struggle to scratch their bums. They think this aerial view is magnificent: "Mezzetinto, from here, from here, you have to see it from here!" (5) The Princess of Zulpetsa has arrived finally and contrives to swirl in great arabesques around the little platform where Don Horacio is perched, seeing him always in great swoops of melodious undulation: "From

here, Mezzetinto, from here!" (6) Eglantine the daughter of Tartaglia
(Emissary of the Doge) still keeps at that hideous song, so her eyes are
closed. (7) Porenzo, Lorenzo, and Credenzo have dug a pit, "From
heeeeere!" and (8) Isabella di Laminafra the public laundress is
catching Don Horacio's dignified silhouette cast with the help of the
blazing sun through the Contessa di Frangipane's newly starched
pillowcases which she is suspending from a creeper vine. Even if
Mezzetinto could pick an ideal point of vantage, however, he'd never
be prepared for what comes next. That barrel of olives Don Horacio is
ensconced upon has traveled for eleven months with the drought,
beginning in Hindustan and proceeding by way of Seville quite as far
as the Golfo di Manfredonia, so that this afternoon, under the Don's
capacious pressure, it simply gives up the ghost. With a munificent
slap the boards disintegrate into a thousand useless fragments and the
great man collapses in a heap upon Filesia's face. Brine everywhere.
Lizard-green olives are forming patterns in the dirt, constellations,
arcane symbols, the symbol of the wounded boar . . . Somebody
hears Mezzetinto muttering hopelessly to himself, "Bring on the
Quattrocento! It can't come soon enough to give us a way out!"

•

Don Horacio Stupenzo has been asked to squat on a rock and the
painting has again begun. But the third and final problem is that
because for weeks there has been no rain Mezzetinto the master
limner can do nothing about his colors. Not a color can be mixt without
arabic water, surely, Gume Arrabecke Watter throwne togethyr from
the watters of the reservoire into whych the reynes doe falle. Nor-
mally it is his practice to utilize a palette both complicated and rich:

> Whitlead (White lead)
> Serusa (Fine ceruse white)
> Cornation (Carnation white)
> Ossium white, made from the burnt bones of a pig still
>   young (or the bones of a Lambe, and of yong burnt, also of
>   some sheels, as ege shells)
> Oyle of whit popy (White poppy)
> Quicksiluer (Quicksilver white)
> Veluet blacke (Velvet black)
> Cherry black, from chery stones (cherry stones)
> Charkecole blacke (Charcoal black)
> Willowecolle (Willowcoal black)

Peach black, from the stones of peaches
Venice lake
Antwerpen murreye (Antwerp murrey, which is not as good
    as Venice lake)
India stammel (a red)
Blacke sugarcandye (Black sugar lake)
Vermelion (Vermilion)
Venice ultramarine
Litmouse blewe (Litmus blue)
Indy blewe (Indigo blue)
Verditer
Massicot
Dull massicot, which be a mixture of massicot and pink
Pauncy greene (pansy-green)
Masticott yeallowe (Massicot yellow)
Oker (ochre)
Oxe gall yeallowe (Yellow gall, which be of gall stones ground)
earth of cullen (Earth brown of Köln)
ochre de rouse
Not to mention the stones, rubye and annatist and saphier
    and emarod and topias orientall

Now he has been able to prepare nothing, noe watter, noe reyne, but he can draw only on a volume of the cherry black, from cherry stones, because the Contessa di Frangipane has caused a cartload of cherries to be dragged from her estates in Squinzano by those two hearties, Ubaldo and Gesualdo, who fear flogging. Fere of flaugynge. The cherry black is a rich one, moistened with pressure of cherries, but it is the only color he has, so the entire portrait must be black, cherry black, a delicious thing to behold and yet impossible to discern. "I am a futurist," says Mezzetinto, painting the black mustache over the black lips upon the black face, and in the distance touching up a black turret upon a cherry black castle upon a cherry black hill. Hearing the word "Futurist" somebody—Imbroglio?—slips in and feeds him chilled spaghetti with poached eggs, pumpkin, boiled liver, peaches, and asparagus.

•

But meanwhile the game of *Asparagus* is being carried forth by Ubaldo and Gesualdo. They've hoarded some very plump stalks of asparagus, also from the estates in Squinzano, and over the many weeks, the many many weeks, of traveling and hoarding, the stalks have softened and gone profoundly limp. Now the trick is to hold your

flaccid asparagus by the base and engage your friend in a spirited duel,
as though the asparagus were swords of Venus, yes, drooping utensils.
The local women, Lady Flaminia, the effervescent Franceschina,
lofty Isabella, lovely Lidia, stand around captivated in whispers and
throaty giggles as, *thwack thwack,* the muted pendulous asparaguses
slap against one another at slapdash angles and finally in a frenzy of
dedication Ubaldo's is snapped in half. "Reward for your virtue!" cries
lovely Lidia, and flings herself into Gesualdo's arms at precisely the
best angle for devouring the man's lengthy vegetable in a single
slurping bite. [Some students later regarded this ritual as a fertility
ceremony and gave it a highly ramified symbology. See Turgood and
Tensen, 1881; Orpington, 1908; Auck, 1923; Richards and Cumberly,
1939; and Craype, 1988.]

•

Lady Flaminia has cut every excess rose to leave a perfect ring of roses
in the Conservatory (especially designed as a cloistered garden with a
springing fountain—from which you cannot drink—surrounded by a
ring of roses) and now she is arranging her freshly cut roses in
Imbroglio's pantry in a crystal goblet. The morning sunlight is drip-
ping down on her, a slight breeze is rippling the tamarisk fronds just
outside the window, she's got some golden clippers and has carefully
selected the roses one by one and snipped their bases for length and
pounded their new-cut bases with the handles of the golden clippers.
Here and there she boldly fights off a low-springing leaf. Rose colors:
There are pallid pink roses like corals, and those darkening by shades
of pink until they are as deep as a cloud of sunset suspended in a
cathedral between the yawning panes of the cathedral's colored glass.
Now the morning sunlight is covering Lady Flaminia with her roses.
She has made the paler roses shorter, the darker roses taller toward
the center. And she's moving on to an arrangement of pink carnations
and lavender tulips, it's pathetic with the pendulous thick green
leaves of the tulips cascading over the lip of the vase. Harlequin is
observing. Secretly. Nothing on earth gives him more pleasure
than——to watch Lady Flaminia——arranging——flowers——
shhhhh. The attar of the roses floats over him. Thinks Harlequin
caught in fascination for the roses, "Now time has stopped."

•

Harlequin and Scaramouche are doing a quadrille to pray for rain. The first, clothed in his puffy cloak of many-colored diamonds, raises his right leg and left arm and cries out, "Yaga polenta! Lapika lapuka!" Then his left leg and right arm: "Tchi, tchai, tchou!" And then, whirling his brittle three-cornered hat each arrogant prong of which is sharp enough to be a stiletto, the other bellows from the vibrant cavern of his entrails, "Hoagh! Foukh!" They move. They move in what begins as a circle and ends as a parallelogram. Black clouds coagulate in the western sky. There is the sound of thunder,

> Koom!
> Kombaraloom!
> Kooma anda dooma!

Filesia and Don Horacio Stupenzo are licking the olive brine from one another's shoulders, whispering, "Pickle! Pickle!" Magnesium lightning sends shudders across Scaramouche's shoulder blades and relieves the descending throes of his lumbago. Nearby, in the cloistered garden with the springing fountain from which you cannot drink and the ring of pink roses, Eglantine the daughter of Tartaglia (Emissary of the Doge) is still squeezing her vocal cords through the impossible apertures of Giuseppi Veronaldi's "Mi credenza di peltazzo per dolor." May the rain fall upon her in boatloads! In all sincerity I must protest that the sound of her voice is an excruciation to gentled ears. She is become a veritable Iron Maiden in the torture chamber of civilization. And because of the catastrophic sound of her, does not each man weep in the singular knowledge that his days and the days of his friends will forever be known with contempt as The Dark Ages?

•

On the vast parterres are great semicircles of horehound, now in the rains become intoxicating again. Imbroglio the assistant chef lies there, the membranes of pounds of mushrooms scattered across his chest. Ravenous for mushrooms after all his mushroom fluting he has devoured all the mushrooms that were fluted. Having sated himself on mushrooms he has the hunger for fiction, Ye hongre for fyxionne. He proceeds in the obvious way to dream the lost legends of Araby.

•

Somehow in the great thunderstorm, so bombastic the magnolia blossoms have all shuddered into the river, the many-colored balloon

bouquets of the Contessa di Frangipane have gone all airless, quite
pathetic, so that now hanging from the lofty boughs of her trysting tree
are only so many vivid bladders unable to stop themselves from
flopping this way and that according to the merest chances of the
breeze. "Any one of those could be me," says a voice from behind a
bush, but as soon as we chase it down, parting the thorns from before
our cheeks, we discover that there is no one there.

•

Porenzo, Lorenzo, and Credenzo are having a little discussion about
the pleasure of the mouth, while behind them on a long table raisins
marinated in gentian, safflower oil, and rosemary are stuffed into the
nostrils of a boar. "How nature manifests itself in everything cooked!"
sings Credenzo, "How the smells of the earth rise up from every
morsel on the table! Why, that boar once roamed the paleolithic
forests of Smagny-Laboisse, and scraps of the very truffles buried
there in blackest loam even now do gleam from the putrid cleavages of
its feet!" Lorenzo is more pragmatic: "I imagine to myself what it will
taste like, when it has been basted a dozen times in shallot butter and
baked in a lake of Paullac and cream. I imagine a glass of Champagne,
and a little dish of roasted potatoes." Porenzo, however: "I can only
say, how philosophically pregnant is the insertion into those critical
organs of olfaction, of objects sacrificed to the all-illuminating beams
of the life-giving sun. This animal, round and perfect, will surely
symbolize intelligence, civilization, conscience, aspiration, truth, and
I myself will be especially attentive to every delicate possibility of
thought and understanding when like a barbarian I hurl myself into
the act of tearing its flesh between my well-ordered teeth."

•

Columbine and Pierrot have been on a hilltop, beautiful hilltop,
overlooking all of this amazing scenario: nothing have they failed to
see or hear. "What do you think? What do you think," says Pierrot
tapping Columbine on the elbow, "What do you suppose? What do
you suppose?" She gives a little smile. Now, "There could still be just
a little more," says she with a twinkle in her blue blue eye, and
reaching into the crazy realm with a cautious hand she deposits a
mouse.

FOUR MEDITATIONS

EDOUARD RODITI

MEDITATION ON "THE TRAVELS OF SIR JOHN MANDEVILLE"

I've traveled far and wide and might
Describe at length the many lands
I've seen, but as the years go by
Their peoples more and more often seem
To live as we, even wearing
The same blue jeans. Of Paradise
I cannot speak, for I have not
Been there, which I regret. But I
Have heard it is, as wise men say,
The highest land on earth, so high
It touches the moon. Even the flood
That covered all lands could never
Reach it, encircled by a wall.
No man can tell of what this wall
Is made. With moss and bushes run over
Its stones cannot be seen. It spreads
From south to north, and there's no way
To enter. Ever burning fires,
The flaming sword of God before
The entrance, still allow no man
To penetrate and reach the spring

From which, in its very center,
Four rivers flow, first underground
For countless miles until they reach
Their second source in distant lands:
Tigris, Euphrates, Ganges, Nile,
With Euphrates the fairest of all four,
Fragrantly sweet from freshly melted snows.

Enough of legends. Now we purchase
Paradise in pills or powders or shoot
Momentary heaven into our veins
Together with dread disease and death.
In a world grown too tight, plane tickets
Are available too to any land
Ever known or imagined, no longer
Shrouded in mystery, legend or hearsay.
Everywhere familiar Hiltons await
Package-tour pilgrims whose purses
Are properly supplied with credit cards
And travelers checks. On charter flights
Senior citizens can visit Katmandu
Or view Cotopaxi in modest comfort,
While guided tours for groups of school teachers fly
Chicago Jews to Eretz or Baltimore Blacks to Benin.
Kilroy has by now been everywhere,
Scrawling his name on men's room walls.
Science fiction in turn supplies the thrills
Of yesteryear's tales of legendary Indies
With hills of gold, which ants look after
As big as hounds here, and no man dares
Go near those hills, for fear that the ants
Might attack him, but men win that gold
By a trick: when the weather is hot
Those ants will hide in the earth, and men
Then come with camels and dromedaries
And horses, and load them up with gold
And leave before the ants come out of their holes.
On another isle wicked and cruel women
Have precious stones set in their eyes. If they look
On a man with angry intent the power

Of those stones will forthwith pierce and slay
As the basilisk does. Elsewhere one can see
Rats bigger than hounds, and geese all red
Except for the head and neck, which are black.
These are much bigger than our geese.

                        Hopes or fears
And dreams follow fads and fashions, at one time
Gothic as a cathedral's porch, at another
More strictly classical, and in our age
As complex as a rocket, a spaceship, a satellite.
We dream of Flying Saucers, then see them
In the sky, and create our own world of marvels.
Encircling all space an ever-receding
Wall of fire marks the ultimate frontier
Of our universe, perceived with several billions
Of light-years of delay, but still valid proof
Of the primal explosion of Genesis in Tohu-wa-bohu.
Can this wall of fire still be the flaming
Sword of God that guards from our prying eyes
And telescopes the Gates of Paradise?
And what can we now imagine beyond this wall,
More wondrous than all that Mandeville described?
I leave it to you, hypocritical reader,
To answer my questions, which are also your own.

MEDITATION ON OVID'S "TRISTIA"

> *"Barbarus hic ego sum, quia non intelligor ulli . . ."*
> Ovid, *Tristia* V. x.

I'm an alien here and everywhere,
Of foreign parents in an alien land
The first-born, taught by them to speak

Two tongues and more, but all of these
With alien intonations, betraying
Me even here, where I can claim
Citizenship of sorts. I'm a Barbarian
Whose accent from another world
My stolid neighbors seem to find
More and more strange as the years go by.

No map leads back to my long-lost home
More deeply buried in the past's ashes
Than Sodom or Pompeii encrusted in lava.
Am I now Lot's wife, so ruefully turned
To a pillar of salt? What Gradiva will guide me
In my lost world's ruins? I'm an exile,
No expatriate here by my own choice,
But banished by the power of the many years
I've lived here or there, a survivor
Haunted each night by dreams of friends
Long dead, landscapes I'll never see
Again, or that might no longer seem
Familiar, should fate allow my eyes
To view them now, with their busy suburbs
Where once I gazed on woods and meadows.

Am I destined soon to seek in vain
To make myself understood by gestures
When words fail me, though I'm still spared
The self-pitying Roman poet's exile
On some distant Euxine's frosty shores
Or Mandelshtam's far more tragic death,
Deported to subarctic Siberia,
Of privations and cold in a prison camp?
Age is my unrelenting tyrant,
Banishing me forever from my past
To this grim frontier of life's empire
Beyond which I view but death's vast realm,
Dim and unchartered and peopled
Only with hoary ghosts beckoning
To join in their savage jamboree.

By nature I'm no graveyard poet
Who sings of the potter's lowly art
Shaping with earth from a prince's grave
And from a pauper's one perfect jar.
Nor have I fingered Yorick's skull
Or sought the tombs of unknown Cromwells
Or dreamed of ghostly Indians pursuing
With their buried weapons their ghostly prey
Beneath their common burial mound.
But I find myself here more and more deprived
Of familiar faces by their death or by distance
And condemned at long last to contemplate
My inescapable fate that is Everyman's.

MEDITATION ON THE "ALCESTIS" OF EURIPIDES

Were I to mourn all my departed
Parentage, lost loves and friends I might
Keen day and night, a grieving survivor,
Until I too would turn stone-cold
And one more voiceless monument
At best in death's democracy.
There all are equal citizens
Of a state that's far too populous.

The past is a vast necropolis
In which I'm doomed in turn to dwell,
Remembered a while but soon forgotten
Like many of its denizens
Whose moss-grown tombs no heirs still tend.
Had I, some sixty years ago
Or less, wed a wife, might she decide
Dutifully now to die in my stead?

Have all my loves whom I've survived
Yielded to death that I might live

These few more years in a world that grows
Daily more alien, ever more crowded
With strangers whose unfamiliar face
And voice can remind me but vaguely of those
Whom once I loved? How long must I
Still live unloving, no longer loved?

But dreams, night's uninvited guests,
Wrest in their Herculean grasp
Again and again from death's embrace
And memory's cemetery the loves
Whose ghosts still haunt me in my sleep.
Day's harbinger at morn then rings
Its shrill alarm. With a batlike twitter
They leave me embracing a lifeless bolster.

Should I seek to postpone the fateful day
When light must cease to guide my steps
While I stumble blindly in the gloom
Of death's vast kingdom? Already the foretaste
Of the frigid kiss that threatens my lips
In that seasonless region makes me shudder.
Death's lips are surely much colder
Than those of any ghost long dead in my stead.

MEDITATION ON DANTE'S "DIVINE COMEDY"

When I'm asleep no Virgil guides
Me through the shadowy labyrinth
That apes my past with punishments,
Shames too that purge and rare rewards
Vouchsafed as ultimate aeons of bliss
In a Paradise proposed as our common goal.
Parents or friends betrayed all haunt
As fiends the Hell to which I'm damned
For sins of violence or fraud.
Of lesser sins I'm purged in dreams

Reminding me with grim remorse
Of all that I once failed to do.

A banshee in my private Hell,
My mother terrorized my childhood.
Her tantrums taught me to mimic death
In seizures, my flight from reality.
In her old age I later failed
To grant her all the love and care
She might have still deserved from me.
For this remissness I now pay
A heavy fine in anguished dreams
From which I wake still wondering
How best I might correct the past
That poisons my present days and nights.

Over fifty years ago I watched
My sick father die at the age of sixty,
An alien in London that had never been
His home. Reduced by a brain hemorrhage
To muttering faintly his childhood Ladino,
He relied on me for his needs, reconciled
With the prodigal son he trusted least.
Did I suspect that I might live
To be eighty or more and likewise doomed
To die in an alien city, all cities
Where I've lived having in turn become
Equally alien to my aging eyes?

Need my whole life remain meaningless
Or else, more human than divine,
A comedy in which I play
But a minor part, never the lead,
And understand at last its plot
Only too late as the curtain falls?
Have I no audience save one that applauds
My pratfalls and clowning, but then shrieks
With derisive laughter when I bewail
My fearful fate in pathetic tones?
Am I King Lear or only his Fool,
A new Dante or one of the damned?

But Doctor Freud now offers to guide
Me as I tread the tortuous path
Of my dreams night after night, a Hell
Reflecting in riddles my whole past.
These I must decipher to free myself
From all the frustrations, fears and failures
That weigh me down and poison my life.
Each level of my Purgatory,
As I ascend from Hell, revives
A different pain, repressed by guilt
Which I belatedly confess,
Driven by timely repentance.

To the fire that refines I know that I
Am condemned to return, remembering
That other poet who once escaped
Briefly from his flame to reveal his name
To Dante, astounded to encounter him there.
As in a set of old photographs
Again and again I meet my past self
Or my reproachful parents and friends
In different settings where I purge
On seven levels as many kinds
Of sins of omission or commission
In dreams that are deciphered as I go.

My faithful guide alone could teach
Me to solve the riddles of these dreams.
Like yours, my days may well have seemed
Peaceful though haunted by news of wars,
Revolutions, holocausts, gulags, famines,
Fears of demographic explosion or else
Of all mankind succumbing to nuclear
Disaster or an incurable new plague.
But why must my dreams remain always haunted
By my own petty sins in a Purgatory that leads
From the Hell from which I escaped unscathed
To no Paradise, only to peace in death?

LOVE WORKER

CHARLES SIMIC

Diligent solely in what concerns love;
In all else dilatory, sleep-walking, sullen.
Some days you could not budge me
Even if you were to use a construction crane.
At work only at loving and being loved.
Tell me, people, ain't it right
To lie in bed past noon
Eating fried chicken and guzzling beer?

Consider the many evils thus avoided
While finding new places to kiss with greasy lips.
Easier for Schwarzkopf to take Kuwait
Than for us to draw the curtains.
The sky blue. It must be summer already.
The blind street preacher is shouting down below.
Your breasts and hair are flying—
Like the clouds, the white clouds.

STUDY IN JEALOUSY

SERGEI TASK

Translated from the Russian by Marian Schwartz

. . . eyes . . .

The windows' lower halves were smeared, only heads poked out. Pale, eyes sunken, women pressed up against the glass, trying to get a look at *theirs*. Today was signout day. Brakes screeched on arriving cars, reception room doors slammed.

Pavel had already reported to his wife, and now, as she buttoned up the umpteenth item of apparel, he paced back and forth in the courtyard, swinging his bouquet like a cudgel. How should he act? First option: smile like nothing's wrong, give her a kiss, hand her the flowers, receive the child . . . or first receive the child, then hand her the flowers? Damned if he knew how it was done, and that was beside the point anyway. So, second option: Lilya, don't think you can kid me—and he chuckled despite himself: that's exactly what she was doing—kidding me. But if she thinks I think the kid is mine, she's got a surprise in store for her. So: Lilya, don't think you can kid . . . No, that's impossible. Just like that, out of the blue. The nurse or nanny's going to be right there. No, that's out. Third option: exceedingly gracious, zero emotion—greeted, gave, received, put in car, not a word en route, polite nod to the neighbor women, door locked in room, and—the whole truth, from day one, the facts, the figures, the lies, the certificate from the hospital, the note—yes, yes, the note too, written in her own hand. Sure, she was going to try to deny it, there might be tears, even hysterics, she'd call him the scum of the earth— let her! let her! The main thing was to get at the whole truth, quietly but firmly, to reach the point where, cry as you might, we're not going to live together. Help you out in the beginning? Gladly. Whatever you need—my pleasure: diapers, food, bottles, stroller, play-pen . . . but the playpen's already bought, I picked it up yesterday, and I got paper diapers, thirty of them, your whole family could wet the bed—in general, any services, but that's what they are, *services*, understand, no sloppy sentimentality, no fatherly feeling, and in a month—that's it, we cut our ties, I go to my parents in Tushino (my father will have a heart attack; my mother will pass out), and . . .

"Pasha!"

He shuddered and turned. Lilya was standing on the landing, holding onto the railing. Next to her a nurse's aide was puffing and holding something large and square-shaped, tied up in a blue ribbon.

"Pasha, what's the matter with you?" shouted Lilya. "I've been calling you and calling you, and you act like you've gone deaf."

He was flustered for a second. After all, he hadn't made up his mind. But it was too late to think it over, so he ran over to the porch.

"Ooh, what roses! Where did you ever get these in the winter?" Lilya presented her cheek to him and imperiously plucked the bouquet from his hands.

"Congratulations, Papa," said the aide, relieved to hand him the heavy aquarium. "You have a marvelous son."

"Thank you for everything, Anna Nikitishna." Lilya smiled, dropping something into her pocket.

"Aw, sweetie, what are you thanking me for?" sang the old woman, dropping her hand into her pocket to determine the amount of the offering. "What are you thanking me for? I feel just like a mother to you, please! Only live in peace. You're young, beautiful, and before long it'll be our time to go."

As they were driving away, the old woman made a cross over them. "University Avenue," said Pavel. "First building." The taxi jerked and water splashed out of the aquarium onto the floor. "This is an official car, too, by the way," said the driver to no one in particular. In any case Pavel responded: "I'll pay."

I've been paying all my life. I often remember what someone said: we make our own hardships so that we can overcome them. That's me. I possess the rare gift of being wrong about people. My first wife, a theatrical makeup artist, captivated me with her domesticity, her almost primordial longing for the family hearth, I would say. A month later she'd run off to Ufa with some touring artist. She offered to exchange the apartment, though. That's how I wound up in a communal on University Avenue, roped up, as mountain climbers say, to some female dinosaurs.

I was always drawn to women who were involved one way or another in the world of art. The reason being that I'm a stage tech myself. No, I'm content with my work, I get to travel around the country a lot, new people, change of atmosphere, what's bad about that? But, you see, there's something missing. You know perfectly well what kind of people are around you. That's why I immediately took Lilya's bait—a designer, book illustrator, no small potatoes. I wound up with her by chance, Vladik dragged me along. Like me, he prefers sensitive, artistic natures, which is why he sticks to high society. In short, he and I ended up on Maslovka, at some artists' place. They'd pulled out all the stops. At one in the morning, having wiped out all our liquid assets, we set our sights on Lilya's room at the Nikitsky Gates. And carried on there until three-thirty. Things settled down only after the neighbor went for a cop. I'd been about to be getting going, but Lilya snatched away my fur cap so I had to stay. They put out the cot for me, and some Sveta and Igorek shared the bed with their hostess.

In the morning Sveta and I drank our tea and left. The others stayed. I don't know what kind of bug bit me, but I wandered around downtown for three hours imagining what they were doing there now . . . him . . . her. . . . I promised myself then and there that I'd never go near her place again. But that evening Lilya called, asked me if I'd gotten back all right, she was sweet, and I forgave her everything. Two days later we arranged to meet at an exhibit. Then we went for a walk. Then we went to her place for tea. That night she was extraordinary. She sat Turkish-style on the couch, so still, and recounted her disorderly life in an undertone. "You've got green eyes," I marveled. She shook her foot and a cloth slipper dropped to the floor. On the other side of the wall, in her neighbor's room, the clock struck twelve. "All right, time for bed," said Lilya, "or else we're going to sit up until morning again." I brought out the cot. Lilya turned off the light. The alarm clock ticked on the table. I didn't feel like sleeping. "Are you asleep?" I asked. "No." "You know what I'm thinking about?" "Well?" "Are you and that Igor having . . . an affair?" "An affair?" She laughed in the darkness. "You're exactly like my mama." The alarm clock ticked loudly in the oncoming darkness. "I can't fall asleep," I said finally. "Can I get in with you?"

That was a strange night. Only once did I accidentally touch her shoulder and snatched my arm back. Exactly like a heathen scared to touch his idol, no doubt. I fell asleep quickly, but she fidgeted for a long time and sighed, shuddering, several times.

We started seeing each other often. We would meet by the monument and walk up the boulevard. When we started to freeze, we stopped in at a café to warm up. Lilya's birthday was in early March. Hoards descended on her. This wasn't the first time I'd seen some of them, but I liked to think it was the last. I already knew which of them Lilya had been close to at various times. She talked incredibly easily about it, whereas I . . . I kept dragging more and more details out of her for some reason. That day Lilya was especially pretty. In her long, floor-length, dark-green flowered dress and her red bugle-bead necklace, she was a real . . . I can't find the word. As was to be expected, all hell broke loose, they were smoking and swearing at the table, clinking glasses. At three in the morning they sang one last "Lechayim, boyars!" and everyone rolled out the door accompanied by a great racket and rumble. While Lilya was soaking in the bath, I cleared two dozen bottles, aired out the room, and washed the dishes. Lilya came out in her robe and those same red beads. She came to me, unbuttoned my shirt, and nudged me toward the bed.

Two months later we were married.

She called the boy Karp. Pavel didn't like the name, and it didn't suit the baby at all, but he held his tongue. So it's Karp. In the final analysis, it wasn't his child. Karp was born pudgy and silvery-scaly, with a streak of green. Like all newborns, he was colicky the first few days, kicked around the aquarium, making incessant gulping movements with his mouth, and calmed down only when Lilya approached. He was hostile to Pavel: no sooner did he get close than Karp turned his tail to him and stood motionless like that in the water, rustling his fins. "What's the matter with you, little one?" Lilya would reason with her son. "This is your papa. Now now, be a good boy." But Karp refused to be a good boy. As for Pavel, he made it quite clear to his wife that as far as he was concerned the new member of the family did not exist.

Thus he chose a *fourth* scenario. Lilya had a good idea as to the cause of the change, noticing how he made a show of avoiding the aquarium, of frowning at each mention of the word "papa," but she was so tired of his constant suspiciousness, of his silent game, that she decided to shut her eyes to everything, whether she thought it was another quirk of Pavel's or out of tactical considerations. Pavel spent hours without raising his head from his drawings; Lilya knitted and watched television. He answered her questions like "Are you going to eat?" or "Aren't you going to the pet store?" in monosyllables: yes— no.

He was meticulous about his trips to the pet store. Little by little it even began to afford him some pleasure. Having always considered fish-breeding a variety of philistine idiocy, he could now stand for hours observing striped guppies go from one wall to another all in a school or a red perch blinking at the visitors. He bought a special baby feed and no more than one package, enough, figuring six feedings a day, for three days. Lilya fed Karp, naturally. At such moments Pavel went out to the kitchen for a smoke. Fully aware of the risk of being waylaid by his neighbor, who would never pass up a chance to inquire into Karpusha's health, he still went, on principle, if only to sting the traitoress one more time.

The day he picked his wife up from the maternity hospital, late in the afternoon, his father-in-law had dropped by. Wearing a luxurious French overcoat and a reindeer cap, he was, as always, irresistible. Behind his father-in-law, grunting from the strain and loudly stomping their feet, two workers crowded into the room carrying a heavy box in import packaging. The wrapping was removed to reveal a glass cube with unusual drain pipes. "A Japanese aquarium," the father-in-law said nonchalantly. "Got it through their consulate, kids. Well"— kissing his daughter—"congratulations, you're great, and you—" slobbering his wet lips on his face—"you're not so bad either, seeing as you're directly involved, so to speak." He'd prepared his jokes beforehand.

The next day his mother-in-law popped in, having paid the young people this honor the last time a year and a half before at their wedding. The audience lasted three minutes. Lilya's mama, that forty-rupee duck, tickled Karp with two expensively ringed fingers, shook a rattle over the water, dropped it with a loud splash and, gasping dramatically, made her exit.

His parents came as well, but they managed without any particular emotions. Neither his father nor his mother approved of his second marriage, Pavel knew that. Nor had they the first. Nor would they all those to follow, one assumed. Talk had probably reached them about Lilya's frivolous life before marriage, or maybe she simply had made a bad impression—it was hard to figure. The fact, however, remained a fact: his folks didn't like to visit them and weren't too anxious to have them over either. In this case, of course, they did come, but clearly not out of any great love for their grandson, but to make an appearance.

Once or twice Marina, Lilya's best friend, dropped by. "What a doll," she sighed. "For some reason I thought it would be a little girl. . . ." And she pulled out of her bag a mass of useless things: a pink cap, rompers, a set of colored bibs, and a massive comb, which in no way would the child be needing for at least another ten years.

Of his friends, Vladik the Handsome and Burshtein came by. Burshtein—a fat, overstuffed-looking clodhopper who was, nevertheless, quite agile and bouncy—stood in front of the aquarium lost in thought, catching watery blips with his round, bulging eyes, the black pupils rimmed in gold, and said thoughtfully: "Good goin', small fry, I mean, little guy." As if he actually appreciated the praise, Karp happily flicked his tail. Vladik dished out the office news and they left.

Everyone left. It seemed to Pavel that they left more often than they came. And his wife was beginning to go out somewhere. . . . That fear that Lilya was cheating on him was always there. When he got back from business trips he often had the urge to grill his old lady neighbors—well, how has my loyal wife been behaving—but his pride wouldn't let him. Sometimes he set subtle traps, slipping in sly questions by the by which she would inevitably cut her own throat on. Zero. She was no innocent bug, and he didn't make a very good fly swatter. By the way, about spiders. Once he read in a definitive dictionary that in the north of Russia a spider is a *pavel*. That pleased him no end for some reason, and that same day he brought Lilya a poem. It ended like this: "Like a gudgeon that's caught on a hook, like a spider whose web never took, I teetered along on the brink—without you." And the dedication: "To my enigmatic Lilit." There was also a hapless sketch—a crooked oval for a face, a little nose, and so on. . . .

Left to his own devices, he would sit up close to the aquarium and watch. Karp would fidget, bury his head in the sand, or else scrawl flourishes in the water. But Pavel kept watching. And—comparing. For this purpose he had acquired a hand mirror. Taking advantage of a moment when Karp, chewing fastidiously, swam up to the front wall, Pavel caught both of their reflections in the mirror and feverishly considered. Not my lips. I have nervous, thin lips, and he's some fat-lipped lout. And fair skin. My eyes are brown, deep set, whereas this one's pop-eyed. Nothing in common. Stop! What about that spot on his right side? Damn it all it is a spot. Pavel pulled up his shirt, checked. No doubt about it: just like Karp's, low on the right, in the exact same place, a black spot. Matching birthmarks, you can't fight the obvious.

Pavel stood up and started pacing around the room. So, was it his or wasn't it? Had she cheated on him or not? And if so, then with whom? He didn't have a clue. No, that's wrong. It wasn't entirely clear whether she'd cheated on him, but it was clear as day that she'd changed. He just had to recall Lilya's first abortion a month before the wedding. Who was the father then? Him? Maybe Igor, that time he'd stayed? There was a whole other story with the second abortion, a year later. Pavel had been called up for six weeks to the army base. Barracks life weighed heavily on him. Moscow was so close, an hour's drive, but they wouldn't give him a pass, and the only respite were conversations on the pay phone before evening roll call. They could have . . . Every time, one of their neighbors came to the phone and with a curt "she's not here" hung up. After ringing off Pavel tossed and turned, imagining the most unbridled bacchanalia. All this in color, on high quality film, the most successful frames—from above, slow motion. The circle of partners kept expanding. There were artist friends, and the bearded neighbor on their stairwell, and Igor, and Vlad, and total strangers, too, whose faces flitted in the crowd. But the heroine was always the same: Lilya, Lilit, his black-haired Magdalene.

When he got back from the base, scrofulous from dust and angry at the whole world, his wife took him aback with the news that, well, she was six weeks pregnant. No sooner had she said that then all his nightmare visions came into focus. His eyes must have made it immediately clear to Lilya. There were no more conversations on the subject, and on Friday, when he came home from work, he found her in bed, exhausted from tears, all the blood drained from her face, and understood everything. For about two weeks she avoided him like the plague, even started talking about divorce. He was eating himself up, cursing his suspiciousness, and tending to Lilya like a baby. Then they went to the Crimea, where they spent a wild three weeks scarcely showing their faces outside their dilapidated cabin, where it smelled of algae and creosote, and all was forgotten.

All right, so he'd made a fool of himself, fine, but this! This was as plain as the nose on your face. After all, here it was one on one, there was no possibility of error. He'd already figured it out on paper a dozen times, recalled the details of their conversations. No, he had it all exactly! Iron logic. Then why not leave her? Silence. Pavel glanced at the aquarium. Karp, standing on his tail, was greedily gulping air. His gills were puffing out like a smith's bellows. Pavel shuddered at the unexpected thought and began pacing faster between the couch and the window. So why not leave her? Because there was one, albeit illusory chance. What if he were wrong? Or if not him—then the doctors? Or if not the doctors—maybe she'd lied? One chance in a hundred. Laughably slight and at the same time scarily great. Once again he sits down at the aquarium with his small hand mirror and looks and looks. . . . And again he tells himself: I've got to get a grip on myself. Fuck all those old calculations, I've got to start fresh.

So . . .

When Karp turned one, Lilya decided to have a small family celebration. Since she had lost all her Maslovka friends by then, Pavel invited his co-workers. Yura and his wife came, the gloomy Burshtein came. Vlad the Handsome stumbled in an hour late, but with fabulous carnations. Everyone "shook hands" symbolically with the birthday boy and sat down to the table. The birthday boy himself was given party food, and now he was lying on the bottom, lazily digging in the sand with his pink caudal fin. He'd put on a lot of weight in one year. His movements suddenly had a kind of substantialness and staidness. Pavel extolled him as no less than a true civil councilor, and going up to him with a bag, bowed low and said: "Will you be so inclined as to dine, Your Excellency?" Karp ate silently, ignoring these attacks. He did not like Pavel and saw no particular reason to hide his feelings.

At dinner Pavel was distracted, drank a lot, and listened with half an ear. Lilya had already kicked him a few times under the table to stop him from pouring himself one after another, but Pavel didn't give a damn. Vlad and Burshtein were grappling. Burshtein had been sitting gloomily all evening, hadn't joined in on the conversation, had just chowed down on Lilya's salads. Obviously, Handsome had stung fat-bellied Burshtein, who'd rolled his black Jewish eyes and talked excitedly, waving his fork with the potato still on it. "All we know how to do is shout!" screamed Burshtein. "Initiative! Energy! But where is it, this energy, I ask you? Raise dust—that we can do . . ." And despite himself he demonstrated just how that's done in Russia. In those moments, raging, with his disheveled beard, and the stolen dormitory trident in his right hand, he looked like Samson reducing the horde of Philistines to trembling with his terrible jaw. Olga and Yura sensibly moved back. "No," thundered Burshtein, "we, ladies and gentlemen, have energy for a ruble, a blow for a kopek, as you know. A mountain gives birth to a mouse!"

"Calm down." Lilya was exasperated. "Look, you've frightened Karp." Everyone turned toward the far corner. And truly, Karp was tossing around the aquarium, flying into the thick walls as if he were blind. Lilya got up from the table and went to quiet him. "All right, boys," Olga intervened. "Time to do the right thing. It's half past midnight, we're getting up early tomorrow."

They started standing up. Pavel came to and stared at the guests. When they all had their coats on, he too suddenly pulled down his coat, tripped, and fell. "Drunk as a skunk." Lilya frowned squeamishly. Pavel wanted to answer with something witty and insulting, but his tongue wouldn't obey him. When they'd rolled out the door, he realized he'd left his cap. "What, are you crazy?" said Burshtein. Pavel waved him off, and the five of them started walking toward Lenin Prospect to hail a taxi. Pavel returned home slightly sobered up, although there was still a ringing in his ears. He couldn't fit the key in the lock right away. Actually, the door was unlocked. Evidently someone had thrown the bolt after he'd left.

There was no one in the room—Lilya was washing dishes in the kitchen. Pavel, still in his coat, walked up to the glass cube, illuminated under four lamps with light blue bulbs. Karp was sleeping, his little nose poking into the sand. Pavel rapped his nail on the wall, but Karp didn't even stir. Then Pavel turned toward the door, locked the room from the inside, got down on his knees in front of the couch, and fumbled for the bucket they used for household chores. He put the bucket on the floor under the drain pipe set millimeters from the bottom and pulled out the clamp that served as a waterlock. An even stream poured out. Karp woke up instantly. At first he didn't understand a thing, being only half-awake, but when he saw his ill-wisher, he could tell right away something was wrong and he started to race about. Time passed. Pavel was sitting on the floor watching the water level fall with a gaze that lacked any expression whatsoever. Another three or four minutes and the aquarium would be empty. Burshtein's idiotic question stuck in his mind: what, are you crazy? "What, are you crazy?" he repeated out loud, to whom he didn't know. Toward the end Karp went mad. It had all become perfectly clear to him. He fluttered his silvery little body and kept swimming to the surface every second to swallow some air. Pavel didn't seem to see him. He was sitting on the floor in his coat and mumbling something. Three fingers of water were left in the aquarium. At that point someone started jerking the door. "Pavel, what are you doing?" He could hear Lilya's voice. "Why have you locked yourself in?" He didn't answer. Didn't want to? Didn't hear? Lilya pressed her ear to the door, and in the silence the resilient sound of falling water distinctly reached her ears. "Pasha! Pavel!" she shouted. "Don't you dare! You're out of your mind! Don't do it, you hear!" Scrambling was heard on the other side of the wall, it was one of their neighbors waking up. A door slammed somewhere. Another. Slippers started shuffling. The last drops were pouring out of the drainpipe. Karp was lying on his side, his mouth gaping unnaturally and his tail flipping desperately against the glass. The door to the room shook from the weight on it. The old ladies' shouts and an incomprehensible whining reached him. Whether the old ladies were begging or threatening, he couldn't tell. Although, what did it matter anyway? At the bottom of the aquarium lay a silvery heap that looked at Pavel with glassy pupils. Suddenly Pavel, who until now had been sitting like a statue, began rocking slowly. Forward and back, forward and back. It was like a hypnotic trance. An incredible quiet fell, like after removing the seventh seal. And in the ensuing silence, somewhere far far away, at the other end of Moscow, the bells of Lykovskaya Trinity began to peel. What marvelous bells! the thought occurred to him. He smiled. And then he remembered. It was all so easy, just look: the same, round, bulging, the black pupil and golden iridescence, huge, biblical—

OWL

MARTHA COLLINS

Owl leans into the tree and disappears.
A friend disappears down the long concourse,
Palestinian scarf over his thin
shoulders, thin legs, thinned blood,
and we wonder, his former lover and I, how long.

The eyes of owl see better because they cannot
shift, the ears of owl hear better because
they are wide, owl seems wise because of these features,
I learn the day my friend leaves, but we
fear owl: the bird of night by day means death.

The next week, while I'm writing this poem, a notice
arrives that says I'm not to *promote* or *produce*,
and then some words and *homoerotic* and more
words, and I wonder if this could be homoerotic,
a friend embracing a former lover, and could

the disease be homoerotic, could this woman's pen
on this woman's page, snow falling on snow,
hand over hand? Eye to eye, death
on death, could feather on feather on owl's gray back,
check on check on the silky black-and-white scarf?

Like to like, except in sex: to attract
an owl we hooted like owls; to attract a woman
a man may hoot and howl, while the woman coos.
Before he left, my friend let me choose a drawing
from his sketchbook. The woman I chose, nude,

hangs on my wall, while my friend waits and we wait,
everyone waits, day after day, for news—
words travel, in written or silent lines.
Owl makes no sound when he moves at night,
but just before dawn he may answer if you call.

GENERAL LASALLE'S LAST HORSE AND OTHER STORIES

CYNTHIA ZARIN

> *"Now we must think of everything beautiful"*
> *—Paula Modersohn Becker to Clara*
> *Westhof Rilke*

In the oceanographer's house,
    a game: *Waterfall Ring Toss.* A
    book-sized vertical pinball toy.
    Propelled by a trigger, tiny
multicolored plastic rings in gel
launch like seahorses from their starting
    gate. A natural rule: when coffee

in the cup is shaken, its tango
    mirrors the bay's oscillation
    during hurricanes. Two miles away,
    perpetually scribbling, the
tide-gauge running on packed nitrogen
and a pen quill foretells
    storms by local disturbances

in spidery writing of the old
    school. Imagine. Gerneral LaSalle's
    last horse had four white feet; an ill
    omen, described so by Delacroix,

who also mentions, that same morning,
a broken mirror, a broken
    pipe, his wife's likeness smashed. Astride,

the General was shot. The horse,
    discounting other auguries, was
    blamed. An honorable misfortune,
    or as he explains, necessary—
stifling weather needed for Mersault
is death on wheat, the white-footed
    horse cantering past the assassin

draws feet through its own focal eye
    and stamps approval at the trough. From
    this, Mary first shrank back. A gilded
    plate, the angel's splendent countenance
hove in and out of painted clouds.
Mirror writing on the future's glass,
    her wavering took five stages.

July 19th, eighteen-fifty-four,
    "We wish for a certain state of
    happiness . . ." By accident, the page
    is marked with a footprint. Fifty
years later, the painter a woman:
"Now we must think of everything
    beautiful." Samples of (inexpensive)
flowered wallpaper, gold frames, a house
    with a "regular confusion" of
    stairways, a few windows with low
    sills, "wide ones you can sit on."
Views? The cleft mouth of the small bay
emptying is the lip of heaven
    Children? The child who lacks a mother

does not lack her oath, the outgoing
    tide pulls away the bulwark but has
    the spit to come back to, the land is
    exposed to shipwreck but does not
shipwreck. Ten years later, July Fourth,

and electric storm ruined the fete
  she hadn't gone to, kept home because

of a fever. Creeping downstairs, bored
  with her book, she, a girl of nine
  alone but for the sleeping cook, saw
  a fireball, sparkling and whirring, big
as a sunflower, roll through the kitchen
screen, down iron pipes, and douse in
  a sink of green peas. Which scorched.

The sleeping cook, the burning smell . . . Her
  father, returning with his sodden
  firecrackers, believed her. *Such
  things happen.* Carried her with her bare
feet upstairs, beneath the upturned
horseshoe in the stairwell cove, lost
  or thrown to be nailed there, abrim.

ENTR'ACTE: TWELVE TYRANTS BETWEEN ACTS; OR, MUNDANE MOMENTS AND INSANE HISTORIES

from *The Walls Come True: An Oratorio for Spoken Voices*

DOUGLAS MESSERLI

The Walls Come True: An Oratorio for Spoken Voices *is a three-act performance for theatre. Voices, speaking in recitative and choral rhythms, retell in a nonlinear narrative the story of a young French boy and his family during the Nazi occupation of Paris in World War II and its aftermath. Part II of a trilogy collectively titled* The Structure of Destruction, The Walls Come True *explores evil and destruction and its effects on the individual and society. "Twelve Tyrants Between Acts" is a vaudeville routine interleaved into this work as an entr'acte that recounts the insanity of twelve of history's greatest tyrants. The last action of Act I, just previous to this, has been the following word broadcast upon a light board: "It is always the mundane that reveals the insane in history."*

[*A performer, heavily made-up and dressed in the costume of a vaudevillian comic, finds his way through the curtain part.*]

Good evening Hades and Recompense. Lovely to be, hear the one about Mussolini? [*delivers the "Twelve Shticks" in the style of a stand-up comedian*]

[*A woman with little on puts a placard upon a stand:* MUSSOLINI SHTICK]

Mussolini was on the soap. His face promoted perfume. His fists clenched in anticipation for a chocolate. Bare-breasted his likeness was attached to swimming trunks. A man paid a fortune for a chair in which Mussolini was said to have sat. Scraps of his hair went to museums. A church in Fabriano encased his spaghetti fork in glass.

"To what do you attribute your immense popularity?" an unwary journalist asked.

"I am the populace!" Il Duce screamed back.

"Well, then, how come you to be such a favorite of yourself?"

"You may put away your pen. You won't be needing it again!"

[*a rim shot and cymbal crash*]

[*The woman puts the placard upon the stand:* THE DOWAGER EMPRESS SHTICK]

When escorted into the room, and her eyes have become adjusted to the dark, the artist sees the Dowager seated upon a teakwood throne, circular in shape, carved with birds and Buddhas and fruits. Her Highness holds in the palm of her hand a lotus into which, as the artist goes forward, she plunges her nose as if to suck in the essence of it.

The artist raises the hem of her dress ever so slightly and bends, imperceptibly almost, from the neck. The Empress does indeed appear to be an empress in the manner one, at least an American, filled with fables and disgust of such potentates, might expect. Yet the Empress Dowager, she reminds herself, has been kind to the visitor during these first months. Two eunuchs behind Her Highness hum an unharmonius hymn. Everything is pleasant.

38 DOUGLAS MESSERLI

Suddenly dogs, three Pekingese pugs and a sort of Skye terrier, splutter across the rice-mat floor and fall in pants at Her Highness' feet. Their heads are patted. The artist delightedly taps the floor, but the pugs pay her no respect. Only the terrier advances shyly toward the hand held first palm out and then turned gradually in to pet. The dog accepts.

In an instant, the artist looks back to the recalcitrant ones, who hover still beneath the green nail sheaths. The artist smiles, following the curves of the finger and hand with her eyes up the arm of the Empress to witness a face flushed, furious, the flower furled to the floor in apparent disgust. The hand of the artist instinctively pulls back from the beast, who growls in fear of its sudden jerk. Now the Empress is smiling again.

[*rim shot, drum roll and gong*]

[*The woman puts the placard on the stand:* FRANCO SHTICK]

On the wall, backed by a tapestry in black, hangs an ivory crucifix, training all attention to the desk on which, in utterly ordered stacks, sit piles and piles of papers. In the center the Caudillo sits, writing a scenario for motion pictures.

The camera pans the room. Focuses on desk. A hand. Hits the inkpot, spills. It is blood. Camera zooms back. Victim lies dead, head across the blotter, hand outstretched.

Enter the detective.

His pulse is checked.

[*drum role, cymbal, a couple of machine-gun blasts*]

[*The woman puts the placard on the stand:* DIONYSUS SHTICK]

My mother and I sometimes were invited to share the company of Dionysus. The guards brought us always into an outer chamber where they stripped away our clothing. One held me close; another my mother, fondling us in the excuses of a search. Might we not hide within our folds destructive weapons?

When our bodies had been thoroughly looked into, we were awarded white robes and entry into his presence.

He kept us at a distance, terrified that some secret missile might have been missed. He spoke little, for he feared that anything he told us might be useful in a plot.

And so was my mother hidden from all others, and I from anyone save tongueless nurses and toadying servants. Except for gold trinkets, heaping platters of lamb and apricots, and the pleasurable sensations of the male and female paramours pulling at my penis and licking my navel free of sweat, I knew nothing of the world. Like a pet, I was simply "kept"; kept as if all that really mattered lay in the territory bound between my eyes and my ass.

The Academy taught me that I also had a mind and feet upon which to stand it.

[*a dagger plunge, escape of breath and body drop*]

[*The woman puts the placard on the stand:* NERO SHTICK]

In Rome, I attended the pyrrhic performance of the flight of Icarus. Never before have I seen such a glorious event. It began in the dark of Daedaelus' labyrinth, the audience straining to spot the artist at his work. Upon the entry of the son, however, the walls came alive with the lights of more than fifty flaming torches lit all at once, so that they burnt momentarily into our sight. And when we had recovered our vision, we witnessed that the walls were trimmed in amber and amethyst. Rubies hung in ropes as emblems of stalactites against the cave's lustrous walls, where emeralds represented moss.

Now we could recognize the alchemist's art. As the son danced out the message of their necessary flight, the father unfolded a set of wings, white as marble, that spread a full twenty hands. And in a ritual dance, with some sexual gestures, he fit the contraption upon the boy's back.

When his son had returned the favor, he and Icarus rose through the flambeaus into a gold-studded sky of stars and flew off into dark.

Suddenly the black was illuminated from below, at first faintly, but in a suspenseful pace, gradually growing lighter and lighter until it reached the floor over which the heroes were suspended. The sun was a ring of fire, through which, when it had approached its proper height, the father flew expertly. But the son, as in the old stories, was singed by the flames, and unable to keep his balance upon the wires to which he was attached, fell to the bottom too fast. Blood splattered upon Nero himself, who sat in a seat overhanging the stage's apron.

At first the audience could not determine whether or not what had happened was part of the plot. And when a cry arose from the chorus, there was near pandemonium. But the Emperor appeared to be nonchalant as he took a bit of the blood upon a finger and licked it off. And so the crowd was calmed.

[*a round of applause and burst of dynamite*]

[*The woman puts the placard on the stand:* JOHANNITZA SHTICK]

Johannitza, King of all Wallachia and Bulgaria, was irritated with his son who sat with colored cloth crying because he could not cut. The scissors lay at his feet before him.

The King tossed the remaining boot which his equerry had been attempting to remove over the head of his suddenly terrified son, who cried now more out of fear than out of frustration.

"You! It's simple!" And taking scissors to cloth he cut into it deep. "Cut and release cut release cut release cut . . ."

The cloth, witness to his acts, was in threads, which he as suddenly thrust with the scissors at the boy, running from the room in disgust.

The child, observing his own blood, was so fascinated with it, he shut up.

[*guillotine slam and scream*]

[*The woman puts the placard on the stand:* KISSINGER SHTICK]

Dr. Kissinger was most disturbed in Hanoi, detached, even dejected. The Paris Accords were all quite meaningless, given the North Vietnamese distrust of the West. Trying their best, they put him in a large suite. But despite the forest of lights, despite the enormous size of the room, atypical in Asia, he was skeptical yet. Each light, for example, had a different switch, so that when it came time for bed he had to scramble about the place, half undressed, to turn the lights out one by one. And when, in pitch-black, he finished and was ready to return, a host of mosquitoes followed him through the netting, so difficult to negotiate in complete darkness, into the bed. His sleep was fitful. And in the morning he could only wonder was it an accident that the masses gathered beneath his window for calesthenics at five-thirty a.m.?

[*a drum role, flourish of trumpet*]

[*The woman puts the placard on the stand:* HULAGU SHTICK]

It was Hulagu, as we have heard, who tricked the Caliph of Baghdad by charging with a mere column of men toward the wall of the great city.

The Caliph laughed when he saw these ragtag troops and took a handful of Mohammedans down to destroy them. The band took flight and, trailed to the edge of a woods, suddenly turned on their stalkers as a battalion appeared from east of the forest and another from the west, who together with the band of original men surrounded and captured the Caliph and his forces.

So the Tartars rode into that city of such wealth that legends of its golden streets are still quoted in some sources.

But there were no golden streets. There was poverty instead. There were many beggars. The palace was impressive, but pearls compare poorly with what the imagination has wrought.

Hulagu, pleased with himself, sent messengers to his conqueror brothers in the north, the east, the west. But he was disappointed nonetheless. As he sat upon the throne of the Caliph he wondered, momentarily of course, why he had chosen to rule the southern section of the universe. But there is a breeze in that valley at night that blows through the palms and rustles the silk of the blouse. And so he stood with the moon to his face and back to minaret.

[*sword upon sword, metal against metal*]

[*The woman puts the placard on the stand:* BORGIA SHTICK]

Fellow ladies: Dress may henceforth be of worth no more than fifty ducats, to be furnished with gems, stones, and glass equal to. China silk shall not be worn in public, nor velvet, embroidered damask, nor satin. Lace from the Spanish, applied to sleaves and hem, may not be attached to bodice. Gems such as silver and gold may be implanted upon the dress unless assessed at more than fifty ducats, but emeralds, rubies, sapphires, jade, black pearls, and diamonds may not be put on anywhere. Fourteen clasps may be attached to the back, two at the front. Sleaves shall not be more than three hands of your daughters deep, flounce and ruffle no more than ten.

Shall these rules be neglected, I have put in the cathedral and every church boxes into which fathers, husbands, lovers, and those women prim and properly attired may drop a complaint of size, sleave, or superciliousness of style.

Lucrezia, Duchess of Ferrara

[*reports of a firing squad*]

[*The woman puts the placard on the stand:* STALIN SHTICK]

The gardens at Gagra are glorious on summer nights. Above the Tsikherva is a villa where, when the sun lies low upon the canyon, roses light up in ochres and reds. "The air here," the visitor, the Gensek himself, observed, "is almost too sweet to suck up one's nose." Everyone agrees.

Koba, the Father of the Peoples, is taken down another path and another where fuschia and iris are planted in patterns punctuated with imported peonies. "For me," muses the Great Master of Abrupt Turns and Revolutionary Daring, "it is too pleasant to pass another moment in this place." And with that he marches his party about face and out through the gate.

His host apologizes for the humidity that hangs upon the river bank. "But why, Joseph Vissarionovich, in such heat do you wear your boots yet?"

"How can I tell you of the comfort I find in them. Such a snug fit satisfies me as when a child is snuggled to his mother's teat. I am totally secure with them upon my feet, for if anyone gets out of line you can kick him in the head so hard his mouth and his stomach shall never meet again.

[*the drone of a squadron of planes*]

[*The woman puts the placard on the stand:* MOCTEZUMA SHTICK]

He, Moctezuma, was a clean man who bathed daily twice. Dark, as the Indians are generally, he had no stubble upon his chin. He was tall and lean. He walked with great pride, upright in manner that led me to believe he was within as he appeared to my eyes. But wherever he went no one of his men might raise his gaze in that direction, so they could not see as we how a civilized man might look.

His court was richly dressed, each man in beads of shrimp and headgear of green and yellow feathers. Their pottery was as solid as that in Madrid. They sat at supper, he and six or eight others, at a table served by twenty of his wives for that reason selected. There were surrounding him jesters and cripples, dwarfs and jugglers, and further from the central porch, at least three thousand more who ate, after he, of the food remaining. They never again used the same pots.

He ate a wide assortment of meats, fowl, fish, maize, and grains not grown in our imaginations. Green fruits and bright red balls of substances at once gummy and sweet. Some have said he cooked and ate babies. But I have seen none, save, on occasion, the flesh of sacrificed fully grown women and men.

[*sharp whistle, direct hit of bomb*]

[*The woman puts the placard on the stand:* HITLER SHTICK]

Blondi was the only one who aroused him to human feelings. The dog was obedient, carefully taught. At supper she sat a full two feet from her master, but gradually as it progressed so too did she, pulling by inches closer and closer until she had laid her head upon the Führer's feet. Sometimes he permitted her to stay.

But in the morning there were no alternatives. He greeted the dog with a flick of the wrist which sent the beast upon the fetch. She was sent away again. And again. And again. Sometimes he permitted her to whimper and jump at the wire fence for a few attempts.

But then the dog was taken and put upon a piece of wood one foot wide by approximately twenty. And there, while he watched in joy, she balanced upon it above the ground at least six feet in the air.

[*the wood creaks with balance, back and forth, creaks*]

[*Blackout*]

[*To the music of "Les Marseillaise" the following information appears on the screen as in film credits:*]

The preceding fictions were based upon materials from the following sources:

Richard Collier. *Duce! A Biography of Benito Mussolini* (New York: Viking, 1971)

Katherine Augustus Carl. *With the Empress Dowager* (New York: Century, 1905)

S. F. A. Coles. *Franco of Spain* (London: Neville Spearman, 1955)

Plutarch. B. Perrin, trans., *Plutarch's Lives, VI: Dion and Brutus* (Cambridge, MA: Harvard University Press, 1918)

Miriam T. Griffin. *Nero: The End of a Dynasty* (New Haven: Yale University Press, 1984)

Geoffroy de Villehardouin. M. R. B. Shaw, trans., *The Conquest of Constantinople* (Harmondsworth, Middlesex, England: Penguin Books, 1963)

Henry Kissinger. *Years of Upheaval* (Boston: Little Brown, 1982)

Marco Polo. R. E. Latham, trans., *The Travels* (Harmondsworth, Middlesex, England: Penguin Books, 1958)

Anton Antonov-Ovseyenko. George Saunders, trans., *The Time of Stalin: Portrait of a Tyranny* (New York: Harper & Row, 1981)

Francisco Lopez de Gomara. Lesley Byrd Simpson, trans., *Cortés: The Life of the Conqueror* (Berkeley: University of California Press, 1964)

Albert Speer. Richard and Clara Winston, trans., *Inside the Third Reich* (New York: Macmillan, 1970)

FROM AN UNTITLED LONG POEM

Pages from the first section which takes place in a Subway

ALICE NOTLEY

"'I once" "found an exit" "from the subway'" ("the woman told me")
"'I once" "found a staircase" "that led to" "an exit" "temporarily
unlocked" "I opened the door to—" "It was an" "Antarctic"
"light, up there" "As if dawn or dusk, but" "neither" "Everyone

wore black" "black cashmere" "discreet diamonds" "had guarded,
dark eyes" "Was it" "the winter holidays?" "I saw" "crushed-red
    lights"
"reflected" "in snowy puddles" "White lights" "in naked trees"
"For me it" "was frozen time," "from past pain," "from a time"

"when I was young," "before I came beneath," "came down here—"
    "before
I'd willingly" "walked away from" "that upper world," "had left"
"a university—" "I then remembered from long before" ("as I stood"
"near the exit") "a library I'd entered" "in that partial light, in

Spring" "There was grass," "there were blossoms" "Huge windows"
"looking out on grass" "And shelves" "of books" "all the books there
were:" "The books were decayed matter," "black & moldy" "Came
    apart"
"in my hands" "All the books were" "black rot" "Were like mummies"

46

"More body of" "the tyrant" "It is all his body" "The world is" "his
mummy" "Up there, up there" "Down here it is" "a more desperate"
"decay," "as if" "rich emotion," "pain," "could still transform us"
"despite him" "despite his power, &" "tyrannical" ". . . ignorance,"

"passing as" "knowledge—" "And so of course I" "re-entered" "re-
entered" "the subway—" "I can't leave it" "ever" "unless"
"we all leave—'"

•

"Once, ' she continued," "'years ago, the tyrant" "was shot"
"We saw it happen" "onscreen" He was shot by" "a masked
assassin" "at close range—" "Blood spurted" "from his chest & head"
"A mother," "someone's mother" "came & cradled" "his head in

her lap" "There was wind & rain," "wind &
black rain" "His flesh colorless," "he seemed dead"
"Blood—" "his blood—" "was smeared onto" "the camera lens—"
"He didn't die." "A few weeks later, he" "reappeared onscreen"

"Announced he'd been" "in a coma," "then had recovered" "His
white hair was" "strangely reddish" "He'd said he'd been" "near
  death"
"He said he'd seen" "a white light" "forgiving" "all embracing"
"He said he'd shed" "his blood for us" "But it was worth it" "worth it"

"for that," "that light" "which would, he now knew," "embrace us all"
"Which does" "include all" "That's when I knew,' she said," "'light
meant lie" "That's when I knew that" "the Light" "was a lie,"
"& that" "I would never" "seek light" "I will never" "seek light,'"

"she repeated" "before she boarded" "her train"

•

"Awhile before" "I entered" "the subway," "all money
underground" "became diseased" "It seared your skin," "when you
touched it" "& poisoned" "your bloodstream" "Within days,"
"you would die" "Thus all money" "was taken" "by people in"

"special suits &" "burned" "No more was issued" "here below—"
"So money" "became invisible" "Invisible money" "began to
change hands" "Paid" "in invisible" "Things paid for"
"by invisible . . ." "Everyone knows," "everyone knows"

"if you have it or not" "if you have enough or not" "All is
exactly as" "before" "when there was money," "except"
"it isn't printed" "isn't seen" "But it is money"
"just the same" "Thus," "there was a woman" "who kept trying"

"to leave the subway" "She was pointed" "out to me" "at a
station," "in process of" "trying to leave us" "A young woman,"
"curly-headed" "with a slightly" "loony look," "encased"
"in a large" "plastic container" ("people wear them" "when they

leave here") "She passed through" "the turnstile" "The other
side of" "the turnstile" "being obscured to us, as if" "everything on
that side" "were somehow" "blurred for us," "were viewed by us
myopically—" "I couldn't see" "exactly" "what happened:"

"movement of figures," "then" "she was" "returned to us,"
"sent back through in" "the plastic" "They *never*" "let me leave"
"I get my plastic," "I get my money" "but they always" "turn me
back" "There's always" "something wrong with" "my money"
  "Usually

they say," "it's not enough" ("though" "it always is") "This time they
said it was" "too old" "I must have saved it too long" "Old money"
"isn't used" "any more" "above the ground" "'Why do you want"
"so much to go there?' I asked" "'Anyone does,'" "she said fiercely"

"I surprised myself" "by saying" "with conviction," "'*I don't*'"

                    •

"A man" "in a suit" "in the first car the" "front car of the train—"
"This older" "distinguished man" "asked me to" "ride with him"
"join him" "I declined &" "moved back" "far back, I" "joined a
car" "that contained" "women &" "girl children" "women in skirts"

"girls in dresses" "I wondered" "who the man was, why he wasn't"
"above the ground" "He must work for" "the tyrant" "But I forgot him
among our flags—" "we had a multitude" "of flags" "Some were red"
"red & wildly torn" "Some were silken" "almost flimsy" "Some were

spangled" "Some were lacy" "One girl carried one" "with a snake"
"appliqued on it" "And one woman had" "the largest flag" "It said—"
"in gold letters" "that were burning," "in gold that showed through
flame" "which followed" "the letters' shapes—" "on white unburning

silk—" "said *Presence*," "*Presence*" "But the burning" "letters
shifted" "when the man entered" "our car" "the distinguished man
     in a
suit" "He sat down" "Did he only" "want to look at us?" "For he was
sitting" "there, staring" "And the letters" "the burning letters"

"shifted" "& changed" "to spell *Poverty*" "instead of *Presence*"
"He didn't need" "to ride the train" "He'd made us poor" "in an
     instant"
"They walk by" "& make you poor" "They look at you & make you
     poor"
"Surreptitiously I began" "to remove my" "bits of jewelry" "my
     earrings"

"with small citrines" "my ring of" "mismatched garnets" "I put them"
"in my pocket" "They weren't" "good enough"

•

"In a station" "I saw" "a woman crying" "She stood against"
"the wall" "looking dirty" "& exhausted," "crying quietly"
"I asked her who she was" "& why" "she was crying" "She
said: 'I'" "am a painter" "I have been trying" "to find"

"a form the tyrant" "doesn't own—" "something" "he doesn't
know about" "hasn't invented, hasn't" "mastered" "hasn't
made his own" "in his mind" "Not rectangular," "not a
sculpture" "Not a thing at all—" "he owns all things,"

"doesn't he?" "He's invented" "all the shapes" "I'm afraid he's"
"invented mine," "my very own" "body'" ("she was hysterical")
"'Did he invent me?" "I want" "to do something like
paint air" "Perhaps" "I even want to" "invent air" "I've

painted" "thin transparent" "pieces" "of plastic" "They—"
"the pictures on them—" "always turn" "rectangular," "circular"
"I once painted" "on bat's wings" "I caught a bat" "painted
colors on" "let it loose &" "watched the air change . . ."

"He owns form," "doesn't he?" "The tyrant" "owns form'"

•

"A car" "awash with blood" "Blood at our feet" "& I
& others" "have small springs" "of blood from our"
"feet & knees" "There is an inch or two" "of blood"
"all over" "the car floor" "Replenished" "periodically"

"by our body springs" "of blood" "And trickling out"
"the door," "when it opens" "at stations." "The
tyrant" "sends a hologram" "a life-size hologram" "of
himself" "into our car" "He stands mid-car" "& says:"

"'The blood at our" "feet" "has cost me" "so much"
"The blood" "at our feet" "has cost us so" "much"
"To clean" "the blood" "is difficult" "to clean the
car." "There is a litter" "of things" "in the

wash of blood" "I see sanitary" "pads," "kleenex,"
"black-blood-encrusted" "old bandages" "An old black
suitcase" "spills out" "torn men's clothes" "& frayed towels"
"The hologram tyrant" "says, 'Here" "are my tears'" "Holds

up his palm" "His tears are" "small drops of jade"
"Red" "& white jade" "His tears have turned to jade"
"They will be placed in" "a National" "Museum" "There is
something in" "my ear" "I pull it out a" "white cord"

"a long" "silk cord" "I pull it out &" "hear our blood"
"It hums" "a unison one" "note loud a" "sheet of sound"
"It hangs there" "sad insect noise" "insect-like"
"Our blood."

                    •

"I stood again" "on the platform" "of the station" "where the snake
sleeps" "Stood near" "the snake herself," "in the shadows there,"
"thinking" "I felt poised" "to be decisive" "be decisive in some way"
"But only knew" "the same decision:" "Get on the next train" "or not"

"The snake" "the sad snake" "opened bleary dark" "gold-ringed
    eyes—"
"crusty sticky" "around their edges" "Opened eyes" "& opened
    mouth"
("I'd never seen her" "awake") "Extended" "a black tongue" "& said
    in"
"a woman's whisper:" "'When I was" "the train," "when I was" "the
    train,"

"flesh & blood" "flesh & blood" "took you to your" "destination"
"to your life" "to your life" "carried you through your life" "Flesh &
blood were" "your life" "Flesh & blood were" "your time" "A soul"
"was not so naked," "so pained &" "denied" "abused &" "denied,"

"when I was" "the train . . .'" "'You're not big enough,'" "I said to
    her,"
"'not big enough to" "be a train'" "She ignored me" "& repeated"
    "over"
"& over," "'When I was" "the train" "When I was" "the train" "When
I was" "the train . . .'" "until she" "finally" "fell asleep again"

THE APOLOGY

A Version

JOHN A. SCOTT

EXORDIUM

John Pietro Pugliani, his fingerpads criminally smudged with newsprint, turns back from ten to nine another page of *Truth*. Its *Truform* guide rests to his right; the front page ghosted by his recent handheel whisperings across its face. Sandown. All the fields subjected to his scrawl; the horses underlined in blue; their numbers bracketed and checked.

John Pietro Pugliani, dressed suitably enough for the occasion in a red silk shirt with zaffre diamond bands, is hunched across the kitchen table. His sleeves are rolled to just above the elbow; his forearm hair profusely scrambling to the finger's second joint.

The forearms of Gerard Barker from the Board of Censors are also thatched with hair. Flocculent. But, as Pugliani has remarked on more than one occasion, only to the wrist. Below, the hands are seen to hang smooth and puffy like those of a doll.

"It looks to me as if the censor regularly shaves his palms," Pugliani smiles to Julia, to Edward Wotton and his latest boyfriend Philip in *The Emperor's Court.* And he fills their glasses with an early *Redman,* his shirtsleeves rolled above the elbow.

Now, Pugliani turns distractedly from eight to seven. A young girl's brassière is roughly hammocked from her body in the Fitzroy Gardens. Mr Basić has begun to kiss her breasts.

Basic, Pugliani thinks, not gracing it with Slavic pronunciation. With his hand up under her skirt, they fall, struggling to the ground.

"He put his hand between my thighs," she says. "He put his finger into my vagina."

A year ago, he notes, and checks the date. A year next Saturday.

•

This morning he had crossed the Fitzroy Gardens, five hours before. And with his face turned upwards, suppliant beneath the ragged vaulting, it had seemed quite natural his thoughts should turn to questions of latitude. The rotting canvases of elm; sun-pierced, undulant. The problem of so many greens.

Pre-fog, he thought.

Ahead of him the path began its upward slope. Head thrown back, his fingers fashioning a crude frame at the eyes, Pugliani had continued on to Julia's house; the shifting parasols of conifer, their darkened branch-ribs variously opening, it seemed to him, against an early glare.

From beyond his field of vision, distant sounds of screaming came to him, that might be bird noise, but for the occasional fluttering rags of speech that called to him of violation.

But then a man had occupied the frame. And then a pelican. A statue in the park. Before he realized, the screaming had already melted in the sudden light and noises of the ordinary.

•

Like a shoelace, Pugliani thinks. The carry-strap of his transistor radio hangs across the speaker like the huge bow on Sebastian's shoe. He stares directly at the moulded plastic. Its matte-black surface holds his attention; this afternoon has always held his attention. Everything else competes. Everything else is a distraction.

Weight in Gold is the sub, it says, *and the money has come for it, a fraction there, in the seventh in Sydney.*

He glances at the kitchen clock. Subtracts the necessary fifteen minutes. Checks his watch. He pushes back the forearm hair that seems already to have grown across its slowly swept face.

•

By ten, the rain from overnight had cleared. But still the air had managed to retain a dampness, and a warmth. As if one might have overdressed. Now, with late afternoon, the clouds were darkening yet again; smudged, as if they had been grabbed by Pugliani's fingers. Cheaply inked, they threatened like a spoiled, destructive child.

The radio is teasing him. He smiles, experiencing the sense of time. Of doing something within time. It baits him with the need to wait.

Just send an envelope with your name, address and the name of one of the fifty-two playing cards, it says, *to Melbourne's own 3DB, 61 Flinders Lane, Melbourne, by the 12th of February* . . . John Pietro Pugliani. Independent Film Maker from McArthur Place. Beside the spray-canned *Incest* sign. Across from *Introspect* and *Circumspect* and *Retrospect:* the stencil-town accommodation of the Carlton "gutterers." Beside the elms. Across from *Disrespect, Respect* and . . . *then on Saturday the 13th, between 8 and 10, I'll be* . . . "King," he enters.

And they are racing in Sydney.

•

Julia passes by the kitchen door. She sees his arm, buried to the fingers in the thick black hair. She remembers seeing him emerging from the backroom suite at *Eisenstein's* three months ago, when he was barely known to her. The juxta-

position of his forearms with the white editor's gloves un-
likely and unnerving; as much—so Edward Wotton had once
remarked—as if he'd entered wearing fishnet stockings.

The black hair of his head streaked through with grey. His
curling grey-black hair. She sees him turn the page. Sees
him calculate the time from the kitchen clock. Six to five. An
older man, she thinks, my Pugliani. This love I rediscover.
Every moment. How you have enlivened me.

And if she might have wanted from this man a little more—
the instant of an absolute attention; a history; an accumu-
lation—and if she might have sought that consequence, both
evident and irrevocable, it barely diminishes the deepening
sense of recuperation she had found in him.

There is, she understands, a clarity to his vision. A certain
Muybridge stillness redeemed from the incomprehensible
motion of life. He holds a truth aloft, barely for a second,
then returns it to the stream, escaping forever. Irredeem-
able.

And if, amongst his documentaries, there is one of some
particular concern, whose images she carries, cannot rid
herself of, it is the feeding child. Its life-red face pushed hard
against the breast of Marietta, Pugliani's former wife. The
working mouth of Sam: her child to someone else. To Dan.
The feeding child recorded on the slow whirr of his camera.
The suffusion of the areole across the breast, as if the child
itself were staining her. Marietta. How she knows him, even
now, still bound to her; transcending separation; freed of sex;
delivered from proximity. That they are so much more in
love, apart. And Julia thinks about his only son. The downing
face. The daff-down. Pappus-cheeked. Sebastian.

And of *her* children, is it possible? However many things
that means.

But now she has moved on. Attained the stairs. She
changes her direction, ascending to the room. The radio is
fading to a list of names and numbers meaning little to her:
Pugliani's update for the last at Sandown . . . *No. 3 is
English Charm $3.80 and $1.20; favourite, 4, Lalebam on
1.45 and 0.80; 5, Walhalla Girl, 3.75, 1.10; 7, Please Your-
self, 3.45, 1.15* . . . She hears it distancing, as if she were
subsiding to a dream, not simply moving down the corridor

and entering the room . . . *and the others all at 20-to-1 or better. $194,500 in the win pool; $104,900 in the place pool* . . . as if she were not simply pulling-to the door.

•

Pugliani holds the phone tightly to his ear, favouring it against the first at Sale.

Telephone betting, it says. *Your account number please* . . .

"175982," he answers.

And your code . . .

"K-I-N-G," he spells, adjusting the notepad in front of him. He places the bet. Certain.

"Sandown Racing. Race 8. A win bet. No. 7 for 200 units . . ." He listens for the confirmation.

"Yes. And in the same race, a multiple trifecta. No. 7 to win; with No. 3, No. 4, and No. 9 to run second; and No. 3, No. 4 and No. 9 to run third . . . for five units . . ."

Julia has entered the kitchen. She has changed the singlet top for a white cotton business shirt. For a moment she feels herself a stranger in this, her house. The air is veiled across her. Smoke.

"Yes. Yes . . . Yes, that's all. Yes. Thank you." Pugliani recradles the phone.

The time pips sound for five o'clock; he automatically checks the kitchen clock for five-fifteen; looks up at Julia and smiles.

"And are the animals behaving?"

"Tolerably," he says and gestures "so-so." But he smiles again and it is clear the day has been successful.

Julia looks down at the table. The Guides. *Best Bets* bent back at page 15. She looks at *Truth*. How Wendy, 24, has died as she and Julian are married in a park in Central Victoria. How friends and relatives watch in horror her collapse and death, moments after the exchange of vows.

Her father tells the paper that his daughter has been suffering from Friedreich's Ataxia—a hereditary disease affecting muscle control.

In a moment, Bill Collins and the last at Sandown, says the radio.

The facts recall, for Julia, Eurydice. The headline though has chosen "Bride Declares 'I Do'—Then Dies!"

Pugliani reaches for her, draws her close, and then releases her, precisely as the radio assumes the resonance of the on-course call. *They're settling. The light is on . . . ready . . . a bit of movement in the centre . . . Capricorn Star . . . they're racing . . .* Julia moves back towards the table. Here is *Mrs. Dalloway.* She holds the Woolf and stares at Pugliani. And if she might have wanted from this man those inadmissable emotions: fondness, faith, safekeeping . . . *Here's Please Yourself bullocking out in the centre . . .* Underneath his nails there will be tiny eyelash blades of ink: his fingers have left their bruise upon the page. Tomorrow, she will take the Pelikan eraser and remove the mark, holding the section of page taut between two fingers so as not to tear the paper . . . *It's English Charm a half-head in front as they get near the line . . . Please Yourself's grabbing it on the line . . . I think it's got up . . . I reckon Please Yourself might've got up and won a nostril to English Charm; Cathcart Lass third; Cosmos Girl fourth; then Laleham, Princess Zegna . . .*

Pugliani waits, not evidently shaking, but with an expectation which he cannot let himself surrender to, for fear of tempting fate. Julia is drawn into his silence . . . *a screamer for the last on the programme . . . Please Yourself maaaay have got there . . . there's only a breath in it . . . a desperate struggle to the line in the final event of the programme and the judge calling for the photo . . .* She touches Fiona's half-empty pack of cigarettes. Lifts it. Places it inside the fruit bowl. She understands the way in which Fiona's untidiness is a metonym of her depression.

She finds the head and stem of a sliced mushroom: a pale brown-grey model of the female reproductive system.

She hears cheering from the radio . . . *No. 7 the winner, Please Yourself, ridden by M Clarke . . .*

Pugliani waits for the minor placings to be confirmed. Three. Nine. He settles back into the chair, enriched. *Please Yourself,* he thinks.

"My love," he says, turning to Julia. "It is a beast of most beauty. A beast of most faithfulness and courage!"

His description such, that if she had not been a piece of a logician before she came to him, he might have well persuaded her to *wish* herself a horse. Or so she says to him, in other words.

•

From the balcony adjoining Julia's room, a view can be had of the same gardens in which Basić had exposed the breasts of the nineteen-year-old girl.

In these gardens numerous wedding ceremonies are taking place. The brides and their maids move like beds of tall swaying flowers.

At 5:05 the clouds grow dark. The wind begins to shoulder at the things of earth. It buffets. The chains that hang loosely from the crane on the nearby construction site commence their slow percussion.

In the park the inexplicable begins. The brides start to walk with awkwardness. They tend to stumble. Their gaits become irregular and clumsy. Now they lurch from side to side.

When they reach out for assistance, a coarse intention tremor becomes obvious. A titubation of the head appears. Now, one by one, their unsupported bodies start to oscillate.

In the park, inexplicably, the brides begin to fall. Dark-suited masses rush towards them. The cameramen enquire as to whether they should continue filming; whilst the shadows break free from the surrounding flora and range across the lawns, yellowing the blades in their wake.

NARRATIO

—Dis, n'as-tu pas regret d'ignorer à
jamais le sort de ta première bien-
aimée?
—Ne t'en vas pas! Reste!

L'enfant et les Sortilèges

Yet why, within a week of having told him she no longer
wishes their relationship to continue, does she ask him to
return this evening? The six hours that remain before their
rendezvous are occupied entirely with this question. He
reworks the likely patterns of their dialogue. He hears the
endless propositions. He rehearses his response.

Yet he cannot find amongst the possibilities any explana-
tion that is not consequent upon an offering of apology; the
wish for reparation. No answer seems to satisfy, unless it
hinge upon the declaration of her love.

Yet given he has felt from almost the beginning of this
relationship a sense of its impossibility—how can he keep
her, she who is so beautiful?—almost of its necessary failure,
how strange it is that he should seek to find beginnings in this
end.

And yet he knows if love is to eventuate, he must, above all
else, deny its likelihood. Hope alone is capable of destroying
him. Hope, and the unthought-of circumstance, grown ma-
lignant in its anonymity.

Yet today he cannot bring himself to this necessary state of
disbelief. He finds himself, instead, considering Zeno's the-
ory of infinite divisibility: like the arrow which may be shown
to never reach its target, so his and Julia's love remains
impossible in every realm, except experience.

In the face of her self-evident obeisance, he becomes
compassionate. Contrition spawns *largesse*. He finds excuse
for her unnecessary angers and impatiences; he chooses to
ignore the incoherence of her argument; he looks benignly
on the recollected imperfections of her body, finding there,
exemplified, the preciousness of our mortality.

In short, before the afternoon is over, he is once again "in love: (he chooses the *andante* from a favoured version of the *Haffner*—Walter, 1960—playing it some seven times) having come to realize that love itself had never really left him, but had simply been displaced amongst a welter of misunderstandings; this quite mistaken man who, surprisingly above all else, finds it quite impossible to think himself unloved.

•

Jonathan Finch, uncommonly erect, a *Cloudy Bay* (its darkened wrapping rilled against the sweating glass) wedged firmly underneath his arm, stood upon the steps of Julia's double-storey terrace.

He glanced towards the balcony, its railing of meringue-frail stucco mealed beneath wysteria.

Festoons of unflowered green plummeted towards the terraced beds below, the cornucopias of lilac long since fallen.

Behind him, he could hear the quiet movements of the park. The gatherings. He looked towards the trees, so much the curving backs of Millet's *Gleaners*.

He had returned to Julia's house. The house (as he had so often chosen to describe it) that stood between a gynecologist and a burgeoning construction site. The house she shared with Freddy and Fiona. The house where she had lived with Stephen Gissing—the memory of that pale and pockmarked face, never quite eclipsed. (The umber hair; the wire of his glasses.)

The front door had been hooked ajar; the length of hallway narrowing before him, quietly devouring light.

No sound except a singing: distant and soprano; and his own voice, *mezzo*, in response, bursting uncontrollably from his opened mouth.

•

Consider Julia's bedroom as a painting, shaped, informed in every detail by the viewer's scrutiny.

A pale light seeding from the standard lamp across the shoulder of an armchair: the antimacassar permanently yellowed by the years of Joachim's brilliantine.

Near the fireplace, a breast of loosened paper, peeling from the wall: the severed hand of Corydon still seeking Amaryllis.

A bedside table, low, and draped in laceworked cloth (a lap on which a book might rest, a file, a flattish red container . . .) the single inset leaf a growth of hair, profuse and clearly visible beneath the cotton of a dress.

Or so he saw it. Julia, her hair buoyed by the oil-weight of dusk, turning to him from the window.

•

And what, quite unexpectedly, impossibly, if the answer to this question were not "because I love you"?

He watched her close her eyes against the flame. There was a crackling: faint and almost cellophane; a brief explosion of saltpetre as she drew the smoke.

"If I could say this in a way that would be absolutely clear," she said, "I would have failed in saying it."

He listened to the utter incoherence of her words; their contradiction; their irrationality.

He watched the smoke thread upwards to the shadowed ceiling: a loose blue string with which to draw the darkness down.

"In everything I said," he heard her say, "I never promised anything."

But none of this was possible. These words had no belongings to his recently imagined worlds. To whom then, did these words belong? Who had created them?

And why, within minutes of having reasserted the end of their relationship, does she ask if he would like to sleep with her this night. This once and—he must understand—no more.

And he agreeing, in the firm belief that it will happen yet again, as *this* has happened.

•

He was covering her. The missionary. Having clambered to this attitude—which he normally so detested—without the least consideration.

He could recall on several occasions having acted quite against his own desires. As he had often found himself confessing to emotions he had never felt; admitting to unfavourable circumstances in his past that never happened; to demonstrate his honesty and the capacity to talk about himself with openness.

•

Is it this very sense of "openness" which now compels him to relate the details of a previous affair?

"I only mention it," he says, "because I think at times you had a quite exaggerated notion of how reliant I might have been on you."

•

But what is happening? The heirlooms start to drift like barges in their thick brocades, colliding with the walls.

The tablecover's leaf design bleeds out across the cotton.

The shreds of torn wallpaper are swaying. They rear up showing the shepherdesses and the sheep. The rent separating Corydon from Amaryllis becomes a rent in the fabric of the world.

He is in the Gardens, the air grown thick with oleander flies. The trees are gashed: the resin seeping from their trunks.

Owls swoop. Feral cats and opossums bear their teeth and squirt their excrement at him.

He runs across the yellowed grass, the train of animals pouring after him. He has become a bride.

He stops, exhausted, by a Moreton Bay fig: the horse flank of its bark knifed with the name of Veljko Basić.

He senses movement close behind him. She has become aroused. He tears the brassière roughly from her shoulders and tugs it to her waist. He puts his hand between her thighs. He slides his fingers into her vagina.

•

Finch looked up to see her moving from the room. Away
from him.
"Julia!" he cried. But his attempt at calling gurgled from
his mouth. A babble. A mew. He watched her move out into
the hallway, hippic, silent and, from what he could discern,
in anger.

PROPOSITIO

So what has happened?
In a single sentence, this: that Julia's words had rendered
everything he once felt as familiar, suddenly unknown—this
man who held dependence for affection, envy for love.

DIVISIO

1

These subtle tyrannies of women, he half-voiced, angry,
lifting back the toilet seat.
Around the porcelain of the bowl he noticed several coin-
shapes of dried urine. A wishing-well of other men.
He unzipped the fly, held out his briefs' black band with a
hooking thumb, and looped his penis over the elastic.
Above all else, he wanted her. The suffusion of the areole,
as he imagined it; the mound completely shaved (perhaps a
stubble); labia smooth as dog-tongue. He found that he had
hardened in his quite unmoving hand.
He waited for the mild tumescence to abate.
A paperback, bent open into wings, lay beside his foot. He

made out the title, sniffing at the sheer coincidence; nothing more.

Some seven days ago, he had been seated opposite its author. Richard Morris. Novelist. New Zealander.

Carefully shifting his weight onto the right leg, he kicked the book against the wall.

Perhaps she was incapable of grasping how a writer must talk openly and shamelessly about his past.

Perhaps she'd taken it as lies: but everything—the lisp, the heroin, the tiny cones her cigarette had made across the vinyl of the armchair—had been true; even her name.

The stream deliberately hit against the back enamel, well above the waterline, and noiselessly; the odour of asparagus.

But if he was to *have* her—and how the memory of her body could be used again, again; sustaining him within the absences of love—he knew that he must sacrifice this indignation.

Finch began to shake his penis, freeing it of urine. He squeezed the foreskin, and prepared for his apology.

2

She had wanted him too soon: her fingers interweaving with his hair, pulling back his mouth, too soon, from the vagina.

He lay across her, barely moving, staring at her body; anxious lest he inadvertently cause himself to be expelled.

Here is a woman's hand, he thought. The wrist; a chain enclosing it. The forearms, for a woman, darkly flocculent.

Here are the corrugations of the ribs where they first meet the breast; the areole, with its scribbled growth of hair.

He worked his hand slowly and clandestinely, expectantly, against the thickening base of his penis.

He felt her body shake. The torso starting in its oscillations. Coarse tremors became obvious. A certain titubation of the head. She began to talk. A whispering that became increasingly chaotic.

And then she screamed. A ludicrously violent expulsion of pleasure.

He had barely entered her and she was screaming. It was inconceivable that he could be arousing her like this.

He felt his penis slackening with humiliation. It fell from her. He attempted to continue with his fingers, willing her to orgasm; accompanying her with his own involuntary murmurings. His fingers pushing deep inside her, stretching at the webbing, as if he were involved in some bizarre ventriloquy.

"What are you *doing!*" she was yelling at him. "What exactly are you *doing!*"

And, for whatever reason, he apologized.

3

Finch lay in the darkness, staring upwards at the roof.

He felt the need to void himself. It was impossible. The noise. The rich embroidery of human stench. These several humiliations.

And what if in the morning, touching him, she found his anus to be fouled? Or what if he should soil the sheet?

He would hold on, as he had held before: his purpling child-buttocks sucked tight within the pot. His mother leaning in the doorway, backlit by the wash-green sky of the kitchen, its glass roof painted out against the summer heat.

For hours if necessary.

He thought of Julia. Of how her absence had achieved the gutting of desire. His hand sought out his genitals.

"What's the matter, now?" her voice broke out, impatiently, beside him.

Could it be that he had said these things aloud?

He quickly offered an apology.

CONFIRMATIO

Crime Passionel

Jonathan Finch, via the letterflap, peered along an umbrous narrowing of hallway.

He rose up from his knees; volleyed at the door; struck until the hand itself refused another blow; then brought the burning knuckles for examination. A red suffusion. Petalled with tiny scallops of flesh, He licked the fingers wet, then blew upon the spittle.

Satisfied at last as to the house's emptiness, Finch turned back down the steps and trotted through the heat, along the softening bitumen of Clarendon and Hotham; across the cobblestone of Trinity.

Finch, through the buckled, parrot-raucous garage doors, stood a moment in the yard of Julia's house; staring upwards to a cloudless and uncolouring, thoroughly amorphous sky; his body trembling with a fear he recognized as belonging to a childhood long forgotten.

Hands above his head, he blindly trilled along the lintel of the backshed door. His fingers found the key; cold and smooth amidst the residues of matted dust.

What is this madness, he asked of himself, again. As if he hoped this midsummer morning to provide another type of clarity.

Julia's Bedroom

As it was, when he had left it that December evening twenty days before; as it will be, when she stands before "the duchess," Pugliani's races drawling to her from be-low . . . *Race 8, Morphetville, over the line and official now at 5, Even True* . . . the murmuring shoals of numbers . . . *at the boxes, Sale, Race 1* . . . her arms uncrossing as she draws the singlet top above her head; in Julia's bedroom, everything was much the same.

Under the patient watch of their shepherdesses, sheep still grazed about the walls. Near the fireplace, the shreds of paper still hung like dying leaves: the rent that separates Corydon from Amaryllis.

Only now, the curtains were drawn against the January heat; a single *tranche* of light coming from the window, its beam aswarm with particles of dust.

Finch averted his face, stepped back and flicked the main light.

This armchair and this table; this bed—its linen and its floor-pooled quilt; the duchesse and the *chiffonière*.

Her mother's furniture. And with it, the appalling stench of lavender: sharp and ineradicable.

They squatted, a ponderous bourgeoisie, leaching every shadow from the air and gathering it about themselves like shawls.

His image flowed within the dressing table's oval lock, a coin of unsilvered mirror, oil-bright, blemishing his face.

Finch at thirty-five, he thought. A trace of grey that strokes amongst the pale brown curls of hair, or from the gingered beard. Broad shouldered, should I choose to hold myself so. Only I have nodded to the postures of belittlement. This stoop well served by circumstance: half-expected, half-deserved, half-willed.

He turned half-circle, the mirror pouring him, out towards the double bed.

The Race Memory of Bed

The Nooooo————came from Wilma Doesberg's mouth; her cry ending in breath, so that the sound far more resembled that of "Noah"; but Joachim's seed had been expelled. She felt the full weight of his body sink upon her; pinning her; her left leg cramping badly; splayed across the freshly laundered linen. Friday evening. The sounds of the radio coming to her from the kitchen below.

She was in tears, of desperation, of disgust at her husband's uncalled-for vigour, which had struck her as some fundamental betrayal of their Baptist faith.

Only later would she find, to add to that disgust, his act had impregnated her.

Three hours prior to Finch's own improper entrance, Julia—now twenty-eight—had been penetrated by John Pietro Pugliani, Independent Film Maker, in this same bed; and without any precise understanding—other than, perhaps, relief at presence—she had also found herself to be in tears.

Three months before, and for the first time, Finch himself had lain upon this bed . . . and so the mattress can be seen to accumulate these personal histories, like a family sepulchre . . . beside the bolster of this woman, Julia, who had withdrawn to sleep.

In that apprehensive silence (his body aching for release, if at his own device) he discerned the first involuntary gaspings from Fiona's room.

Within a matter of some minutes, the screaming had begun. At first quite faint: resembling the sound sometimes heard from birds—how Brian Proctor had described the dying words of Hazlitt.

The Sheet

Finch drew the bottom sheet scruffwise, grasping it towards his face. Contours of sweat, salt-white. The linen wealed, discoloured in its loops. Ejaculants dried back to starch. He let it fall. He cried. It had been blained and ringed with sex.

P.I.D.

In later weeks, as Julia's health had rendered the description of her previous condition increasingly abstract, he came to doubt the basis of her plea for abstinence.

At best, he viewed it as the means by which she had avoided an initial gesture of commitment; at best, from fear.

At worst, he knew it as a legacy of her previous affair with Gissing—as if that late September she had written in a diary:

I wasn't interested in another of his sex. This made it easier
for me, this lie, for him.

Finch "re-made" the bed, seeking to restore, as perfectly
as possible, its previous abandon; forced in his pain to
recreate, dispassionately, the markings of their passion.

The Search

Bending from the waist, Finch eased out the bottom drawer.
Illegible, he pronounced, peering at the scribbled leather of
her belts and shoulder bags.

He moved slowly upwards, through the gloves and scarves
and straps. Shed skins of stockings, and a cream—*Apply the
cream . . .*—a box of tampons, a single brassière: flesh-
toned and prophylactic. The glint of underwear, silk and
nylon, crackling, catching at the roughside of his index
finger; at the drying unskinned knuckles.

Finch bent to his knees and slid the first drawer of the
second row. He smiled. He eased his weight sidewards,
drawing his legs from under him and sat upon the carpet, his
back pressed to the timber of the chest.

The Metaphor of the Letter

They were gifts.

Her letters, drawn together in their ribboned parcels,
were like gifts. Carola's stationery—a frown of paper—
gathered to the drawerfront.

Pluck it out, he thought, offended by its bloom; its blush.
Out-and-out. And held the wad at bay a moment. *Bitch,* he
spat.

He pulled the ribbon; watched it fall to either side, apart,
as if he had disrobed her; staring at the dark hair of the
writing; the tight black curls of the address.

The protruding edges of the paper had been crushed and
worn to mohair; its deckle softened and discoloured by
touch.

He drew the papers through their slits: each gash-edge frayed with paper-coil, knife-ringleted. He unfolded them, the hard and deep-creased papers snapping; and he gathered them into a book.

October

As for endings, how is it possible to know, now everything seems so determined? So much damage done. Does one go on, enduring these excesses, for just another week, another month? It is shock enough to find someone you've loved (still *love*, despite all this—I hear you say. But bear with me) capable of doing such things. And then there is the problem with forgiving, that it can so easily be taken for condonement. What is loss, that makes it so impossible to separate our *needs* from love?

And what if I should say it *could* begin again, and he be blessed with all the knowledge of his rather singular behaviours: would it be so different? Or would it simply overwhelm him once again? Condemn him. Find him guiltier and guiltier.

And was she speaking of the present or the past? And who is "he"?

The Love He Could Have Had

These episodes with Finch are most unpleasurable. But you already know my feelings about all of this. There seem to be a surprisingly large number of men—and Wotton is another one who springs to mind—who get love confused with power; who mistake dependence for affection; and as a consequence, quite simply tear apart the love they could have had.

The love he could have had.

I have this love. I do not have this love. It reappears only to declare its absence.

These compounded sufferings he feels: who has nothing; who once had, but did not recognize the having; who suffers at his own stupidity; who suffers knowing he has acted in a way that has lost him what he most desires—which had been offered to him, openly: the love he could have had. Who could bear this thought?

Regret envelops him, defeated by the order in which everything has been revealed.

And who is Wotton?

Digression

There are, of course, these earlier questions he has yet to satisfactorily resolve.

Why, for instance, he who has such apparent need for love (has he not searched painstakingly for evidence of love in those who do not love him?) would so fervently deny its possibility in those whom he believes to be in love with him: he, who seeks with such persistent ingenuity the grounds on which relationships will fail; who has hounded love away with his obsessions; needing to be loved so totally—and even by those who are unknown to him—or else wishing it to be destroyed. And totally.

November

I have been reading all that you have written recently, again. Retracing this relationship. And such a flood of competing emotions it releases.

There are so many ways by which we might account for our behaviours; but whether we are envious, or fearful, or whether we are simply inadvertent—the envy, the fear, the inadvertence cannot be ignored.

Perhaps at last, through the confusions and grotesqueries, it seems a sense of purpose has emerged from all of this; that you have come to terms with the relationship after such a long time of (what seemed) unnecessary effort.

Above all else, I am excited that out of this disorder you might have found the possibility of a "new" romance.

With whom? The paper leant towards him in his hand.

The Problem of Inverted Commas

Finch stared at the tendrils of Carola's script, so clinging to the lines he could imagine sweet pea fragrance.

Why, he wondered, had she placed inverted commas around "new"?

An innocent embellishment perhaps.

Or else in error: as a menu offering "fresh" asparagus.

Or was it that the word might simply mean "*not* new"—as in the senses of "rekindled," "re-discovered," or "ongoing"?

These words torn from their dialogue, how could they ever be explained; the answers—Julia's *questions*—irretrievable. The letters had abandoned him amongst this plethora of rivals. These unknown and unknowable men.

Save one of them had taken her away from him within the first weeks of November.

A Phrase from Lawrence

Strange dance, his hands upon the woodhips: Finch is edging back the final drawer in smallish movements, side-to-side.

He stood, legs stiff from squatting; made his way towards the double bed.

The journal was undated, ending (from what little he could gather) somewhere in September: its evenings noted with chrysanthemum, gathered from an earlier season. A rank complicity of pressed flowers.

Somewhere, held beside her now, amongst the coloured pencils and the tissues and the lipstick and the tampons and the text of Pinter's *No Man's Land*, the hairbrush with its undergrowth of scale and dust, there was another history— more recent: the chapters of late spring to early summer

when he was a character named Finch. These women's
thoughts. *Ripe figs!* he spat, from Lawrence.

He took the metal nail file from where it rested on a copy of
My Sister's Hand . . . , upon the bedside table, scything it
around his first and second fingers.

Julia's diaphragm gaped from its red container. As he had
the night of their first sex, he stared in fascination at its size:
the bulbous and indecent tympani of skin; waiting in this
very bedroom, an October evening, as she fed it deep in her
vagina and lay back; until he brought her to that child-voiced
whimper of release.

The love he could have had. The nail file poised above the
membrane of the "cap."

A Pedestrian

Jonathan Finch, his hair sweat-heavied and uncurling, drove
north, away from Julia's house.

Shortly after Gertrude Street he noticed the pedestrian.

At first perhaps it was the shirt, *sans* collar; or else the
fashionable looseness of the trousers, drawn like a dillybag
about the waist.

And then it was the hair's quite umber lankness; the pale
complexion with its slightly pockmarked skin; the steel-
rimmed spectacles evocative of revolution.

Finch, reducing speed, glanced to the rearview mirror.
The man was, for the moment, lost to view.

He snapped the indicator for a U-turn, but a steady stream
of traffic from the opposite direction kept him pinned against
the line of parked cars.

A woman in a yellow 323 pulled up behind him, as if there
weren't sufficient room to pass.

"Go around!" he yelled, gesticulating with a round-arm
motion through the open window. Their eyes met in the
mirror and he saw her shrug.

"Go round!" he yelled again, enraged. "Go round, you
stupid bitch!"

But she remained behind.

By the time that Finch was heading south again, the pedestrian had disappeared. He pulled up at the Gertrude Street lights.

The faces of the women on the billboard gaped vacuously at the traffic; their bodies massive; perfectly proportioned.

The faint pepper trace of dried chrysanthemum moved to him amongst the still air of the car.

The lights changed. Finch swung right, towards the city.

As he drove, he was possessed by the sensation that occurs sometimes in moving cars: that the vehicle is still, and all else is rushing past. As on windy nights, the moon can sometimes seem to hurl itself through clouds, illuminating them a moment.

from REFUTATIO

Quicquid conabar dicere versus erit

Bleak September. Mornings stranded in rain. The slap of wettened gabardine. Twill of. Whip of. Fluttering. I listen to the endless prattle. The scuff and clock of shoe-leather, brisk against the paths. Rain. In its place. Drops. Bulbs of water foliaging the eaves. Like barges all these transports. Punts, these cars. Adrift. Butting on the street's black canal. Drizzle of the radios. Their interwoven voices through the twill of rain. Windscreens misting. Breath and yarn. The wipers screech in their exhaustion. Drop. I turn towards the room. It is how I found it, coming to her house. The furniture shrouded beneath white sheets. Instead, they are my clothes in disrespect. Deranged. The whispering begins. Subduedly from the terraces. Listen. All the voices say. I dreamt that I gave birth to my mother. I hear them rise up from their couches to the diesel smear of traffic. The bay windows chatter. All the women leaning back in the creak of leather. Yes? And that while I slept she came to me. And? And stole my breasts for her own. Too much has ended. Too many

things have been brought to their end. Sharp thrust. The
legacy of his desire. A pain deep in the abdomen. Tender-
ness. Between the pelvic bones, a burden hanging in its
ornamental curve. A terminus. A *cul-de-sac*. The dillybag.
Soft rounded leather, pouching like a belly. Drawn together
with this string. Ridicule. The woman's bag. Brunt of jokes.
At the bottom of the sack I find his cigarettes. The soft pack.
Scrotum. Reticule. And when they slice it open it expels her
half-devoured breasts. These intensities that verge into ob-
session. Why is it so hard to free my mind of him? His face.
Pale damaged skin, brushed with stubble. Umber lankness
of the hair. Escaping through my fingers. Why does this
description seem so necessary now? It grows dark. It is
another night. The telephone has woken me, shrill within
the sleeping house. I cradle it. Where is her husband now?
His fingers rasped with oil and blackened by the metal.
Rough and penis-thick. A visitor, he says. At three o'clock. I
hold him to my body. Feel the stubble pierce my legs. He
moves upon my body. Proving something to himself he has
already long forgotten. I see the taxi pulling up outside. I
hear the treble voices of the radio. I hear him saying mate.
His pockets spill across the vinyl bench. His cigarette has left
a mark. I hear the door slam. Dressing quickly. Hurrying
down the stairs before he wakes the house. Again. My love,
he says. His drinking accent. Foreigner to me. I say his
name. He tells me everything I say is verse. And how can I
not love him now? The purpose of his visit never surfaces. To
simply stay. Or simply leave. I watch these shapes unfocus-
ing. They turn from me. Retreat across the room. These
presences. These absences. I stumble to their arms as if a
drunkard. My walk, irregular and clumsy. As if my nervous
system dies away from me. The consequence of ending. Now
I fall. And everything begins its falling. Through the dark.
My fingers comb the air. Everything is spilling. The ink runs
from this pen. The rain. I hold him. I kiss inside his mouth.
My fingers woven in the lines of hair. Subordinate. I see him
peel his glasses from behind the ears. Both hands held to the
wire. I see his naked, hipless body. Scar lines faint across the
lower belly and thighs where the bands have gripped his
flesh. A piebald birthmark. Blue-white mottled skin. A

willow pattern. Inks. I need to cry. I cannot find a reason for these moments. Unless it is a general sadness. A pity. For the sadnesses of living. I see the tight fist of the scrotum and the penis draped across it. The breast of this penis he has stolen. That he might deface me. Feed me. Smear me with it. I have closed my eyes to aid him in this absolution. To free him of uncertainty. Against my lips. I smell the trace of urine held beneath the foreskin suddenly released. The mouth prepares for speech. Condemned to these ventriloquies of loss. And I condone. I find myself. Pretending interest. He visits me when I can smell her on his hands. I have found myself caressing her. My tongue inside her mouth. My fingers weaving through the curling lines of hair. My sex with him is lesbian. I take his breast. It comes to me that he was present at my birth. I try to recollect our days together only finding they are memories of something else. I am running from the river's edge. Late autumn. Voices from the playing fields come drifting through the whitening, ribboned air. The sound of feet a tantrum on the dark and trampled earth. I turn towards my family. My sister. I have made them small and porcelain. I lift them from the view and I return them. I tug my panties inefficiently to the side and squat to urinate. And I had thought instead I was positioning myself for penetration. The *I* makes paths, but has no idea where the possibilities might lead. Confession or redemption. I grow frightened. Not enough to bring about the numbness of inevitability. This stone. I am exhausted by its weight. These fears of what it is. Of what I may have caused this thing to be. Of what it might have been. These tenses. Everything flies from the edge. As if for once I understood the speed at which the earth is turning. I am terrified to be disfigured by these accidents. An hour before the end. I stand upon the railway footbridge. The curve of track emerging from the cutting. I watch the train approach. I see a woman leaning outwards from an opened carriage door. Her hair exploding at her face like some Medusa. Sister's hair. I see her leaning out towards the mirror of the duchesse. Her dress is rolled down to her waist. I watch her tape adhesive strips across her nipples as if they might be wounds. The train passes by beneath me. Everything becomes still. I must return. I must focus on this bleak September morning. What is it that I have written? I move towards the balcony, listening to the traffic and the sounds of people running by below me in the rain. As if I were afraid to compromise these moments with the trace of poetry. As if I felt it a betrayal. From the balcony it is possible to see, above the trees, a single white building. And yes, cathedral spires. A car horn sounds below. A distant band of trees, swaying, dull and unfocused by the weather. The front door closes. I return to the view of the street. The gutters white with rain. A car door slams below. The black reflecting roof of the taxi shoulders out into the traffic from the curb. The rain a pencil, shading in a presence to the empty air. I watch him come to me. Lean over me. His pale torso moving across the light. I feel his shadow weight. The tremors of intention as he sways above me. I love you, are his words. He says. I hear him say. I watch the bruising of the sky. At first mistaking thunder for a furniture arranged in an adjoining room. It speaks to me at length. In time. There are half-sentences. Half-truths. Nothing I can be bothered taking task with. Eventually I fall into this troubled sleep. I am lying in the shadow of my mother. I take the nipple to my mouth. This presence and this absence. Take it here in gratitude. But do not move to hasten it. I feel the semen separate. Melt into its pools. Within the socket of the eye. The corner of the mouth. The hollow of the collarbone. This confirmation. Love. I crave a language based entirely in the present. An act of reading that erases all that has been written from the page. An act of speaking that erodes the memory. Our conversations riddled with a sense of *déjà vu*. A door that opens to a darkened hall. These stairs ascending. A room that opens to a balcony. And there would be no more of love. I am tired of this dangerous word. Let us be rid of it. Be free of its atrocity. Its hour arrived in any case, it says. It says, to stay, I would go on doing this forever. Surrendering more of myself each time to you. And now it chooses to break free. The door opens. I watch it sink into this bleak September rain. Its mouth opens wide. Wide enough to scream. Its teeth bite abandonedly into the streaming flesh of separation. And there is an exquisite pleasure there it will not be let heard.

DIGRESSIO

In one sense pornography is a literature about the tasks of beautiful women; about their infinite capacity for abandonment.

It tells their love of the spectator (the contract unequivocally sealed with their regard) the very proof of which is demonstrated through excess: their capacity to accede and to surrender without question.

In particular, the opened mouth of Ankar had come to represent this view. I love you so completely, it suggested, there is nothing I would not gladly do.

Ankar was a young German girl, whose breasts, whilst not large, were remarkable in that they were almost totally suffused by the areole. She was a blonde and her genitals, as he preferred, were shaved. She had been photographed in two separate sessions with a total of twenty men.

Below each photograph her words were reproduced; their emphases clearly indicated by the use of an italic face:

Ja. Schieb das Ding in meinen Mund.
Schiess, los, *schiess*. Ich werde *alles*
schlucken, was die zwanzig Säcke zu
bieten haben—und mehr!

This speech had been translated thus:

Yeah. *Shove* that dong in my mouth.
Shoot, go on, *shoot*. I'll swallow *all*
that twenty ball-sacks have to offer—
and more!

In one particular photograph, the molar teeth were easily visible. The fillings, the plaque. The slightly coated tongue was pushed out, causing the bottom lip to pout.

"Mein Schlitz pulsiert," she gasped. "Ich laufe aus, ich *komme* immer wieder . . ."

My twat is pulsating; I'm *coming*
down there; *I never stop coming.*

". . . Ah, ahhh! Oh, war das fantastisch! Was? Es ist
vorbei? Oh, nein. Bitte, *bitte*. Nein!"
He gazed upon the final moment, frozen in its motion.
Chalkmark. Whiplash. The ejaculant winding from the penis
like the scarf of Isadora.
    "Ah, ahhh! Ow, was that fantastic! What? It's over? Oh,
no. Please, *please*, no!"

•

Dryden, in his *Ovid and the Art of Translation*, suggested
three basic approaches to translation: *Metaphrase*, or "turn-
ing an author word by word, and line by line, from one
language into another"—that is, the translation of the signi-
fiers; *Paraphrase*, "translating with latitude . . . his words
are not so strictly followed as his sense"—that is, the transla-
tion of the signified; and finally, *Imitation*, "where the
translator assumes the liberty not only to vary from the words
and sense, but to forsake them both as he sees occasion"—
one thinks of Pound's Propertius, for example.
    "All translation, I suppose," wrote Dryden, "may be
reduced to these three heads."

PERORATIO

from A Conclusion

To the perpetual embarrassment of her daughter, Virginia
Cathcart had chosen a salad made of mignonette, tomato and
shallots.

•

"You're not in the Writing Department, I gather, Peter," Hadleigh Laleham made enquiry of Wren. "Those who can, *do*. No, I'm what's known as a fractional tutor in Literature." And he reached for the decanter.

"I think what Peter's hinting at," said Cosmo McBride, editor of *The Eleven Hads: A Journal of Postmodernism,* "is that he's recently had his first novel accepted for publication."

"That's the ticket!" said Laleham. "What's it called?"

"That's the Ticket," Wren replied, pouring out an inauspicious serving of Chablis.

"That's a coincidence."

"No, you're thinking of Grant Phillip's first novel—or was it *That's a Pity?*"

Laleham watched him nod a "cheers" to McBride and Zegna Horvitz and drain his glass.

Wren was a man in his mid-thirties, with light brown curling hair and a beard with ginger trace. His body seemed already gripped with intensity, closing in upon itself.

"That's the Ticket," he continued, "is about a Creative Writing Department staffed by insular elitists with no interest in their students beyond the possibility of consolidating sleeping arrangements." He glanced across at Georgina Musić with a blandly innocent smile.

"Yes, well one can only hope it also chooses to address the rather desperate plight of the nontenured or the wastage of talent and the contempt for achievement by the native born," said Dr. Horvitz. "I would think these are the real issues at stake in Australian academic circles."

"Here, here," said James Cathcart.

"Actually, I've heard that Peter is attempting to put the 'dirt' back in the *roman à 'clay'!*"

"Cosmo, tell me why it is your *jeu de mots* always end up sounding like cryptic crossword clues."

McBride paused momentarily, then announced:

"Initially, because all lecturers love striving for bouncy rejoinders. Five letters."

Wren swung in his seat, his finger pointed straight before him: a weathervane impelled by some sudden shift in breeze.

"Georgina, as a student, as it were, I imagine you must find Cosmo's Graduate Diploma absolutely chock-a-block with snappy comebacks . . ."

Laleham watched Wren's attention lapse towards Georgina Musić's breasts.

". . . not to mention all the snappy come*ons*."

"Ah, 'balls'!" exclaimed Virginia Cathcart with a beaming sense of pride in her achievement.

"Talking of which, Hadleigh . . ."

Laleham caught the pinkening smudge of Wren's face veering back in his direction.

". . . what's that *other* Hadlee-type New Zealander up to these days?"

"Richard? Oh, his wickets and my book sales are pretty much neck-and-neck, numbers-wise."

"I was actually at the Carisbrook Test when he broke Dick Collinge's record," offered Cathcart. "And he started out that game nine wickets away! Do you know Ian Donelly's *Tribute?*"

Laleham shook his head.

"Pakis, poms and ockers,
From Boy's High to Bombay,
They've all been smitten by the barb
Of our top dog—'R J.'
So if in the life hereafter,
The visitors are short,
Perhaps the great scorebook will read:
'J. Christ bowled Hadlee, nought.'"

"I can honestly say I've not come across that one before, James."

"James is somewhat of a connoisseur of contemporary verse . . ."

"Did you manage to get to the session on the function of Australian poetry, Mr. Laleham?" asked Zegna Horvitz.

"No, unfortunately. I was scheduled for a reading at Ormond College."

"It was a vivifying debate," she continued, placing her cutlery soundlessly to the Wedgwood. "After the sterile opportunism of the so-called 'Generation of 68,' it was refreshing to discover a commitment to the clarification of the unknown . . . to explain our world with some renewed sense of moral urgency . . ."

"And so the exceptional is once again reduced to the commonplace. Greek cliffs suddenly appear as 'scones' . . ."

Wren's elbows clattered to the table, his head resting in the "U" of his palms, pushing his cheeks upwards and narrowing his eyes into a World War Two caricature of a Japanese. His stare had fallen once again upon Georgina Musić.

". . . The Colosseum is become a vast vagina."

She glanced twice. Once to McBride and then briefly to her lap. Wren seemed to follow her gaze.

"I would have thought the aim of poetry might rather be to make the familiar as *unfamiliar* as possible, wouldn't you, Georgina?"

"And is *yours* to be familiar with everyone you can?" she barely uttered.

"Is everything all right down there," came Cosmo's voice. Wren checked his fly.

"Have no fear, McBride. Musić hath charmed the savage beast. Or was it *breast?*" His eyes returned to Georgina. "*Breast.*"

He looked wistfully about the room.

"God save us from the *savage* breast. Bring on the *good* breast, that's what *I* say!"

The table paused as Cathcart's fusty daughter Mignonette, stooped as if in perpetual contemplation of the miseries of her name, filled her glass from the decanter like some nervous urination.

•

"It has been a busy year for you, 1987?" Zegna Horvitz enquired.

"Not at all, I'm sad to say. Apart from your *Spoleto*, there's only been the conference on Commonwealth Literature in Lecce."

"Then you have been privileged to see the Southern Italian light," said Horvitz. "Such luminosity! The stone gleams and the dust is white! What is dark is dark. And what is darker is blacker without mitigation!"

"Did you manage to visit the Colosseum whilst you were in Italy?"

"Peter," Cathcart cautioned.

"I actually spent what little time I had hunting down the carvers: Alberti, Gorgione . . ."

"Have you read Stokes on Hadleigh . . . on *Gorgione*, rather," he corrected.

McBride was smirking.

"Have *you* read Stokes, McBride?" he swung. "On anybody? *Stokes*, McBride. Art theorist. Went to couch with Melanie Klein in the 1930s . . ."

"It's not the lecture theatre, Peter."

"Are you particularly opposed to the carving tradition?" Laleham asked Wren, quite without side.

"'Neither a carver nor a modeller be' . . . mind you," he nodded to Georgina, "I'll do the carving, if you'll do the modelling."

And he returned to Laleham:

"I take the same view Stokes himself came to in his later work. Art is an attack on the material and the constant struggle to repair the damage."

"Yes, well I would think by *those* criteria," said McBride, "you've been quite an artist yourself, tonight."

"And I'll have that white wine back when you've finished with it," said Wren.

"I believe our Cosmo's talked you into giving him a piece for next year's *The Eleven Hads*," Cathcart came in, firmly.

"Only on the condition that he confesses where he got his title from," smiled Laleham.

Cosmo McBride placed the decanter on the table and recited:

"'John, where James had had "had," had had "had had." "Had had" had had a better effect on the teacher.' The schoolboy conundrum meets Gertrude Stein!"

"A toss-up between that and 'Had Enough,'" said Wren.

His gestures seemed to have become increasingly adrift: the hand as if it somehow lacked a cigarette.

"And what's the *latest* number got to offer, Cosmo?" he enquired, glancing back to Georgina Musić. "Cosmo?" he persisted.

Laleham caught Cathcart's nod to McBride. He was to take the question seriously.

"We have an essay re-evaluating the notion of indecency . . ."

Wren kept his eye on McBride whilst delving in a pasta sauce.

". . . the argument is actually a counter text to a lecture of Trollope's—'English Fiction as a Rational Amusement' . . ."

"'A lecture of Trollope's' sounds like the collective noun for prostitutes."

"In my department, Peter, we prefer the term 'An anthology of Pros,'" said Cathcart.

There was a brief outbreak of laughter. McBride waited.

"Georgina and I have also managed to negotiate a detailed review from Dr. Horvitz . . ."

"*Horvitz* was an imprint I've always associated with pulp," said Wren.

"Would someone pass that rather special sauce?" asked Zegna. She dipped a mitten of Italian bread into the dish that Wren had previously been using.

"Personally," he continued, "I prefer reviews that transcend a personal attack upon the author because they happened to read for a press which said 'no' to a collection of poems several years before . . ."

Whatever this might have meant, Zegna clearly understood the reference.

"Is it I?" she asked rhetorically to the silenced room.

"Actually, Dr. Horvitz has given us a detailed article on the new Grant Phillips . . ."

"It's remarkable, isn't it," Wren uttered, "how once upon a time one needed suicide or a decent overdose to be canonized in Australian Literature before one's sixtieth. Now the wheelchair serves the purpose admirably for the under twenty-fives."

"And how are the *under*graduates shaping up, Cosmo?" Virginia tried.

"Optic atrophy present in about one third of cases and ten per cent have recently developed sensorineural deafness," he offered back.

"You see, it's catching on! Cosmo, do you actually *tell* them in your lectures that the secret of success is currently disease?" asked Wren, laughing loudly, plucking a wad of dressing-stained salad from a bowl and letting it fall back.

He turned his tremoring head to Hadleigh Laleham. Perhaps he felt that somewhere in the saddening face of the guest he had so thoroughly disdained all evening, he might find the necessary support. But there was little Laleham could now do. It was clear to everyone, and now it seemed to Wren himself, the damage had been done. The company watched him slowly talk himself to death, thrashing in his repetitions and his slanders, waiting for the final blow.

"Now Hadleigh . . . what *are* things like across the Tasman? Have you any well-respected up-and-comers with all their limbs intact? My God, if we had had, Hadleigh, half the . . ."

"That's shallot!" broke in Cathcart.

The room, silenced, turned to him, his face beaming, holding the tiny green tube of vegetable between his thumb and first finger.

There was a moment of embarrassed laughter. The next sound was that of Wren's chair scraping on the polished boards of James and Virginia Cathcart's dining room floor.

He stood up shakily and moved to behind his seat. It was a gesture that jettisoned Laleham back to memories of boarding school in New Zealand: the lad about to thank his prefect for the necessary thrashing.

"If you will excuse me, a moment," Wren enunciated.

He raised his eyes to the group and stepped backwards from the table.

"I'm sure you can please yourself in that regard, Peter," answered Cathcart.

And with what considerable charm he offered "Please yourself." English charm.

Mignonette, Georgina Musić, then Laleham himself and
Zegna Horvitz . . . one by one, the faces followed Peter
Wren.

He attempted an apology, but ended merely blundering
from the room in the direction of the bathroom, or the street.
Nor was there any move to stop him.

"'Had had Hadleigh'!" Dr. Horvitz amusedly repeated for
the benefit of the table.

"A toss-up between that and 'had enough,'" said McBride.

Richard Morris

BLEEDING HEARTS

EILEEN MYLES

Know what
I'm jealous of?
Last night.
It held
us both
in its
big black
arms
& today
I hold
between
my legs
a shivering
pussy.
Bleeding &
shaking
wet with
memory
grief &
relief.
I don't know
why the universe
chose me
to be female

so much beauty
& pain,
so much
going on
inside
all this
change
everywhere
coins falling
all over
the bed
& death
is a dream.
Deep in
the night
with thousands
of lovers
the sucking
snapping
reeling
flesh
deep in
the cavity
of endless
night across
mounds
of bodies
I peer over
is it
love or
war. The hollow
creeping
cheek
where
I was
born.

SIX POEMS

FIONA PITT-KETHLEY

DOGS

Young men, like pups, can be somewhat unformed.
Unless you're certain of their pedigree,
it's hard to see how they'll mature and grow.
(Alsatians will fuck dachsunds now and then.)

A man who has some mileage on the clock
in theory would be best. You know the worst—
how much his hair is likely to recede,
his face to fold, as "character" comes out.
(Furrows look better on the land than skin—
the worst one is a constipated frown—
laughter lines are the most forgivable.)
Auden grew wrinkled as a shar-pei dog.
Most only reach the pug or bloodhound stage.

I've tried "the older man"—the problem's not
the looks. It's the god-awful temperament.
Rottweiler-grumpiness sets in with age.
I'll stick to pups who're younger than myself—
they've got more stamina for exercise
and better natures, willing to be trained.
I'll whistle and they'll come, fetch, carry, beg.

Of course, I wouldn't take on one *too* young—
I'd certainly prefer him weaned from Mum.

Old dogs, it's said, *cannot* be taught new tricks—
and those they have are all predictable.
They guard their kennels self-importantly,
mark out their territory in wind and piss,
bark righteously for any trifling cause,
follow the pack in every bloody thing.
All their affection's of the boisterous kind—
they're awfully free with dandruff, spittle, hair.
The eviler ones are snappish with young kids,
chase those who're weaker than themselves (like sheep),
seize you and won't let go, roger your legs,
lose socks, worry old bones and bury things.
And *all* take leaks at frequent intervals.

Don't get me wrong—I'm partial to a dog.
I blame their breeders for the way they're trained.

BED TIME

Sex in the afternoon is always good—
it's honest lust, not lodgings for the night—
no one's too drunk or tired to manage it.

The afternoon's discreet, ambiguous,
a time when no excuses need be made.
Each enjoys each—they know as they are known.
There's no concealment—daylight's always on.
And when it's time to leave, the night's still young—
home, food, TV all wait—and best of all,
the peace of being alone in your own bed.
Solitary sleep's less disillusioning.

Night sex is often far less pleasurable—
a tired, furtive, fumbling in the dark.

Objective vision comes with morning's light.
(I have the knack of always waking first.)
I dreamed of friends but find a stranger there—
his mouth gapes snoring wide; yesterday's style—
the careful, blow-dried cut—is now on end;
one duvet-clutching hand has dirty nails;
and, something ludicrous, the modest sod's
managed to get his pants back on in bed.
He wakes and things get worse. I must wipe off
the grin those pants inspired and try to talk.

The in-built problem with a one-night stand
is how to handle things after you've slept.
How many lovers' moods are synchronized?
An early-morning surliness in one
undoes everything tender done or said.
I'd advocate pre- or post-breakfast fucks
to show continuance of last night's desire—
proof positive that neither has regrets.

EQUALITY

Some argue feminists shouldn't like a fuck.
The fact that men are oftener on top
is taken metaphysically. They're seen
as dominating while the woman submits.
Like Hell! That's what they think . . .

You feel abused? A doormat underneath?
The answer's simple—change it all around—
roll over, get on top and milk him dry.

There's a third path, where neither dominates.
Why don't we settle for equality—
my favourite way—and do it side by side?

NO SMOKING

Lent is the time for cutting out what's bad,
I'll give up going to bed with men who smoke—
for that *and* other seasons of the year.

Is it the taste? That's not *too* bad as long
as I don't put my tongue into their mouths.
The tiredness of their skin? Their bloodshot eyes?
Is it the smell of fag-ash in my hair
next day? Not really. That can be washed out.

Post-coital light-up is what worries me.
We've had each other, then the smoking man
turns desperately seeking something else,
scouring the bedside cupboard, pockets, drawers.
He sighs on finding what he really wants,
then's silently unfaithful with his fag.

Some keep their little weapons to themselves.
The worst kind start a sort of troilism.
I don't feel easy with a naked flame
too near my vulnerable naked flesh—
you, me, a cigarette, a smoky kiss.
Out of the corner of one eye I see
a toppling inch of ash above a stub,
while lover-boy is fiddling with my tits—
foreplay designed to set the bed on fire.

BLOW JOBS

You'd get more protein from the average egg;
the taste's a tepid, watery nothingness—
skimmed milk? weak coffee? puréed cucumber?

Fellation's not a woman's idea of fun.
Just doing it as foreplay is OK.

You kiss me, I'll kiss you's a quid pro quo—
but carrying on until the buggers come—
suck, suck, suck, suck for half a bloody hour!
(I haven't timed it but it feels that way.)

There's nothing in the act for us. Our mouths
are better stimulated by a kiss.
The sucked lie back (with beatific smiles),
forget our bodies in their private dreams,
while we grow cold, detached, unloved, untouched,
our heads like 3-D sporrans on their groins,
bored out of mind, with aching jaws and cheeks,
like kids that Santa gave a plastic flute,
still trying to get a tune on Boxing Day.

"Toothless George" sucked all comers to the rocks
in a secluded Jersey cove each June.
(He'd come from Blackpool for his yearly treat.)
Men love the act, sucking and being sucked.
Most women wish they'd keep it to themselves.

ROMANCE

I hate romance. I hate all Mills and Boon.
And Barbara Cartlands really make me sick.
I loathe the trash that people push as love.

A husband talks to me about his wife,
calls her "a real bitch." She sounds one too—
the sort you only can laugh at not with.
(Her jokes are purely practical.)

He closed the shutters, sat there opposite
last time he called me round and told me that
the treatment had got worse. I wondered how.
(The trip before, I'd heard he'd come in tired—
she lay upon the sofa on a sheet.

He saw the writing on the wall beside—
her message for him—DEAD OF BOREDOM—scrawled
like blood in bright red paint across the white.)
He seemed to think *her* words could still be seen
beneath *his* several coats of vinyl matt.

Society pities the faithful wife,
the bruised and battered wife who waits at home
while hubby has his office-party screw.
Yet men who're knocked around are just a joke.
And he whose wife's a whore is thought a pimp.

I'm not society.
I'm really *really* sorry for this man—
right up until the moment that he says
he's stuck it all for love.

Love? Shit! that's abject masochism.

Her tapir's profile triumphs from the wall.
(He has to have pictures of her around.)
This one's surrounded by a glittering frame—
cemented shards of broken mirror-glass
Madame de Sade, I think, probably made
him walk across them first.

Note: Mills and Boon publish stereotyped romantic novels. The heroine is always
seventeen to twenty, the hero thirty to forty-five. Barbara Cartland is almost an
English institution. She has written more than two hundred novels and was
recently made a Dame.—F.P.K.

WRITING AND EXILE

DAVID ANTIN

when i was invited to talk at a tikkun conference i was a
little surprised because   unlike most people who identify
strongly with their jewishness   i dont think about it much
and when peter cole called i hadnt been thinking about it at all
      though there are claims i could make   ive been
anthologized as a jewish poet a couple of times   not only in
  jerome rothenbergs *big jewish book*   but also in a french
anthologie   de la poésie juive du monde entier   along with
  king solomon max jacob bobby dylan and jerome rothenberg   so
i supposed it was reasonable enough to try to think about it
      and what i thought i shared   in a way that i hadnt really
thought about enough   with a lot of people who took their
jewishness more for granted   was a sense of exile
                                                though my
experience of growing up in the united states might not be what
  most people would think of as exile   because i grew up at
  home and in exile at the same time   or maybe at home in two
worlds   one inside the house and one outside the house

      i was brought up in a house where people spoke four
  other languages besides english   which they didnt speak much
in the house   and in the street i was a native american   if i
can borrow the american indian term   i spoke the brooklyn
language or dialect   whatever that was at the time   and that

was my native language and i spoke english the way anyone born
in my neighborhood spoke it   and inside the house i spoke a
variety of other languages   as well as a child can who learns
them from trying to eavesdrop the conversations that people are
trying to keep from you by shifting to another language   and
you learn them so well that after a while the people inside the
house expect you to speak them correctly and are somewhat
offended when you dont address them with the correct polite form
and think it shows a lack of respect   when the only forms
youve overheard are the intimate ones used by adult friends and
relatives to each other   but after a while you'd pick these up
too   and the point was
                              i was at home in both worlds   which
didnt often come together   so that i wasnt aware that i was in
exile   and i had no problem in either world   though there
was a clear separation between the two worlds   and even then i
must have been aware that there would have been a certain
difficulty in bringing the two of them together

          the world of the new york streets of the 1930s was
almost rural in our part of brooklyn   those tree lined
streets of boro park   were not urban or suburban the way we
know them now   they were sleepy maple and sycamore shaded
streets lined with two story wood and brick houses sheltered
under gabled rooves and set back behind small gardens and
windowed porches with little stoops   filled with lots of little
kids and small animals   and we lived around the corner from
the local police station   where one of my great childhood
joys was watching the policemen come out to start their shift
marching out two by two in their bright blue uniforms with shiny
brass buttons   and i used to go around every afternoon
it didnt rain and watch them come marching out   it was like
watching a peaceful little parade at about two in the
afternoon   just before the older kids came home from school

                    but inside the house things were different
and not so peaceful   it was like we lived in europe and
everybody was worried about the way things were going   franco
was moving on madrid   the nazis had control in germany and were
taking over austria   mussolini's fascists were invading

abyssinia   and everybody had heated opinions about what was
    happening and what roosevelt should do   and most of this
was brought home to me by pictures in the newspapers and most
    weirdly by a photograph i remember seeing in the sunday
supplement   that must have made an even greater impression on me
because i couldnt really read the newspapers   i'd just
learned how to read well enough to stare at the photographs and
    figure out the captions   and this one image i had to struggle
very hard to understand was a picture of these elderly italian
    ladies in black dresses crowding around an army truck and
weeping and throwing their gold wedding rings into a common
    basket so they could be melted down to buy bombs and tanks for
their heroic war against the ethiopians   who as far as i knew
had no tanks or planes and rode with spears and horses against
    italian armor   so this image of italian heroics made no sense
to me   and i remember struggling long and hard to understand it
and thinking then that my trouble in understanding came from my
just learning how to read   and i didnt know then that this kind
of not understanding was the beginning of my exile

        now there were lots of things i didnt understand then
        but i thought that was because i was a kid and i would understand
    them later when i grew up   one thing i didnt understand was
    the cheerfulness of the house i lived in with my grandmother
    and my three aunts   because everybody was poor in the 1930s
way and everybody was worried about the fate of the jews in
    austria poland russia   where we had relatives   but living
in boro park with my grandmother and my three aunts was like
    living in the middle of one long ongoing party   where
uncles and cousins dropped in continually to eat and talk and
    sing and play chess and cards and argue all night long   and
in the house i felt like i was in europe but i was happy there
    and in the street where i played tag with my friends or
marbles or hide and seek or went shopping with my grandmother or
    watched the big kids playing punchball   or even when i walked
with my aunt betty on the days she was out of work all the way to
    the open air market on 13th avenue   where the smells of
hanging cheeses salt cod and barrels of sour pickles were so
sharp they brought tears to my eyes   i didnt think i was
    in europe and there was no collision between my worlds

till one sunday afternoon in early december when i was
sitting on an ottoman in the living room of my aunt sarah's
   comfortable overstuffed house listening to the radio with my
aunt and my cousins when we heard the news of the japanese attack
   on pearl harbor and my two worlds seemed to come together
because everybody got very inspired   my cousin started jumping
on and off chairs to strengthen his arches so he could be a flier
      another cousin volunteered for the army engineers and my
   downstairs neighbor   the pianist from music and art   joined
the marines
            apparently jumping on and off chairs and eating lots
of carrots got my cousin into the air force because he wound up
   in italy bombing the ploesti oil fields and german factories
and managed to survive some twenty-four missions no one knows how
   while losing two crews along the way   so that he could come
      home to a partnership in his father's dress business at the end
of the war
            the japanese attack on pearl harbor was the
      inspiration for all of this   and i was excited by it like
everyone else was   you can hardly imagine the degree of
   excitement   and inside the house we all knew how dreadful the
   nazis were and the italian fascists but now everybody else knew
   and now we knew how treacherous the japanese were the way
everyone else did   how they were treacherous little yellow
   people with funny eyes and buck teeth who made loud shrill
noises when they were shot or bayonetted while americans died
with stoic barely audible grunts   they would say "ugh" and die
   heroically while the japanese would scream with lots of vowels
   before they died   which i understood was not so heroic because
this was a time when i wasnt in exile   this was the moment of
   union between the two parts of my life   my home and the street

      we practiced bayonetting people in the street   we imagined
we were all going to be drafted eventually   i was merely
   waiting my turn   all of my cousins were in the war   one was
an engineer putting a bridge across the rhine at remagen   the
   other was the flier and my downstairs neighbor was at okinawa
   everyone was doing heroic things   and back at home we
   collected scrap paper and tin and frozen animal fat for
explosives and waited to be called up   i had a map of the war

with pins and i knew all the cities that fell and the islands
i knew how we were slaughtered on wake island and trapped in the
kasserine pass and   i followed it all as though i was on the
    general staff

            but at a certain point   at a certain point in the war
after italy and germany had surrendered and the japanese air
force had been destroyed and the regular bombings had started
over japan   something odd happened   i used to listen to the
news on the radio every day   it was the beginning of summer in
1945   it was before the atomic bomb it was the time of the
incendiary raids   and i can still hear that radio report today
    "the rain of fire continues over japan for the thirteenth
    day"   "the rain of fire continues over japan for the
fifteenth day" because we were dropping fire bombs over japan
and i was a   smart little kid like all jewish kids and i
knew that the cities   of tokyo and yokahama had many wood and
    paper houses and i knew   that these flotillas of planes were
        dropping fire bombs and i   had an image of kids being
incinerated and i was beginning to have trouble sleeping

                now it was a hot summer and we all knew that
the japanese tortured their prisoners and disemboweled them
        but we were incinerating pet dogs   i didnt know then that
the japanese didnt go in for dogs   i figured they had little
    dogs and cats and old ladies   and the radio said cheerfully
every day "the rain of fire continues over japan for the twenty-
    third day   the rain of fire continues over japan for the
twenty-fourth day"   and theyd give you the number of planes
    the only thing they didnt tell you was how many little old
    ladies and cats

                one day i had a nightmare   i imagined an american
    bomber flying over new york and colliding with the empire state
building   and then it happened   the next day an american
    bomber flew into the empire state building and was stuck there
or part of it was stuck there for several days   and when it was
    removed it left a gaping hole and there were pictures of it in
the newspapers   and now i'm not sure it happened that way
        but the way i remember first i dreamed that an american bomber

like my cousin's b-24 smashed into the empire state building and
  got stuck there   and then i woke up and it turned out to be
true

          so this seems to mark the beginning of my exile   and my
  sense of exile was then beginning with an examination of what i
was exiled from   i was exiled from a certain kind of enthusiasm
        i remember there was a children's costume contest in coney
    island where the costumes were supposed to be based on a theme
  and the first prize went to a six year old in commando clothing
  with a blackened face and twigs on his helmet with a rifle and
bayonet called "dawn raid"
                              and this was a figure of a national
  allegory that celebrated innocent american violence   which was
    part of what i regard as the native experience   a
construction of images for which we have an unqualified
    enthusiasm because   they project a deeply satisfying sense
  of an "us" corresponding to a deeply threatening "them"
whoever   they may happen to be   and in both of which we
    thoroughly believe

              now people are often threatened   by circumstances by the
  uncertainty of the future by unemployment or war   but for the
    native experience wars are the most convenient because they
  provide us with a "them" against whose threat we become more of
    an "us" as they become more and more of a "them"   which
  becomes very other   as i remember from a wartime *new yorker*
    cartoon   now the *new yorker* is a sophisticated urban magazine
  thats celebrated for its elegant and witty cartoons   but this
  was the time of an intense national experience   in which wit
  plays a very small part   and this cartoon depicted a scene from
    the pacific jungle war   a platoon of american soldiers were
scattered along the ground firing into the trees that were filled
  with monkeys and japanese soldiers   and the platoon leader was
    shouting to his men   "shoot only the ones without tails!"

          now the humor in this seems to depend upon the very
  exaggerated sense of community and is the consequence of what ive
    been calling the national experience   and it was this
  hyperbole of community from which you always exile the other and
  from which i seem to have been departing as the war wore on

        i didnt lose my american accent   i didnt lose my
understanding of american pop   i could still eat hot dogs drink
    coca cola and go to the movies   i liked everything american
kids liked but i just wasnt as enthusiastic any more   and
there were doubts   that came up after the war
                                        suddenly the
    russians werent our friends any more   all through the war they
were our great friends and now they were dangerous potential
    enemies   for four or five years we sang "meadowland"   in
movies we watched as "over tall fields smiling came the youthful
    heroes filing"   and maybe they werent our great friends after
all   they were going to need veto powers in the u.n.   and
they were going to need poland and czechoslovakia and hungary
    it all became very dubious

        judaism always seemed dubious   the religion i mean   in
my experience it was a drunken hebrew school teacher
    drilling kids to pronounce hebrew in a hebrew school nobody
wanted to go to so you could take part in a dreadful ceremony
called a bar mitzvah to which people came to give you idiot
presents that you wanted to retreat from out of sheer
embarrassment because you considered them offensive
                                        you know i'm
    a dedicated atheist   when i hear jews say god i dont know who
theyre talking about   i should say "what theyre talking about"
        when you say "who" its even more shocking   the idea that
jews can address an omnipotent   an omniscient figure
        an all powerful all knowing being localized with intention
        and do this with reverence strikes me as preposterous but also
offensive   so my experience of that sort of judaism   raunchy
old men with earlocks who drank too much and read from books of
prayer that when translated into english became more offensive
    than they sounded when you only had a vague notion of what they
meant   this was my experience   from a few distant elderly
    relatives   and there were not too many of them
                                        my family comes
from a kind of left wing of the jewish tradition   the haskalah
    background   my grandfather was a hebrew scholar turned
spinozan   and there was a family of marxists   chessplayers
    hustlers   the part of the family i liked   so to me

jewishness was the sense of refusal   all these refusals   but
   i didnt put it together with what i was losing in the street

      the great enthusiasm   i was losing an enthusiasm and i
tried to cultivate a new enthusiasm   but i wasnt so good at
enthusiasm any more   i tried to become a marxist   i figured
marx might explain some of the social and political issues i was
   having doubts about   but i made the mistake of reading the
texts   and while they illuminated some things they sometimes
seemed dubious themselves   but mostly they made me lose my
enthusiasm for marxists   who were mostly stalinists then whose
discourse was dominated by the national interests of russia as
understood by stalin and the party   and i couldnt find any
sensible way of connecting stalin or russia to what i understood
of marx   and i didnt have any enthusiasm for the american
right   which was mobilizing then and all through the fifties
      for a while i tried to be a trotskyite because i thought i
had found a hero of opposition   at least he'd been killed
            but i wasnt too good at heroes   and trotsky was almost as
lethal as stalin but just didnt get a chance   so in a certain
sense i was a failure at joining   and i thought this is like
being anarchic and isolated   but somehow i felt comfortable in
   my violent disapproval of all the things that became meaningless
and went away from me   and i thought that maybe as a writer
   which i was becoming   that there was a different way of
looking at this   a different way of looking at experience
   even at religious experience

            now i'm not interested in god   but at onetime my
   friend jerome rothenberg and i were talking about starting a
press   with the aim of opening up a kind of counter
   conversation in poetry   a kind of counter writing   that
would stand in   opposition to the placid suburban
affirmative of the 1950s   when i hear the word affirmative
   action   i know it means something different now   but i
still think it means moving to the suburbs and having a lawn
            at the end of the fifties the idea of affirmation was
something that gave me the creeps   and   it seemed to me that
   the idea of a counter version a counter poetics and a counter
consciousness was what we had in mind   jerome and diane

and myself as we sat around in their apartment on 163rd street in
upper manhattan   and one of the first books   we thought to
publish was *tales of angels spirits and demons* an early book by
martin buber   because we thought it offered a serious
suggestion for a move away from the banal naturalism of our time

                we had a kind of affection for buber   he was a jewish
philosopher with a kind of existential strength and a way of
    addressing religious experience that made it   if not
persuasive   at least serious in a way my own sense of jewish
    religious experience was not only not serious but plainly
offensive   so we translated the stories in the book and jerome
    published it   and it happened   since jerome was in
correspondence with buber   that we learned he was coming to the
    united states and we had a chance to meet with him at the union
theological seminary   and since the stories we had translated
    were in german we thought the interview would also be in
german   which was all right but as it turned out buber's
    english was faintly accented and extraordinarily good   he was
    an intensely energetic little man who seemed to have learned
    english a few years before around the age of 70   and all
through our conversation   which had the gentle banality of an
old man speaking to two very young poet admirers of a work he
    had done when he was also in his twenties   there was one
question i wanted to ask him about his hasidic tales for an
oddly personal reason

                in terms that normally dont mean a great deal to
me   i come from a highly distinguished hasidic lineage   an
ancestor of mine   of my mother's father   bearing the rather
    marvelous name of wolf kitzes   was one of the closest
associates of the baal shem   and in writing the tales of the
    hasidic masters   buber had included two stories concerning my
    ancestor   who seemed as i read the stories to be mainly
distinguished by his absent mindedness   so referring to one of
    the tales   i asked buber what distinguished my ancestor
and the tale went like this

                the baal shem for some mysterious reason sent my
ancestor off on an expedition that required him to travel from

bialystok   or wherever he was in the indeterminate space
between poland and russia   to the shore of some sea   across
    which he had to travel for some time on board a ship that was
    caught in a storm and wrecked   and clinging to a spar he
    drifted ashore on what looked   like a deserted island
        exhausted and dripping wet he crawled up the beach
        creeping along in his soggy clothing   perhaps having lost
his stremmel   looking for some sign of human   habitation
    which appeared on a distant peak or crag   to be a lone castle
or manor   and he painfully made his way up the mountain to the
manor and rang at the gate   hoping to be admitted with the
    servants   but nobody came   the gate simply swung open
as did the great door of the principal building   that opened
into a grand central hallway   where wolf found himself at   the
    end of a huge table that seemed to stretch an immense distance
into the interior of the castle   which appeared so dark and far
    away that he couldnt make out the head of the table   and this
table was set with a heavy tablecloth shot through with gold and
    silver silken threads   on which were set wax candles in golden
    candlesticks and goblets of venetian glass among dishes of
chinese porcelain and knives and spoons of beaten gold   and
    there was food on the table in such measure it seemed as spilled
    from some great horn of plenty   nuts and fruits   grapes and
peaches and persimmons and melons he had never seen   and great
    trenchers   loaded down with roasted birds amid decanters of
    ruby wine
                but there was no one at the table   all the places
were empty   and he was afraid to begin to eat   so he looked
    around the room and up toward the other end of the table   but
    the head of the table that was dark before now seemed to be
enveloped in a sort of luminous fog out of which a powerful voice
    spoke
            "wolf   how is it with my people"
    and wolf   who was at first terrified to hear the voice
reflected and then answered as any true jew would
        "so how should it be?"
        "so be it" answered the voice and the light dissipated
from the head of the table   wolf lost his fear and took up the
    decanter of wine nearest him poured out a goblet full and
pronounced the blessing over it and proceeded to eat and drink

till he fell asleep at the table   when he woke up he was out
at sea again clinging to a spar in the water   from which he
was picked up by a fishing boat that carried him to the port from
which he eventually made his way back to bialystok or wherever
he had started from on the polish lithuanian russian border
        and he went to his beloved master the baal shem and reported
what had happened
                when he got to the part about the voice the
baal shem couldnt contain himself and demanded   "so wolf what
did you say?"   and wolf told him and the baal shem got very
depressed   "so what should i have said?" my ancestor asked
        "if you had told told him the truth he would have made it
better"

                now realizing that my distinguished ancestor could be
regarded as responsible for   the troubled fate of all the
exilic jews   and not imagining any other distinction he might
have had   i asked martin buber   how do you understand this
        and buber said
                "he had fire"
                and i had accepted this answer   i was talking with a
seventy-seven year old man   a jewish philosopher about an area
of experience in which i am to say the least   not expert
        but i know my relatives   and i've been thinking about this
a lot since then   and now i beg to differ with you martin
        you were wrong   the story says something else   and
martin buber didnt understand the story well enough because he
    didnt understand my family well enough   what happened was
this   my ancestor   wolf   in the spirit i know well from my
family   heard a voice   coming to him from the distance and
asking what he would have had to consider   if he considered it
critically as a serious religious thinker   an obscene question
        because any omnipotent omniscient boss knows how his people
are   and it is a stupid and offensive question asked by an
obscene power
                if you believe thats what you're confronting
        wolf   knowing that he wasnt confronting this obscenity
realized he was confronting his own delusional system   his
terrible fear and pain and hunger and thirst had gotten the
better of him and produced the delusion that he could ask for

his situation to change   and that there was some addressable
being with the will and the power to change it who somehow never
had the will or the power to change any of all the other
      terrible situations of the jews throughout history   my
ancestor realized the ludicrousness of this situation and turned
on himself the mockery that has become the true mark of the
jewish tradition by answering in response to the question
            "how is it with my people?"
            "so how should it be?"
and when he got back home and went to visit his beloved master
of the holy name and the baal shem tov asked him "what did you
say?"   he realized with a feeling of pity as deep as his love
that his master had so profound and excessive a love for the
numinous that listening to the story he could momentarily believe
in the absolute status of this event   and taking pity on his
great teacher he answered once again in the jewish tradition
      "so what should i have said" and left it at that   because
there was nothing he should have said   because there is nothing
you should say when youre addressed in this way   it is not an
address fitting for an exiled human being at all   essentially
you must refuse this question because it is imbecilic   and my
ancestor was distinguished by rejecting this degrading delusion
even in the optimistic power of his love for the baal shem
            because he must have realized that exile is inherently
written into the humanness of the jewish tradition   which is
      the human tradition   and my ancestor must have known this
and martin buber would probably have known this too if he had
thought about it enough   if he had connected it with all those
      situations that buber had to have thought about in this reading
of jewish history   in his immigration to israel   where jews
have become a nation and there is no exile   only a national
experience and a community that creates an exile for everybody
      who is not part of that national experience and happens to be
there   like the arabs   or the jews who are not part of that
      national experience because they havent yet learned how to hate
the arabs and dont want to behave like a nation   which will
      behave like any nation   or writers   who as writers cannot
afford to be part of any nation

STYLE

HENRY H. ROTH

When I was little, I was always surprised to see my father return home daily from work. I was certain he had better places to go. Mumbling to himself, dialing frantically and shouting orders into a phone, impatient with everyone around him, father seemed restless and never happy in our spacious apartment.

Eventually, a small unused bedroom was converted into an office where he paced back and forth like a caged animal, devising plans to increase the productivity of his thriving men's sportswear firm.

My older brother, Charles, and I never ventured too close to our father. And we were never invited into his new office. We did garner much loving attention from our gentle mother, but she was to die before she was forty. With her death, we lost our only ally.

Mother smiled a lot; father occasionally grinned but rarely smiled and never laughed because he considered the world serious business. He'd shake hands, bid goodnight, and march off to his lair, happy to be rid of us. I can't recall relatives or friends dropping in to visit our parents. It was a somber childhood. Charles always had great difficulty sleeping. And he'd keep me up late at night tossing out pessimistic comments about our chances of survival.

"Pop would pay us plenty to run away and keep away. Mom won't let him of course, so he can only dream about his master plan."

Now my father is seventy. I am forty. My brother is forty-six. Father calls me once a week for a briefing. Once every two months, he strolls over for dinner with his third wife, a timid lanky woman, with thick glasses, spindly legs, and a harsh voice, to dine at my cluttered apartment. As always father, though charming to my family, is mostly distracted and annoyed whenever locked in a family situation.

Years have passed. Charles is completely out of the picture. Father will tolerate no mention of my brother. Jailed twice for major financial indiscretions, Charles is about to be prosecuted in Denver on new embezzling charges.

I long to bring up my brother's name at our infrequent gatherings, but my family has been won over by the old man, who brings flowers to Laura and thoughtful toys to Tom and Gregg. Father would have a major tantrum if I revealed Charles' latest mess, and I'd be judged by all present as a cruel bully. So I grumpily make small talk and impatiently wait for him and his skittish wife to leave.

I rarely call my father. He never invites us to his apartment a few blocks away. Everything is acted out on his terms. We both appear satisfied with this relationship.

Laura strongly disagrees. "He admires you, but he can't say it or show it. You give him no easy openings."

I usually counter, "Look, I'm an assistant professor of philosophy. My fate is far better than poor Charles', but father can't possibly admire me."

"You're wrong."

"He'd never take the time to find out who I am."

"Your father's afraid of you."

"He fears no one."

"He's sure you don't really like him. And he doesn't know what to do about it."

"Oh, a man of action can always act out his feelings. Let's stop debating!"

She pursues, "He's old and he loves you."

I shrug, "Father always warned that you always get what you pay for."

She continues, "You circle each other like prize fighters? It's so sad."

I didn't respond anymore because if we keep sparring a real fight will ensue. Usually I pick up a book and begin to scan it. Laura makes a lot of noise stacking dishes into the dishwasher. The boys are asleep. Once I've calmed down, I'm proud and astounded that somehow I've come up with a family, a predictable life.

It's only by default that I'm the favored son. Charles' jail sentences propelled him out of the family chronicle. Father treated my brother as if he'd been an orphan who by good fortune lodged with us on Madison Avenue and eighty-eighth street. But when he erred, and for very good reason lost favor, Charles was banished forever from the kingdom.

Besides his vindictive wrath, father never accepted loss. Mother's death stunned him for several weeks. Then father pranced away from pain and sorrow blaming everyone for the violent cancer that galloped across her body. Father sued the surgeon; he accused the hospital staff of indifferent care. He lectured to Charles, then twenty, how mother had been devastated by his criminal antics. Father revealed how much mother worried about my daydreaming and refusal to admit there was a tough and lousy world out there.

After mother's death, we all lived an uneasy truce. Father kept writing checks to defray Charles' latest handiworks—slashed tires, busted school windows, and illegal sale of firecrackers.

I'd concealed my loneliness and excelled in school. It was a feat which did not impress Charles or my father. I would end up teaching philosophy in half-empty classrooms. Though appalled by my profession, father never severed relations with me.

Charles was never fortunate. He is a pain in the ass and many times I've wished he'd journey further than Denver. But he is my brother the only witness and true companion of my childhood. He was kind and protective of me. He is all I have of the past. I need him. Since father knew nothing of Charles' recent troubles, I have posted the bill for the defense lawyers who will fail my brother just as we all have.

Just after my eighteenth birthday Charles pushed open the bedroom door, flopped on my unmade bed, and pulled out a joint. I shook my head in annoyance.

"Don't be so negative," Charles squinted at me.

"Right," I said disgustedly, "and get your shoes off my pillow."

Charles was a chubby spoiled-looking young man. Pimples crisscrossed his wide forehead. He still looked like a rumpled teenager.

"You're not a bad kid at all," Charles admitted, "still, pop doesn't care much for you either."

"C'mon," I said nervously.

I couldn't wait for my last year of high school to end. By late summer

I'd be in a college far away from my joyless home. And be free of Charles' latest misdemeanors and having to bear father's new wife. Unhappy and uncomfortable being alone, father had married six months after our mother's death.

Mabel was a tiny bewildered woman who spent most of her time out of the apartment shopping or serving on committees. Father had strongly hinted Mabel was on the way out. We neither cared one way or the other. Father was very disappointed in this wife who yessed him to death. Father demanded acquiescence, but enjoyed some zesty combat to attain his goals. Charles was not surprised by any of father's actions.

"First mom, then poor Mabel! See, pop writes people off easily. He's a first-class hit man. Out of sight out of mind," he said bitterly.

I became uneasy.

"That's really taking it to the max, Charles."

Charles replied in a half whisper. "There's no room for love in him or anywhere he lives."

When Charles began to sob, I turned away. Then he ran out of the room.

With Charles more determined than ever to cheat others, shrewd authorities began to pay closer attention to him. Cursed with a sloppy thieving style, my brother was easily snared and dealt harshly with.

During my senior college year I flew home to join my father as glum spectators to Charles' first incarceration.

Charles, tiny and very frightened, was dispatched to Rikers Island for nine months by an oafish-looking judge in wrinkled robes. We darted from the rank-smelling Bronx courthouse and entered the first dingy restaurant we saw.

Father, already denying the event, and beginning to plot Charles' permanent exile, said nothing about what had just transpired. He stared furiously at his chicken salad platter. His hands twitched.

He shouted at me, "Now Charles is a jailbird. He must be very pleased!"

I felt dizzy, sipped my ice water, and hoped to wait the tirade out. But father's outburst was quickly over. Now he ate quickly. He left no food on his plate.

After I ate half my tuna-melt sandwich and drank the good coffee, I announced loudly, "I told Charles I'd stand behind him. He kept asking where you were, why you hadn't visited."

Father pointed a finger at me, "Your brother will hide behind you. He'll feed off you. And he'll steal. Don't be as fool."

"I'm not a fool," I yelled back.

"Good," he snapped.

People stared at us. We didn't care. My father was livid.

"I won't tolerate fools or criminals," he warned looking much older and weary and dangerous.

He left. Leaving me to pay the check and having to use more mundane transportation than his fat Cadillac back to Manhattan. Charles' future was clear. Father would be his failed son's hit man. Everything had changed. I would never return to my father's apartment. Father would remarry again. I would find a woman who loved me. My brother, who had no options, eventually headed west once released from prison.

I sat at the chipped table in the noisy restaurant and hastily scribbled a poem about my father, my brother, and me. I wrote it on a stained paper napkin my father had left near his empty plate. I could barely read my shaky handwriting. I was trembling. I knew the poem was corny and unfocused. Father would've mocked my sophomoric impulse. But it was the best I could do. It was the best I could ever manage.

Recently I saw my father walking along Madison Avenue. He walked briskly, never delaying half a step to admire a store window display or an attractive woman. He was as usual on a specific mission, and there was never time for stray considerations.

On a whim, I followed him. Then I noticed father was preoccupied; he didn't try to beat the light. He studied the faultless blue sky for a moment and patiently waited for the light to change again. He kept looking at his watch, but was daydreaming. He kept patting at his sports jacket as if reassuring himself he still had a heart. I called over to him. He walked swiftly away, pretending he hadn't heard me. Something was awry. Perhaps he was meeting another elderly woman. Deceit and betrayal had been added to the baggage. I was the child suddenly being granted insight and power that were always there for the taking. I kept calling out.

Finally, my father stopped. He was a little confused. I almost expected him to throw his hands up into the air.

"What's the big hurry?" I challenged.

He suddenly smiled. Since it was an unnatural grimace, it seemed to pain him. Still, he smiled again. Startled, I was sorry I'd pestered him.

"Well," my father confessed, "you're right. I'm running late for class. He coughed nervously.

"Class?"

"Yeah," he said sharply.

"What class?" I asked, in sudden annoyance.

"Fiction writing," he said.

"You're writing fiction," I almost shouted.

"I don't like the essay form," my amazing father declared.

"Oh," I said dumbly.

"Fiction is so much more open-ended," he insisted. "We read a lot of Chekhov and Babel. What great writers!"

I nodded sadly.

"I've written a story," he confessed. "I'm bringing it in today to class."

He patted the jacket again and reaching inside it pulled out a folder. Then he delicately hid the work again. I waited as I often have all my life.

"Class is over today," he blurted out. "The teacher is very professional. We're all beginners. He reads all our work out loud and we discuss it in class. Today my story'll be discussed."

He rubbed his dry lips.

"Congratulations." I tried to shake his hand but he pulled it away.

"Not yet," my father cautioned. "I want you to read the story. Invite me and Margaret over on Thursday," he gently bullied, and then instructed, "after the main course we'll have small talk and you'll go into your study and read my story." When my father snapped his fingers, I saw him years ago moving back and forth in his makeshift office, like a prisoner suddenly getting an idea and hurling himself across the room and fiercely dialing the phone number of some underling. And I resented his game plan this afternoon.

He said, "And we'll discuss the manuscript, over coffee and the chocolate mousse cake I'll bring from Dumas."

We shook hands on it.

Laura said cautiously, "Just be kind. Tell him writing a story is a romantic gesture."

"He often told Charles and me never to bullshit a bullshitter."

"I think he'd accept praise from you."

"And I think he may be daring me not to praise his fluff."

Before storming out of the living room Laura asked, "Why are you so furious, he wrote a story?"

Until Thursday I was in rotten spirits. I taught my classes indifferently and dismissed them early. I was impatient and short-tempered at home. I suddenly found my sons far too noisy. I resented Laura always taking the old man's side. She had real sympathy for the primitive power broker of my childhood. I slept poorly. I wrote a letter and sent a check to Charles, but I had no intention of flying out to Denver to be with him. And I wondered how different was I from my father, unwilling to ever be compassionate.

On Thursday evening he arrived punctually, bearing a bouquet of roses for Laura and baseball gloves for the boys, who dashed about the apartment spearing imaginary line drives. My stepmother, Margaret, sat down on the couch and began smoking. Father had once told me, sadly, that cigarettes were her only vice.

Father in an expensive light blue silk suit exuded self-confidence. This meeting was a done deal. There was predictable aimless conversation and drinks refilled, while Margaret eyes half-shut grimly smoked. Pollution was her sole contribution to any evening.

The game plan was to be appetizers, followed by prime roast beef and Yorkshire pudding. Then intermission until I returned with gaudy news about father's first attempt at fiction. I felt like an aged toddler, anxious to make awful mischief and able to contribute only negative news and sounds. Not even brave father (Laura's phrase) would be spared for what he dared to write. I felt distant from everyone in the living room. Tom and Gregg had drifted to their rooms and homework and whispering, and I thought of Charles and me in times of adolescent despair. Laura tailed my father like a wise nurse anticipating a great man's fall. Father sipping countless white wine spritzers was oblivious of problems. He was accustomed to applause and success, but I owed him plenty for the poem I'd written years ago lamenting the morning Charles was first locked up.

Father, ever impatient, roared, "I certainly anticipate better news from you about my story than what I just learned about Charles."

I was thrown off balance.

"I don't understand. What's happened?"

"Charles tried to kill himself last night. But of course he failed."

"You're disappointed?"

"Facts are always simple. Your brother never stops looking for the easy way out."

"Is he ok?"

"Aside from a bruised throat, Charles is the same," father said wearily.

"You spoke to him?" I asked still unsettled to hear father even say Charles' name after a dozen years of willful silence.

"I did not," he said, churlishly adding, "I did talk to his lawyer, whose fee I understand you paid."

"Why didn't you call me last night?"

"I don't know. And believe it or not, professor, I'm glad Charles didn't succeed."

"Of course you are," Laura interrupted.

Father did not bow out gracefully; it was not his lusty style.

He added, "None of us should be surprised by any of Charles' many failures."

Furious, I left the room to make sure the boys were getting ready for bed. Laura and Margaret were serving the appetizers when I strode away.

When I returned, Laura had put aside a platter of pâté and saga cheese on flat bread. Father had been eating nonstop. His suit was unwrinkled. I always considered him of average height, but occasionally, I correctly perceived how tiny and fragile he could appear to the innocent eye.

We were beckoned to the dining room by Laura and served excellent roast beef. I was not going to say anything more to my father until I read his damn story. "The salad is tasty," my father praised too loudly. I ate very little. Laura couldn't take her eyes off me.

As Laura and Margaret took the dishes away, father removed the manuscript delicately from his inside pocket and offered it to me. It was a graceful gesture, the second time in four days I'd seen him almost courtly.

Father tried not to look nervous. He certainly seemed thoughtful. That's his business look, I thought, the overconfident ambiance he loves to create, as an edge. Without saying a word, I turned my back and walked into the master bedroom and shut the door. I read my father's story standing up.

It was in the first person. The narrator in the first three pages was a boy of ten and in the last three pages the narrator was now sixty years older. The voice in both segments was perfectly believable. The piece was intelligent, carefully blocked out, ironic, and well done. I didn't dare sit down; I read it again.

The young boy was a mischievous bully determined to challenge a society that needs to be pushed around. "They expect it," the boy decides as he lies at will, cheats on tests, and charms his victims.

The narrator becomes a valued advisor to the President. He tells how he is honored each year for his intricate skills at lying and deception. He may even have once prevented a war.

He claims, "I am the natural result of the American Dream."

And he concludes, "How can someone like me ever be chastised or jailed or not be absolutely necessary?"

Every word has a weight and meaning. There was passion in the writing. It owed a lot to Hemingway and Sherwood Anderson. I read it a third time and was still impressed.

It's for Charles too, I thought angrily, but he'll never see it.

They all turned to face me when I came back. Margaret was now loudly chewing gum. Laura rocked back and forth on the couch. Father was flushed and attempting to judge my decision. He seemed uneasy and I was glad.

"It's good, it's very good. I was surprised."

Laura clapped her hands softly.

"But you're not happy," father said grimly.

"It's not your story that's making me unhappy."

"But you have a problem I can tell, damn it! What's wrong with it?"

"I just said it's first rate."

"Should it be longer?"

"You could tell more. There could be a few detailed scenes."

"Our teacher said if the voice is good, you believe it all."

"I do believe."

"Then what do you want?"

"Dialogue, too, more dialogue."

Father stamped his feet on the carpet. He was very frustrated.

"It's probably publishable in a literary magazine," I said.

"Which one?"

"I don't read them. But I'm sure it's in the ball park. Ask your teacher."

"I told you the class is over. The class is dead."

"That's a little dramatic," I smiled thinly.

My father whispered, "The teacher said it was the best story in class."

"I'm sure that's true."

"It was hard as hell. I'm an old man. Writing got me very tired. Let's have dessert and call it a day."

"Night," I corrected.

He didn't smile. Neither did anyone else.

After dessert, father yanked Margaret away. Both barely muttered good night. Father kissed Laura and nodded curtly to me. I strolled into the center of the living room and began cleaning up the cake crumbs.

Laura said coldly, "That was awful; you were so stern and unyielding."

She scowled.

"I treated him as I would any promising student."

"He's your father!"

"I'm his son. Much that I am is owed all to him."

"No," she said, "you were annoyed and a little jealous. You wanted to punish him, but he had skills you never imagined."

"What do you want?" I asked.

She pleaded, "Go after him, please. He was shaking."

"You're wrong," I said.

But I left the apartment and, once in the deserted lobby, swung open the entrance door and ran outside.

They had only gotten as far as the next block. Father was leaning against a parked Honda. His head was thrust up toward the pale sky. He was gasping for breath. Margaret was crying.

Both relaxed when they spotted me. Slowly, my father straightened up. He began breathing deeply and seemed ok. Margaret blew her nose several times, searched in her purse for a cigarette. Instead she came up with a piece of gum; but she seemed satisfied.

My father confessed nervously. "Too much wine, and meat. And then that killer cake. I felt queasy, wasn't my heart. Relax!"

He clearly wanted to ignore any other questions of health.

"I must apologize. I was pompous and tried to be the neutral reader. That wasn't fair."

"Forget it."

"You wrote a wonderful story, took chances with the narrative, and it held up."

"Look I admit I could do better."
Now I leaned against the car.
"Don't worry," my father said. Forlornly, "I won't write any more."
He touched my hand. I gripped his hand firmly. We both stared at each other in surprise. Margaret chewed her gum patiently.
"What grade would you give me, professor?"
"A."
"Not B + ."
"No."
"What about A–"
"A."
"Have I talent?"
"Oh, yes."
"*This* time I have talent, right."
I nodded.
"You were warning me, you gotta do it again and again to be a real writer."
"I'm not sure what I . . ."
He interrupted impatiently. "You were complimenting me. You just weren't handing me any prizes. You were taking me seriously. I appreciate that."
"I overdid it."
"You're probably a great teacher."
"I used to be, now, I'm not sure."
"No, you're a pro I see that."
Father was restless. His suit remained firmly pressed. His gray eyes were weary but clear. Father didn't even try to smile.
"It's late. C'mon, honey, I have a power breakfast at eight."
"Let me walk you home."
"No, don't be silly."
"Call a cab."
"It's only five blocks. Go home and teach philosophy," he ordered good-naturedly.
Father almost reached out to me again, but decided against it. Margaret walked slowly behind him. I followed them. Abruptly, my father stopped and permitted me to catch up.
"Here," he said peevishly, and treating me as if I were a panhandler, offered instead of loose change, six folded pages; then grabbing his wife firmly, he waltzed home.

FIVE POEMS

GEORGE EVANS

A DAY

It is a filled bowl, a wide-angle San Francisco from the streetcar
    above Dolores Park and my wife who has quit work to go to school
    and become a teacher has broken down
    and bought a new pair of shoes but we seem quite happy
    in the poorhouse

Iranians are streaking the Straits of Hormuz on little
    motorboats loaded with nuclear bombs and switchblades
    —the bombs will not work because Iran has no plutonium
    but I admire such innocence wishing we were all just streaming
    around rivers and oceans on water skis or rafts merely wishing
    to get even
            then visions of holocaust interrupt:
    visions of oppression, grief, terror and everything difficult
    about life—such as rent, direction, purpose, meaning—are
    erupting like human-sized volcanoes but I'm suppressing all of it
    for the sake of looking at the sky, looking at a man on the car
    who is looking at me and resembles a friend from years ago
    I used to run into on streetcars after work and take home
    and who is now dead from AIDS   but I can't stop looking
    and hoping, though I know he is dead and suddenly
    I would like to see him again more than anything

and take him home, whip on some Texas Blues,
throw a chicken in a pot or roll burritos
and joints so the three of us—our friend, my wife and I—
can go crazy with sound and call up everyone we know to come over
which we do, and they do . . .
                              how suddenly I'd like to see him
again and will suppress anything to believe it's possible it is
a typical day because I am always suppressing one thing
or another during the day for the sake of something and am yet
to hook into the fact that life is terrible, difficult and so
should be enjoyed as terrible and difficult but the facts
are yet to sustain me through one day though I am open,
and work to be open, very open in spite of distractions
and all the fears of distraction

Just give me an anesthetic, my brain pan aches,
    my hidden tumors ache, my histories are aching why
    do I like it pure and untrammeled—my testicles, no: my
    balls are aching my cock is aching my eyes my hair
    my fingernails: aching and I seem to like it because one day
    I want to wake up to a terrible world which will be my element
    and all the bombings murders lies and hellstorms be my home
    which will be home sweet home if I could only be miserable
    and like what is happening

Otherwise it's a typical day and I pay no attention to that
    which will crush and concentrate instead upon fruitstands
    in the Mission, memories of strolling Manhattan
    in a dream state entranced by everything the homeless the
    hustlers the suits and all the women
    who thrill me as no man could   I wouldn't lie
    even as social amenity about that about wanting them
    it's not the uppermost thing in my mind
    but it is something

EARL AND MADGE TAKE A TRIP

Cut every coupon and used every one.
Saved everything, even soap bits,
and didn't waste money on the lottery
which anyway Earl calls tax for the stupid.
Then we joined a travel club and went to Hawaii
(still caint *believe* that's part of this continent!),
Hong Kong where they shop all day and we spoke the language,
Bangkok where they got hundreds of filthy rivers and air
that you caint breathe but the cutest little kids, and . . .
well, I caint recall where all, but then—and get this—we
went to Japan for godsakes. Well I'm here to tell you,
Tokyo's one big pinball machine, but that Kyoto's the cutest
little thing . . . and all those people . . . they got Japanese
everywhere, just *everywhere!* They like us though.
They ought to, we keep em in noodles as Earl says.
Anyway, then they flew us down to Nagasaki for free
cause their trying to build up the tourists, you know.
I caint hardly begin to tell you what all, but
that place used to swarm with Christians?
They made a big point to show us the churches, and museums
filled with Christian things (they killed them all
of course, so all they *got* is things), but you know what?
I never *will* forget where they dropped that bomb.
Early one day they took us to a park and said:
There it is; that's the place.
And there it was, no bigger than your eye.
I looked up at the sky, and I looked down at that dot . . .
well I still caint believe it. And they were so nice!
Earl said: "You're gonna always be nice to somebody
can drop all *that* shit on a little dot."
I maybe might agree, but aint slept right since.
Come over the house. I'll show you things *you* won't believe.

TO WHO SAID HE WAS ONCE A PAINTER

I remember many things like times the electric
    got switched off plunging us into dark
    but we'd light nickel candles and make it
    on the rug those were times which inform
    the very sound of land yes and I
    wouldn't let her go for anything or one

    but she did go and I will say
    and always   that was

where I built the road
by what I know   and listened all night
and listened all day

to love's commotion

WHAT IT IS

Crossing the snow line we walk a white bridge
arched and frozen over a rushing river
and if we fall we get sucked into the mountains or snow,
sucked into other lights, other but similar things
happen at the track when you bet a longshot no good
beautiful losing horse then wind up weaving traffic home
but hit nothing though you stopped at the Turf Club
for a stiff one and floated out into the freeway space
thinking I am of another time, and it's *not* yesterday,
and certainly not today

but mainly all
that is yet to happen.

PUNITIVE DAMAGES

The owl rises   feathered moon

hooking black air rises

apart from everything   scandal, love, electricity

and all that

                            following blood shades

by wind-lift, drought, fire, shotgun and divorce

over mountain bones of earth
face spread
across darkness plucking mice from the field
changing air
from an acre to a mile
the owl pounds air then glides
its beginning and end
this bird which is no bird this lightning

                                        cracks and splinters

appears as contours on my skin
which is also lightning
and has been from the instant of my mother's pain

breathing me into this storm
and earth   its poverty and grace

                                        where only traces

                  electrical branches   crack the dark

exploding underground   under skin where the owl maneuvers

alone

endlessly

rushing nowhere
                  with purpose   while I'm jumping

ribbon tracks towards Ohio, Georgia, Idaho maybe, rocking
by wallboard shacks
which pass for the great house of America

with radio sounds, music rising
chicken bones rattle
rattle
goes a bastard with tire chains in the corner
of the car and says come here you little white
slick as a wet chicken
skin motherfucker
gonna show you
gonna make you,
                              but I fly over the great continent
breaking his eye slashing
at other tramps with half a pool cue on the railroad while I dream,
throwing one off near San Antonio
because he didn't understand about what is small
is miserable and death itself if you prod it worse
if you make light
riding the great American train
following its electric blood
reading Bo signs on cars and fences
blood in leaves
and the sound of iron scars
rib by rib where I first was last
breaking my own heart under moonlight
where a great owl floats
without family
and I slave without shame over bread

THREE POEMS

ANTHONY ROBBINS

RED STICK GHAZALS

1
Selves in exultation at the potential of indirection, as they lay
there together their feet began languidly copulating.

In that parish he was taken by fecundity and the cooking, but much
helmeted against golfballs and the constant heavy rain of oak.

Riot of cricket, forest of frog, mosquitoed muliebrity nightly,
the center of the universe has his ear. She is munching on it wetly.

I got up this morning, put my beard in sink. Outside streams
of diaphanous aerial plankton sortied off pine stump into sun-stream.

Inside, cabbage-pepper-onion-chicken-basmati rice soup. Outside
        the jay
maneuvers the acorn into a knot-hole where he can hammer it easily.

"Festooned"? A luxurious word in a time of precision. Heroic. But
by the time he acceded the wisteria was over.

2
The egress of polychlorinated biphenol drawn up into toe-white
fibers, root, bone—imagine a molecular morgenstern.

He lifted them gently over one of life's chasms, whispering, "The
shortest distance between two points is through music and lava."

When the air is cold the sky is blue from the north an Exxon stench
and the cat lurks in the bushes behind the beautiful impatiens.

A clear relation. Lack of respect for poesy quinsies environment:
When we don't listen we do things make earth withhold laurel.

Riding my bike it all comes back: all my life hounded by Schnauzers
of the merely and now by the Rottweilers of the filthy rich.

In relative fact the wino on the street is a clear relief. He has
at least the heart to wear his monkey on his sleeve.

READING, NOT SLEEPING

just before light the heaven
is dark self-engorged blue
expectancy   soon the champion
crammed with his accustomed
vacuity comes   I see what
the stars do not express   nothing
that has nothing to do with . . .
is it me   I think   stars did
shine on dreamers before
body or *soul* whatever dreams
may sans god sans internal sans
combustion have been . . . some of me
left behind the deep red rip of
beyond even the knight born of
love and stirrup   stars are tenseless
but embossed by my defect my
loss into patterns above my
seminary   Devil's Bagpipe
there there the Cloven Fontanelle
spewing back at me   a bright brain

blood   I'm dreaming I've been made
to love in a hollow
tree trunk   The treetop hole is notched
with fluted crenellations   How
beautiful the moon kiss that
awakens as it moves past
the hole with its cold astringent
clarity   how fell the
sun kiss that puts to sleep

THE CIRCLE GAME

There deep between the goal tines, his frozen aesthete's face
under his brown knit cap, passive, ataractic among
the spray of twisting features convened to make circular
and complete and full the sentiment of the colossal
public closure, of "arena," wherein frictions and excitments
are kindled because of the inching, imperceptible loosening
or tightening of the grounds: flux in field's nape, depth of grid
mark, sheerness of slope center to side, and acoustics,
weathers, grudges, surgeries, probation status, blood
toxicity. Not the formal, but another, shadow
government—not of taste or law, but of drugs and lawnmowers.
It is early and the franchise has been knocked out. "CORRO,
CORRIDA, CORRAL." Louder is one way of not saying
what it means. Silence likewise signifies that he has been
abused to the point where he can no longer be bonded.
If they lose, he will carry on his face the standard
heel mark of having worshiped. If they win, he will flow out
with the torrent, brick a car window, kick a wino, grab
tits, filch eye-level drinks in loud, fan-freaked bars. At midnight
he finds himself near home. He walks up to the room. Everyone's
asleep. It is cold. It smells of kerosene. He falls
asleep on a mat in the corner. He dreams a play that he means to kill:
down and out. It works too well. Corro. Corrida. Corral.

THE LAST OF THE MAIDU

E. M. BEEKMAN

"Damn it, I feel good," Wort shouted into the wind, "I think I'll lay off the Eskatrol this weekend and stick to this crazy sugar as the Maidu call it. Wild Turkey is still the best there is." He passed the bottle to Morgan and flipped the clip-on sunglasses up and down on his spectacles, but the strobe disoriented him and the MG began to weave.

"Watch it Bob, if a trooper catches us," Morgan said under the wind that cut across the windshield, slumped back in the shotgun seat as if in a recliner, his sunglasses slipping down his nose, two brown waves of hair fluttering over his ears like Mercury's wings.

"They call an automobile a wind vehicle. Boy, do I feel great since we left sea level. But it's the getting away you know, away from Sue and work. If I could just keep on going I'd be all right. It's a damned shame no Maidu communities are left because I'd join them, be their memory stenographer or whatever. I could stop feeling tired." The car bumped over a dead squirrel as if merely an irregularity in the road.

"Yes," Morgan answered, "yes, I know what you mean. Must be the altitude and the booze, but it feels as if I'm all lit up inside."

Bob Wort was a decade older than Morgan. He was a large man with a huge stomach that sagged over his belt like a solid awning. His girth made his mincing hands and feet seem incongruous, while his size forced him to buy loafers, have his clothes tailor-made, and made

127

getting out of his sporty two-seater a laborious excavating job. Wort ate to mock his father. Wort senior, the prosperous owner of a Ford dealership in Los Angeles, disapproved of his son. In high school Bob didn't do enough sports, in college he didn't study enough science and business administration, and after college he didn't show enough interest in selling cars. Junior went on to earn a doctorate in linguistics at the Berkeley campus of the University of California, an institution that now employed him. He specialized in the vanishing languages of California Indians, people his father considered irrelevant scum.

Wort's scholarship was excellence nurtured by hatred, while his linguistic salvaging operation began as an unconscious attempt to find something utterly useless to fly in the face of his father. His intellect was also his nemesis because Sue had showed him that his entire academic career was meant to irritate his father. At times his mental conflict translated itself into compulsive movements and tics that animated his face and insensibly energized his limbs, while on a professional level it meant that teaching was torture to him. He could only face classes on a steady diet of Eskatrol, a pill that was supposed to lift his depressions while tranquilizing his mania. Eskatrol and liquor kept Wort going and provided a daily reason why Sue, a psychiatrist he had lived with for over two years, could not leave him. There had been talk of marriage, though it would seem that only *he* would profit from it.

Wort's resemblance to Samuel Johnson went unnoticed until Morgan Evans mentioned it. Once revealed it was so obvious that even Wort consented to read the exemplary life and was soon repeating Johnson's mockery of the Scots, distrust of marriage, even the lexicographer's fetters and padlocks which, in the shape of a used straitjacket, he entrusted to Sue's care as Johnson had done with Mrs. Thrale. He felt kin to the great man's spleen and his fear of solitude, his love for drink, even found a motto for his own work when Johnson stated in Scotland: "I am sorry when any language is lost, because languages are the pedigrees of nations." But Wort lacked that intrepid core of moral stamina which gave direction to Johnson's difficult existence. Wort tried to whet his wit as well but had to concede defeat and be satisfied with memorizing responses to events California society would never entertain.

Instructor Wort met Morgan the janitor in his office one night, engaged him in conversation, and they'd been arguing ever since.

Became friends, even though Wort championed Chomsky and universal grammar while Morgan felt that Whorf and linguistic relativity was right.

"Whorf's warped. If you push his notion far enough you wind up with closed systems that are mutually incomprehensible to each other."

"Whorf's the Wallace Stevens of linguistics, and you only subscribe to a universal grammar because you've got to keep yourself going. American optimism, that's what it is, an optimism that hides terror because you can't stand being alone, either physically or linguistically. Chomsky is your mental Eskatrol."

"You stupid Welshman, you want to lock people up in linguistic cells and throw the key away. We might as well pack up and leave right now if that's true."

"It's far more realistic. Come on Bob, no one can ever know the real secrets and subtleties of any other person. It's like the metonymies of lovers, no one else can ever understand their special resonance. Imagination thinks it can invent them. But I doubt it."

Though linguistics granted certainty to his daily life, Bob Wort lacked a center while Morgan Evans had drifted onto a steady course plotted by the letter M and imagination.

At the end of the eighteenth century some of his ancestors had emigrated from Cardiganshire to Pennsylvania, the Welsh heartland of America. The Baptist farmers settled in Philadelphia and soon dominated the dairy business there as they had in London. Growing up in Philly, Morgan learned to fight, to drink, and to memorize his mother's favorite passages of verse and prose. He was burly, with a broad chest and heavy forearms, muscles developed from loading crates of bottled milk for his father. Tough and street-smart, Morgan's ambition to be the first Welsh pitcher for the Phillies lost out to his heritage of bawling bards. The Welsh have been called a marginal people, but Morgan took his liminal past as a sign of strength, the way a limb can be stronger where it was broken. King Arthur became his liege, he sailed with Prince Madoc to a new continent, he read the *Mabinogion* and returned again and again to that Celtic past of fluidity, a confluence of magical dreams and stirring reality before the Teutonic onslaught that brought certainty and precision. What Wort measured Morgan dreamt.

Morgan's mother, Mona, became purblind at the age of forty, and after dinner Morgan often read Welsh literature to her. From her dim world of milky shades the son remigrated his mother to a bright realm of vivid colors, lovingly noted details of animals, hills, and flowers, back to a circumspect world intimately known, where nature and the supernatural were at ease with one another. Mona asked her son to help her grow herbs and flowers in window boxes, and he had to describe them to her in detail so she could gauge their progress. By the time she died Morgan was of age. She left her son with a finesse of vision which disclosed to him the spell of reality that only enhanced the dreams language had fostered. The Welsh gift of placing a natural gem within a collet of words allowed Morgan to negotiate with ease from the realm of fact to the land which is both of and beyond reality. He became a penumbral man, and one contented, for in this region ideas become material and walk.

On his way to Evangeline's home in Lafayette, Louisiana, Morgan stopped in Mobile, Alabama, and made a pilgrimage to Fort Morgan on Mobile Bay where the Daughters of the American Revolution put up a plaque in 1953 to commemorate Prince Madoc's landing. Prince Madoc discovered America in 1170 and is said to have left a nation of Welsh Indians. Properly speaking the States should be known as Madocia, and it was through the latter continent that Morgan trekked, fully aware that he was moving through a geographical grid of the nation but also pleased to know he traveled through that other region behind his eyes. He was harmonized by it.

The Welsh Indians were never found because the white man allowed only memorials in the names of states, cities, and rivers. Yet the Indians had trekked onto pages of books, and since for them time was like a glass marble without demarcation of tenses but clearly present in its opacity on all sides, Morgan felt their kinship with the early Celts, for whom time was also fluid as memory, a different order created by the imagination, when a word is more potent than history.

In 1796 John Evans reached the earth lodges of the Mandan Indians who lived along the Missouri. Though they were not quite bearded, blue-eyed, and red-haired, the Mandans were very fair and had light hair that turned gray. The bullboats they used to cross the Missouri were remarkably like the coracles of the Welsh, and they had the unique gift of being able to make beads from blue glass. Mandan women were known for their beauty, friendliness, and amiable chatter which was not even silenced while they made love. Lewis and

Clark wintered among the Mandans in 1804–05, built Fort Mandan on the banks of the Missouri, and witnessed their buffalo dance when the old men were enjoined to have sex with young women who stood there naked inside robes of skins. The last of the Mandans died in 1837 during a smallpox epidemic, and so the entire nation had vanished from the prairies to take up lodging in the underground village of the dead.

In 1806 Lewis and Clark came among the Flathead Indians in the Rocky Mountains. The Indians flattened a child's head from birth until its profile formed a straight line ascending like a hypotenuse from the tip of the nose to the center of the skull. Lewis noted down a brief vocabulary of their language because their gurgling speech sounded like Welsh to him. Or had the Yucatán Maya once traveled to the great mountain chain in the heart of Madocia? They too admired such sloping beauty. There was a link. In 1595 Sir Walter Raleigh claimed Mexico for his Queen because, in fact, that realm was the Empire of Madock, settled by Welshmen. Edward Thurlow had known this before Raleigh. In 1568 he came to free the Mexicans from Spanish tyranny because the Mexicans were like his own flesh and blood. The beauty of the Mexican women was proof. "Fashioned for love," the "Ancient British Beauty" and their "Welsh Pedigree" could be traced on "their fine, round, apple smooth countenances, and fat, plump, cheeks and bodys."

George Catlin learned to paint in Philadelphia and became famous for his paintings and descriptions of the Mandans. He was convinced that Madoc's people had made a landfall where the Mississippi disembogues into the Gulf of Mexico, although it may also be possible that the Prince had entered Madocia in Florida, that peninsula where the only flowers of note are pink flamingos. Morgan never tested his harmony against the crudity of Florida's Gold Coast, but preferred to follow the route of William Bartram's magic travels.

Fellow Pennsylvanians, John and William Bartram were very much alike in their dedication to nature, baroque style and thought, and intrepid independence. But the son was also a poet. Morgan knew some of William's pages by heart. He could easily recall "the daughters of the sun" who lived on a solar island in a labyrinth of bogs and swamps as if a Merlin were protecting them from sullying. Exhausted Creek hunters had been fed oranges by these wondrously beautiful women who told them to be aware of their ferocious husbands. And the hunters were obsessively tormented by this paradise island clearly visible at the horizon of their fingertips but which, when reached for, dissolved tremulous and slow like a lazy Fata Morgana. This fabled island was near St. Mary's River, which has its source in the huge Okefenokee Swamp that spills over both sides of the border between Georgia and Florida. Swamps are a dangerous attraction.

On the train to California, coming after Evangeline, Morgan withdrew to that Madocian pastoral when Bartram came upon the Cherokee maidens in North Carolina. Amidst magnolias, azaleas, Philadelphus, and surrounded by gentle hills and diamond creeks, the Cherokee beauties were picking strawberries among gleaming knolls bestrewn with flowers. Around them flocks of turkeys and deer darted like shriners across the glaucous meadows. While Bartram the Quaker spied on these Elysian Fields, nature won over reason and he went down to join them. After the tumult had died down he was allowed to sit, and he ate strawberries with the Cherokee colleens in the vale of Cowe. Rocked by the rail Morgan stilled the scene, watching the Indian lips enclose the ruby fruits, a pacific joy sparkling with innocence and beauty. And when the Quaker poet mounted again and rode off slowly and surely blue, perhaps he knew that America's grave was dug in these strawberry beds and those flecked fragrances can only ripen again in Madocia.

Bartram's daughters of the sun and the strawberry girls were kin to Melville's Marquesans who reclined naked in island groves, adorned with floral jewelry, idle. Melville's Faraway delicately eating a "love of a fish," smoking her pipe, conversing with her "labial melody" like a trilling bird, was like Rima in her green island mansion, innocent of the death that struck its sails in the bay. Faraway playing a flute with her nose, or standing nude in the head of a canoe with her robe billowing behind her like a spinnaker, a nutbrown and sunlit body carved golden against Pacific blue. All sisters, all doomed.

Sharing an apartment with Evangeline in Oakland, Morgan mourned for Madocia. He was content being a janitor since it was a labor of no consequence to anyone. It left him time to walk his idea, to be a custodian of something more than dust. Evangeline did not approve. She wanted him to *be* somebody, to *make* something of himself. He was smart enough, had a college degree, read books, wrote stuff about

Indians, was good-looking and polite. Morgan was weird, but perhaps a job with the Bureau of Indian Affairs . . . It was the one time he exploded. Evangeline was two feet off the floor, dangling from his right fist, his left cocked. His mind already saw her mouth a smashed fruit with white lips mottling the red, and when it registered he opened his fist and let her drop. She crumbled onto the cocomat, and with his shoe he swept her long brown hair aside and looked into her face. He had dropped her in time. She was not hurt, just white with fear and her eyes black with hatred.

This was the Cajun girl he had traced back from a finishing school in Philadelphia to Lafayette in Louisiana, to a bayou, to a swamp. Her father had made good money as a timber merchant and was proud to descend from the original Acadians who the British had deported from Nova Scotia. Their country of origin may have been Acadia, but Morgan thought it more likely that it came from acadie, a word in the language of the Micmac Indians, meaning "fertile land." Evangeline had discovered talent on her body and tanned it, trimmed it, stroked it, and offered it to commerce. Their fights energized a zone of Cajun hate, with Morgan often refusing combat, intent on strawberry fields, Polynesian mermaids, and Madoc disappearing into that large Indian continent. His paycheck did not suffice for her training, he was a hindrance to her modeling career, she hated his guts, he was a Richard Burton of the slums.

"Are you going to marry Sue?"

"I don't know. It'd be nice to have my own private shrink, and if I had to divorce her she makes enough money on her own so that she doesn't have to sue for alimony. She doesn't want kids either. Too busy. Which is the truth. I don't know. And how about you and Evangeline?"

"That's finished. She moved across the bay and has found an apartment in San Francisco. That talent agency is really getting her some work, might even get her some commercials. Last week I moved the last of her stuff out of my place and brought it to her in a U-haul. You know what that idiot did? She painted the whole place black. Black, I tell you. It's not a large place, really like one long and narrow room. It looks like a goddamn gondola."

"Maybe she'd better see Sue. Did I tell you? After my grammar and dictionary is finished and I have tenure, I'm only going to do Indian death tales and descriptions of their spirit land, *kul m k dom*, and their ghosts or spirits, the ones they call darkness people. Sue doesn't like it at all. She says that it's not particularly healthy for a depressive personality. But she can go to hell. You say I look like Samuel Johnson, but I'll never equal that man. But maybe I can be a Boswell to the Maidu."

Morgan looked at Bob, searching his face for the tic that would indicate he was entering a depression. But Wort laughed.

"Bit my tongue, damn it, better sterilize it. Pass me the bottle, will you? Aren't you glad you came along?"

"It's a hell of a long drive," Morgan noted, "where are we anyway?"

At the next sign Wort saw that they had gone too far.

"We're in Paradise damn it. Completely missed the turnoff. Now I've got to turn around and drive all the way back."

"And that's just for today, right?"

"Yup, just to Oroville. Got to get up early tomorrow and drive another eighty miles or so. Then we'll stay for the night and drive all the way back on Sunday. But I don't care because I hate to go back."

It was already dark when they drove into Oroville and looked for the house of Dixie, a middle-aged woman who some years back had helped Wort find informers. Dixie was Indian and Irish, she'd lost her husband during the war in a logging accident near Timbered Mountain. They ate, which dimmed their glow somewhat, and then sat by the fire with the Wild Turkey. Dixie sat in a rocker with the case of Bud that Wort had brought next to her.

Morgan was aware that when he drank it did not make him drunk but enhanced a glowing effortlessness, a cool joy, like a winter sunburn. As if he had draped his skin from a nimbus which floated over him like a parasol, keeping the worst rays out. A luxation which had left the impostors Wort and Evans in Berkeley, to give these levity brothers a chance to rise to the mountains of the Maidu. Things were possible, no restraints, no embarrassments. But he had to ask about Oroville.

And Wort told him about that summer some sixty years ago when sheriff Webber was hauled out of bed to arrest a savage. Two miles from Oroville he aimed his flashlight at the last wild Indian in North America. Not even a Welsh bard could have imagined a sadder dirge. The last of the Yahi was held at bay by dogs in the corral of a slaughterhouse, emaciated, his hair burned short to indicate his mourning, the last of his tribe, speaking an unknown tongue. The Indian left Oroville on Labor Day and spent the last five years of his

life in a museum of anthropology on the Berkeley campus, in the end
dying from tuberculosis because he was not immune to civilization.
He died a stranger, for the name Ishi he went by meant no more than
"man." No one ever knew the real name of this Ishmael exiled to a
modern wilderness near the Golden Gate. One of his favorite phrases
in English was "evelybody hoppy?" And though he taught his crafts to
the museum people, he never told them about the past he had left that
August night when, by disclosing himself to the white man, he had
committed a kind of suicide.

"You have to remember," said Wort, "that the twenty-one nations
of California Indians lived in very distinct territories which to us seem
very small. They spoke twenty-one different languages, and there
were around a hundred and thirteen dialects. Ishi, for instance, did
neither speak nor understand Maidu, even though his Yashi nation
bordered on the land of the Maidu. They lived in a small world, but it
was one they knew intimately, and they had no desire to travel outside
of it. The Yahi were not really fierce warriors. But they resisted
aggression, and that made them ferocious savages. The white settlers
called them the Millcreek Indians or Digger Indians. In those days
'digger' had the same force as 'nigger.' The Maidu were afraid of the
Yahi, but in 1864 some three hundred Maidu were hung, shot, or
scalped by white vigilantes, because they were accused of Yahi crimes
and because they were far easier prey than the Yahi. There are more
ghosts than acorns in these damn mountains."

Dixie lifted the pall. She wanted some fun. She made Wort recall
stories about Coyote, that ubiquitous trickster of the North American
Indians. The Maidu called him W pa, and most of the tales told how W
pa managed to have sex with as many females as possible. He went to a
dance where Brush Crane, Blue Jay, White Root, Shitepoke, Tad-
pole, and Kingfisher were singing, and Coyote went three times after
the most beautiful woman there and got her, only to discover that each
time he had slept with Frog Old Woman, his own wife. Or the time
when he used the stink-ant orphans for an elaborate deceit so he could
sleep with his mother-in-law and begot a whole litter on her during
the night, but the next morning she threw all that offspring in his face.
On another day Coyote made female genitals out of the aromatic l kbo
root and attached them to his body, while he pretended to be an aging
woman. He put his prick in a pack basket and disguised it as an infant.
When the women he was after told him that the child looked weird,
Coyote said that the little manchild had fallen on its head and the

accident had caused its head to swell. Taking pity on the two ugly things, they let the disguised Coyote sleep with them, and during the night he sprinkled sleeping powder on their faces and had his way with all of them.

As in the legends of other Indians, the Maidu W da could die and come back to life again. The stories' limpid narrative style erased boundaries, creating a magic zone where chance and necessity were interchangeable. It was like a lucid stream that presented ordinary pebbles as bright jewels but that also showed that a severed head rolled along like any other rock. There was the hunter who heard the white owl sing and went crazy. While he danced a crazed jig he began to eat his body, first his arms, then his feet, then his legs, his entire body, until he was only a head rolling around and he frightened his people away and he had to live from hunting small game. And that was how the world knew craziness. Or Coyote's strange encounter with the Devil, who refused to talk to him. When Coyote kicked him his foot got stuck to the Devil, as did his hand when he hit him, but the Devil just kept on fishing and dragged Coyote along because he wouldn't let go. Coyote yelled that he would stab him with his prick, and the Devil said go ahead, and so his prick got also stuck, and Coyote died while the Devil kept on humming his Devil song.

But Dixie didn't like frightening stories in the flickering darkness of her living room. She popped another can of Bud and repeated funnier tales about the insatiable Coyote who could never get enough of what a woman's got between her legs. And Dixie laughed, and the three of them drank, and then Dixie sang softly and out of tune until she was humming to herself. Wort said that he admired the freedom of the Maidu and betrayed the intellectual's envy of frank earthiness which can only remain so when it is not known as such. Though drunk, he did not reveal the bizarre skits he put on for Sue, using his manic phases to excuse license. Sue thought they were revealing. But he did mention to Morgan that he had joined the students and their free-speech movement, how he had carried a placard on a long pole with the Maidu word k s on it, which was their stongest term for the male member. Abuse from the spectators was directed more at him and the strange word than at the other demonstrators who lofted more familiar ones.

Dixie thought both the company and the beer had gone flat and went to bed. Her guests slept in sleeping bags in the living room. Morgan listened to Wort snore, his chattering lips almost planting kisses on the tote bag that contained his tape recorder and legal pads. He used it as a pillow. What a job, Morgan thought, to go and find an expiring language, transcribe stories, legends, lore, a religion. A salvaging job. If Benjamin Lee Whorf was right that a language reflects a particular reality, then the Maidu lived an existence of flowers, happy copulation, and had a keen and precise knowledge of their natural environment, which they saw as boundlessly circumscribed. And they showed the Indian's characteristic ease with matters mystical or magical or supernatural, not without a touch of fear, but not without familiarity either. And when he dreamt that night in Oroville he was reaching for a Madocia that faded to a present reality of a head eating its body, singing a night song, angrily plucking at flowers and plants which grew through its skull, its hair cropped by fire, craving acorn mush, its mouth mounted by a prairie wolf.

The next morning they got up early and left for Paynes Creek, up Route 99, then down a back road to the east. The effect of altitude was now even more noticeable, and Morgan felt giddy as if drunk on air. They had entered Maidu country. Slopes and bluffs against a peerless blue with a dulcet light that lacquered everything in sight with a high gloss. And it may have been the altitude or it may have been the booze, but both men saw everything far more clearly than they had ever by the bay, as if they had been finally fitted with the proper lenses and saw the world for the first time.

Morgan asked Wort to tell him the Maidu words for things they saw around them, and the words were as inevitably right as when Adam went through the garden and named it. The words seemed better than English and priceless like antiques, not because they were old but because they were better made.

"Why hasn't somebody written the poetry of names?"

"You're nuts."

"No, I mean it. The words you mentioned or the names on this map. This morning we've gone by Chico, Paradise, Vina, Los Molinos, and Red Bluff. If we keep on going on this road we'll pass Mineral Summit and wind up on Lassen Peak, while further to the right is Honey Lake."

"The Maidu maintain that the white man stole that name from them. And by the way, I'm Bap now. That's their way of pronouncing Bob. We're over five thousand feet. My Mary went to school in Quincy. O I love that woman. I had her mother first, but she died, and

Mary felt it her duty to continue feeding me. She's the best informant I'll ever have."

"You people should come up with a better handle than that."

"She had no children. She was married to George Meadows, a white with some Atsugewi blood in him, a tribe the Maidu call Snow People. I've known her for eight years now, and she has been patient as hell with me, talking into my mike, getting other people to talk to me too. Even a shaman once. He's dead now. I never quite figured out what he said. Mary Meadows is the last to know Maidu fluently. Learned it from her mother and was determined to keep it alive. But she has no children of her own to pass it on to, and everybody around her has less and less Maidu blood. Her stepfather was white, and that's how she got to learn white. She also went to a white school in Clear Creek, and when she went to high school in Oroville the stagecoach driver tried to rape her, but she turned his own shotgun on him. She started that trip in Humbug Valley and had to cross the mountains to the town where Ishi appeared. You'll hear the craziest things around here. Her uncle had a crooked arm all of his life from a Yana arrow that hit him when he was a kid. She had another uncle who was an opium addict, and her white stepfather panned gold on the Mosquito River. Her real father told his children Coyote stories when they went to bed, and he played for them on his elderberry flute and sang Indian songs. I've got it all on tape."

To go on like this, running the MG on something other than gasoline, going up and up, past timber, past time, to a snow redolent with rubies.

"They call a bog like that there pak n."

Morgan looked at the disarray of skeletal trunks mired in black water that was edged with tule and leafless birches. The way it should be. Not a sun island in a swamp, but a dead bog in a solar meadow.

"They call this autumn season semenkit, the time of acorns. The Maidu were never farmers because nature provided abundant food. They made cone-shaped baskets from birch and bunch grass and filled them with the six edible varieties of acorns and with wild currants, manzanita berries, elderberries, black-, rasp-, buck-, and gooseber- ries, pine nuts, wild parsnip, bulbous roots of a variety of Queen Anne's lace, wild grapes, and white clover. They hunted such small game as ducks, geese, rabbits, and gray squirrel, relished a grasshop- per stew, and roasted earthworms threaded on a green twig."

The MG turned onto a dirt road, and after rounding a curve they saw a modest house built from buff pine boards, unpainted, etching its profile sharply against the turquoise noon. Bap parked the car, and when he came up to the door a woman stepped into the sun and embraced him. Though past sixty, the skin of her face was smooth and nutbrown. Her head was larger than her body warranted, the dark hair pulled back from her face into a tail. She kept her head tilted up with a proud thrust of her chin, the curved nose flanked by the high cheekbones which were emphasized by two deep furrows which grooved down to her straight and thin-lipped mouth and stubborn jaw. Mary Meadows wore glasses. She had a simple calico dress on, short-sleeved, with umber floral designs on black. Her arms were muscled and firm. Her voice was light, and she smiled readily.

This was the last of the Maidu. Not a fabled warrior but an ordinary Indian woman, aging, nearsighted, with an engaging laugh and a measured warmth. Custodian of her mother's tongue.

Wort seemed to have reached back to his youth despite his Johnsonian girth, a lighter mass now, laughing, tossing Maidu words back and forth with Mary, his glasses flashing. Sue could not have seen him like this very often.

Wort had brought Mary some yards of cloth, canned goods, a case of beer, three bottles of bourbon, and several bags of groceries they had bought in Paradise. When Morgan helped him bring the goods and their gear into the house, Wort told him that he had to work and that Morgan better amuse himself with Lena, Mary's niece, who was feeding Gerber to her infant son in the kitchen. Lena could not have been older than early twenties, plump, shy, with a soft smile and a round face. Wort took his tools into the living room, poured Mary a beer, and began to explain to her that he had to check his phonetic transcriptions of earlier tapes, record more glottal stops, perhaps add some more reminiscences if she would, and verify dictionary entries. Perhaps they might even get into something about the k kkini, the benevolent spirits, or anything at all about kul m k dom or dark country, also called the above meadow.

Morgan walked through the sere grass around the house. There was nothing else on the plateau except a tarred toolshed and utility poles. This was acorn time. Acorns were to the Maidu what huckleberries were to the Iroquois. The acorns were cracked and shucked, the kernels pounded and winnowed until a fine acorn meal was left. Then the bitterness was leached from the meal with the help of cedar boughs, and you could taste the cedar even after the cooking stones had turned the meal into mush, even after it had been wrapped in maple leaves and baked. He felt dizzy, as if his entire body had been sucked down to the pit of his stomach. Would Madocia die with him? Should he cease his custodial care, join a talent agency, live in a Venetian coffin, go with the flow and drown? Boswell had it easier: he was saving something concrete, committed to snatch wisps of sound from the past and register them. But Morgan was, as Wort had told him, h kitsa, lonely by nature. It would be good to have nature dictate your days, have that inexorable ritual order your solitude. It is easier to be alone when you're looking for sokom roots, when you gather attacus cocoons to make the shaman's rattles, when you fashion twigs of the service berry into arrows for small game, or when you're fishing for trout and salmon in the streams. Bring back branches of the pepperwood and whip the sick house to drive out Bad Coughing Man. Look for the redbell and the wild pansy, fill a basket with the bark of the cascara buckthorn to soothe stomach pains. Have a headband made from yellowhammer quills. To live that life needed perspicuity, but you always knew which task you had because it depended on the way things looked.

Softened by the setting sun the fierce sky was turning mountain blue. Skeletal trees rattled in a breeze. A penumbral man must live in his head, for he can't claim any country of origin and must collect his dreams as wages. Boswell was finished. He came out and called Morgan back to the house. Mary and Wort laughed about the things they had shared, and Morgan thought it peculiar to be jolly at a wake. Lena had started dinner, and Mary went to help her. Wort and Morgan drank some bourbon and went outside to watch the sun go down. Wort's large body disturbed the pageant.

"Jesus, I feel good. I'd swear you could drink this air. Feel the nip? Mary said there'll be some hoarfrost tonight."

They ate dinner, and for dessert there was shortcake topped with the frozen strawberries Wort had bought in Paradise. The men drank more whisky, and Wort rediscovered his mania. He whooped and hollered, bandied snatches from Coyote stories, while Mary chuckled and bobbed her head up and down. Lena smiled and looked at Morgan.

"She thinks you're handsome," Wort shouted at Morgan, "and soon k will come and the pass will be closed. But spring will come after. And the Maidu have the loveliest festival when things turn green. They sing and dance at the w da. Tell him Mary."

And she told him that when the wormwood looks tall the w da is held, that when the dogwood blossoms they hold the w da. And the women rub wormwood on each other and they dance and they sing and tell Coyote stories. When the dogwood blooms and the wormwood stands tall. And they sing a bear song and they sing a coyote song and things are green and the sky is blue again. And beflowered they dance and they sing w da lul, j myni lul, that is the rite of spring lul, when flowers bloom lul. And Wort got up and hoisted Mary to her feet and he began to shake and shimmy and shouted the spring song and his informant pealed, their spectacles flashed, Wort shook the walls, and the dishes rattled on the table. The child began to cry in the other room and Lena went to soothe him.

"Now we are five," Wort bellowed, "and five is a sacred number. And h hla is a badger, and h j is to follow, and h jwito is to fuck or what is called follow your other one in. And Coyote got his prick stuck in the Devil. And goddamit Morgan, this is it. There is no more left. W da lul. Fetters and locks." His body twitched and his glasses were blind with vapor.

"Crazy sugar they call this. Sue lul. Spring isn't good for me she says, makes me want to kill myself she says. I'm not a nature boy and I had to have Mary show me all the words, I mean the plants for the words. I better stick to darkness people. They say that flowers and whistling attracts the spirits. Evelybody hoppy?" He hugged Mary and told her he loved her and begged her pardon for using her. Lena looked at Morgan and beamed.

When the Wild Turkey was gone Wort stretched out on the sofa and pulled a blanket over his naked face. His damp glasses were on top of his legal pad. Mary had retired to her room off the little hall, and Lena and her boy slept in the narrow room next to the kitchen. From under his blanket Wort mumbled to Morgan that he felt like a criminal and that he was glad he'd be miserable when they'd arrive in Berkeley the next night after the long and tiring drive.

Morgan snugged the sleeping bag around his body and listened to the house squeak. Wort snored. Through the window came the light of the harvest moon, a light the color of the boards on the outside walls. Morgan shrugged off his sleeping bag and got dressed again. He stole to the door and tiptoed outside. No doubt, the moon had built the house. The toolshed had vanished in the shadows. He searched with his foot for stones. He found a pebble and held it in his palm, a Maidu fetish-stone to get him through some time. The moon would occasionally light on something, make it dart like the little shiner fish in the creeks. He whistled and hoped for flowers. There were no more w das. It was only a text now. Near the bog in the mountain meadow the salt tule prospered. He wished he could recall going to sleep while an ancestor played an elderberry flute. He scuffed up some dirt powder and felt his dead parents near. His blind mother who had taught him to see nature, the father who got tired of milk bottles, retired, and died within a year. Evangeline living in blackness. And then Bartram occurred to him, and for a shining moment he rode with him through incarnadine fields, scattering turkeys and deer, and saw them once again sink lunar chips into the rubies flecked with gold until the tooth meat and the fruit could no longer be distinguished.

Morgan stole back into the moonbox. He stripped down to his shorts and teeshirt and heard her behind him. She peered around the doorpost, wondering. He took a step toward her, and she widened the space for him to enter. The infant boy slept and made a noise like soft and warm mudbubbles bursting. She was plump and soft, and the darkness beamed. Nothing dramatic, just entering a warm smile. No passionate ferocity but a hushing mouth near his ear. And he followed himself in, into a docile stream tepid from a long afternoon of sun, and he hoped to wiggle in the shallows as a fish when spawning, dart like a shiner, leap like a salmon. But he could not, and Morgan retreated from this sweet normalcy, this kind dream, this fulsome night.

Back in his bag he wished it did not bother him. That to his left yet another world, yet another language was sleeping toward death. Mary was in good shape, to be sure, but she was aging, and when she fell silent her words would be gone forever. Except for Wort's grammar, but that was hardly a substitute. Another world extinct. And if time is organic, as the Hopi believe, then a time would decompose with her. To flourish again perhaps? But language is not a body of atoms that, after annihilation, recombine into another energy. When Maidu died no other speech would presently bloom on the shores of some remote and frozen Asian sea.

Morgan mourned in his sleeping bag. Envied Wort who, when loss threatened to drive him crazy, measured it, indexed it, graphed it. All Morgan had was a whirl of worlds in his head, worlds no one really believed in. Like that lonesome rolling head that demonstrated lunacy to the people. To steady himself he looked at the shape the moon made in the window. A form that might be construed as a map. A map of Madocia for instance. Write a map of it, it said in his head, the way they used to have narrative maps for mariners. Add Maidu to the realm. There are many provinces in Madocia. It might not be exact, but it would be a likeness. Start in spring. Winter is brief on the shores of San Francisco Bay.

THREE POEMS

PETER PORTER

BRIDES COME TO THE POET'S WINDOW

Birds, it should have been, but pleasure quickens
As the white and peregrine performers land—

Such chattering of all the hopeful starts,
Like trees renewing their hay-fever wraps—

Cool shadows, straight and ordinary,
to startle the recluse's whisky dreams.

Each bride is decked in her uncertainty,
Her jokes are uncles, sex a limousine,

And in the ride to the abyss she hears
With doubtful face the radiant hymn swell up.

These are the frescoes of a fallen world,
The flocks of sulphur-crested cockatoos,

The parrots which don't read the City Pages,
Corporate worms indifferent to Darwin—

Where else, how otherwise devise a world
Where God is in his place and heaven's a sight,

Where boredom does the artwork, misery
The economic planning and petulance

Sends the invitations? Our daughter's wedding
Was the day we decided to separate.

The poet in his cell is sneezing with
The pollen of the breeding world; he blows

His nose on sheets of multi-stanza'd white—
Is he obliged to fizz his own champagne?

O Brides of Solomon, did no one tell you
You're merely symbols of a loving god,

That high erotic temperatures are just
Visions of paradise on fading silk?

In the painted garlands of the Farnesina
The melons, halved, glisten in future light.

TRICKY LITTLE MAGDALENE

The membrane separating this world
from its other is wafer-thin
and only sex sustains it.

The Lost Past and the Last Post sound together,
childhood through the rain-swept queues
shows dogs fucking at your trouser-cuffs
and Uncle Mick leaving Circular Quay
with Resch's Dinner Ale and a bottle of oysters
wrapped in the evening paper.

After the light shows and the Edwardian whiskers
a gift for drawing—grandeur and decline
are chiaroscuro,

the knights ride on the ice
and here a drunken woman falls to the ground
masturbating through her skirt
outside our chic Belphoori.

This androgyne Belshazzar
giggles as a hefty Rapunzel
curtains his genitals with her hair.
What's going on behind? Certainly
he's got his toes in her ravine:
it helps the ecstasy to find sex funny,
then you can put these things where they need to go,
in the hole created for our trickiness.

No, we are not doing the dirt on sex
or finding it repulsive,
but considering Freud's pet vulture
as she parts our lips with her tail feathers
and brings us to the world's workface.

Is this the Obscurity Principle,
the laziness of imagination,
a doing-without significance,
or is it instead the Obscenity Principle
where all the happy tales of hobbits
and witches inside mirrors
are pornography for men afraid of women?

The sex-chain is a food-chain.
Eat your mother till you are her,
steal from Daddy's well-stocked plate
and go down greedily on Goldilocks.
The chants of cannibalism
float down from a cantoria
so quattrocento, such a frieze
of angels proudly edible,
The Last Supper everlastingly laid out.

Of course, the best course is Repentance
for which you need a feast of sin.

God's little joke is in two worlds,
and coming from the other
we have no memory of it
and going thither once again
we will not know what we have been
once back in that occluded air. The scene's
a football crowd, an orgy, a party
at the zoo—the caption reads
"They shall not die," and Magdalene
stands up for Jesus, your parents show you
the picture books of history,
the cruiser Aurora fires her salvos,
jacaranda moulders on the garden path
as Granny Main, stiff in her lacy black,
lifts her veil and shows you down the steps
to the dark places of inheritance.

LISTENING TO SHAKESPEARE

I was at school with him,
that Will Shakespeare,
carved his name on his desk,
pissed on it to make it shine,
edited a magazine called *Nova*
the name of our river spelled backwards—
he said we should always remember
that words were the way you told lies
and got out of a walloping—
he got us to compare our penises
and said one boy's was Small Latin
and another one's Less Greek,
he kept us entertained with faces
and wrote endless essays
when he wasn't courting.

When he went to London
I was really sorry. Or was it Lancashire?

Anyway we heard of him in London,
then his Dad got into trouble about church
and his Old Woman sulked at home
and we had several discontented winters.
One day I met him in the High Street,
he seemed a bit furtive,
said the chap loitering on the corner
was a government spy,
"haven't I got trouble enough with Coriolanus?"
I loved his stories from the classics
but it only made him gloomy,

"You know what Marston told me,
all Penelope did in Ulysses' absence
was fill Ithaca full of moths—
why come back when the moths at home
are never going to change to butterflies?"
I showed him a review in the local paper,
"Stratford author's sour-note sonnets!"
He wasn't interested and talked
about the price of real estate.

But he was big in London,
you heard about it even here.
And all the time he bought up property
and made himself a gentleman
like his father had tried but failed to do.
Then he came home, old and tired,
saying if life's race were run from eleven to ninety
he was at the ninety end
though all of forty-eight.
Once at an Open Day he said mysteriously
"Congratulations, you have just invented
a new art form—let's call it Local History
and hurry it along to Heritage."

We listened when he talked to us,
I used to love his high haranguing
but it died away. He died too,
quite suddenly. Managed a good tomb

before the altar and no digging-up
and stowing in the ossuary. I've kept a note
he passed me under the desk once
during a long grammar lesson.
"No man may know a neighbour closer
than his own defeat. The unfolding star
calls up the shepherd. Soon there'll be
nothing of the world to listen to."

IN THE SAME BOAT

JOSIP NOVAKOVICH

A white sailboat rattled through the waves of the Pacific, with the North American continent as a rugged blue shade in the background, like a distant and violent oceanic storm. The thumping of the boards against the hissing waves mesmerized the two men in the boat. The sunshine permeated their skins and warmed their bones; they had surrendered themselves to the sun, the god of the Incas. Peter, blond and pink, with his large translucent blue eyes, produced an impression of trust and honesty. Francisco, black-haired, with his dark, narrowly set eyes flickering through long eyelashes struck you as clever and warm; and his thin aquiline nose portrayed him as refined. They both wore white tee-shirts which didn't hide the lines, curves, and teeth of their muscles.

On the second day of their journey they woke up as the sun was buoying out of the ocean. Francisco sang *Gracias a la vida*, stretching his arms wide as if to embrace the sun; his armpit hairs sprouted out of his shirt, and thick blue veins calmly branched from his biceps over the elbow into his forearm. Peter rubbed his thick eyelids and ejected his night-spittle overboard.

The fish they caught in a net they grilled on a propane cooker. They separated the flesh and the bones and threw the white comblike skeletons with slanted ribs into the water of grape-juice color. The sun scattered its bronze radiance over the sky and water, slid behind the ocean, and Francisco and Peter fell asleep, dreaming the second day and the second morning were good.

On the third day they fished, ate, worshiped the sun without looking at it directly, just as Moses could not look at God's glory but only at the radiance that went after Him. The water sprinkled over their skins now and then, enough to soothe them against the sun. No border patrol was in sight. They felt the day had been good.

The fourth day the tranquility became boredom. They no longer noticed the sun and failed to worship it. They told anecdotes, jokes, memories. They went over the details of their friendship the way lovers would.

They had become friends in Gillette, Wyoming, playing pool in a bar where laid-off oil-rig hands hung around—some missed their fingers, and some clenched beer cans in artificial arms and fists of steel. "What are we playing for?" Peter had asked. Francisco had replied: "For your SS#!"

"Gladly, if you want my IRS problems and my debts, go ahead!" Peter had dropped out of Baylor Medical School after his first year, with his student loans exceeding thirty thousand dollars. Without an SS# Francisco as an illegal alien from Mexico could not hold a job for more than one paycheck period, fearing that the Immigration & Naturalization Service agents would track him down. So Francisco worked on Peter's SS# on an oil rig as a worm, splitting his salary with Peter. They stayed together in a bunkhouse, drank vodka, and shot pool every night, and every dawn Francisco, badly hung over, put on his gloves and a cracked, orange plastic helmet, and pushed drilling pipes dangling from the derricks, one over another until one struck him in the head and knocked him out with a brain concussion. He had refused to be taken to the hospital, scared that after his papers were scrutinized, he would be tossed in jail or over the border. So he recovered with Peter in the bunkhouse, drinking Coke, and reading a *National Geographic* report on the Incas. He fancied himself in Machu Picchu, in golden robes, glittering in the sun, surrounded by lovely bronze maidens, supplely dancing, coiling around him. . . . Did they sacrifice the maidens? Did they eat them? He had talked about the Incas so much that Peter had said, "You must have been an Inca king in one of your previous lives to have these vivid dreams, first thing as you recover from the brain concussion!"

Francisco had suggested they should go to the Andes and live like poets on the beauty of the mountains. They were sober when they decided to go to Peru, and in a genuine Persian manner, they reconsidered their decision when they were drunk, for three days later, and liking the decision in both states of mind, they adopted it. Peter dreamed of collecting the ancient pottery and selling it to Sotheby's in London. They chose the cheapest form of transportation with the fewest number of borders: the wind and the ocean. They had stolen a sailboat named *Kon-Tiki* in Santa Monica, California.

Now, on the boat, they went through their story many times, and they told each other many anecdotes. Peter told this one: During the Great Depression in Berlin it was not advisable for well-fed provincial girls to get off the train at the Friedrichstrasse station, looking for work, because they could reappear at the station as sausages sold to the hungry passengers. A butcher who had employed them slaughtered them and processed them through sausage-making machines.

On the eighth day of their journey they ran out of stories. The image of the high jungles and icecaps of the Andes was paled in their minds. They fished, ate the chunks of flesh from the ocean, and yawned.

On the twelfth day, they were still on the seas, with the tilting horizon and frothing water which protruded sharp like millions of broken teeth cracking once again while the new ones rose through the dark indigo gums. Seas, seas, always the seas. All you see is the sea, ever and ever, ever and forever. In the evening a great wind plunged into the ocean and the ocean leapt into the wind to drive it away, but the wind only grew windier at that. Lightning flashed, and the high long waves carried the boat high and laid it down low, in a railless roller coaster. The scene looked like the famous Japanese painting with the wave about to bury a twisted boat. The waves screamed and howled and hissed like thousands of lions and snakes, but they did no harm to Peter and Francisco. By the morning, the tired storm lay down on the ocean, thin, prostrate, and the ocean became as calm as a glacial lake. The sun, the Old Man of the Sky, warmed the ocean.

They lost count of days.

One day, perhaps the thirtieth, Peter cast the net into the water. For a long time no fish hit the net, and Peter yawned. All of a sudden something big smashed into the net. The ropes cracked and would have pulled Peter overboard but for Francisco's grabbing his hand. A shark dragged the boat the way a horse drags a sled over the blue snow. Francisco fired from his gun. Some red mixed with the salty foam, resembling a strawberry shake. The shark convulsed and pulled so vehemently that Peter and Francisco and the gun fell overboard. The men quickly swam to the boat, which floated away from them just as quickly. With the image of the shark jaws snapping their feet, they plunged their arms into the water, splashing. Francisco reached the boat and extended an oar to Peter and lifted him aboard. They gasped and when they grew hungry several hours later, they realized that they had lost their net, their food. Peter had once fasted for three weeks, drinking a gallon of spring water a day, and when his mother saw him after it, she burst into tears. Peter smiled at the recollection. They had to ration water, down to three gallons. They sliced the sail, to make a net. They managed to catch nothing; another big fish tore the net. Five days later they lay in a stupor, no longer hungry. Big ocean liners and tankers noiselessly passed by at a great distance, and Peter and Francisco at first stood up and hollered, and later, as they watched ships slide noiselessly over the line of the horizon like setting suns, they gave up.

Francisco missed the earth more than he missed women. When he got a morning erection, he masturbated, as if his sperm had promised life; and he imagined not luscious women but grassy ravines and rivers. Ejaculating, he watched his sperm fall onto the boards and ooze. Peter shouted: "You idiot! What a waste of energy!"

"Trrue, may be a hol whorr of my life."

"Maybe your whole life because you could be short of the shore that one hour. But what am I saying? We'll make it. We've got to believe it."

"Pover of positive tinking, ha? I don't even know for sure what the coast looks like." He kneeled and licked his sperm the way a cat laps milk.

Peter said: "That's some improvement. If you have to do it, at least eat it. But, your body can never restore the energy you lose through the sperm. At best, the body can use only about thirty percent of energy from food."

They both dozed off and neglected to steer the boat. Peter woke up and shouted at Francisco. Francisco seated himself and steered.

Peter was falling asleep again, falling adead. His body was stringy and dry, and his blood moved slowly. His every breath, every motion, was slow; he felt his body as precise, with a sensation of bodily control stemming from the opposite, the lack of control; he felt the struggle for control as precision. He admired his minimalistic bodily economy, feeling pure, nearly abstract, a spirit with hallucinogenic visions:

waterfalls, filled with luminosity of the sun, splashing over him. He awoke with his throat parched and sore, and thought, I can have only two glasses of water a day. If Francisco weren't here, I could have four! When Francisco fell asleep, Peter poured himself an extra glass of water, water stolen from Francisco's blood. Peter's hand trembled. His Adam's apple leaped like a stone in a rough brook as he gulped the water.

Francisco groaned in his sleep as if aware that his plasma was being drunk. He awoke and touched his face, eclipsed by bones. His eyes glowed, and he kept them closed because the platinum sunrise was too brilliant. He squinted at Peter; Peter's eyelids were nearly fully drawn over his eyes, and his eyesacks were creased and purple.

They stared at each other with an acute, shared consciousness. What were they now? Still best friends? How could they be? Friendship is the highest form of being human, and they were no longer human nor animal; they were dying life, and dying life like a wounded lion knows no mercy, no friendship, only struggle and revenge. Neither could seek vengeance on his own self. They could not attack a shark, they could not attack the ocean, and they could not attack the sky. They could attack only each other.

Peter appeared to Francisco stranger than any stranger, slowly disappearing from his sight and mind, and his sight and mind were slowly disappearing also.

Peter's heart thumped against his rib cage at the thought that Francisco was flesh, meat. He could kill Francisco, eat him, and live. But how could he, his best friend? A raspy voice kept repeating into his ears, somewhere from within: "Kill him, kill him, killim, killim, killm, kill!" He shuddered, and thought that it would be better to kill him or be killed by him than that both of them die. He thought about the Incas with their human sacrifices. They would have the Andes right on the ocean; two hungry men with nothing to eat but their flesh. Flesh is singular. There are no porks, sheeps, fleshes; it's all one. Peter lustfully stared at Francisco's *musculus gracilis*, the graceful and lean muscle crossing the inner thigh.

Peter's blood cried, like the spilled blood of Abel, except that Abel's blood shrieked against murder and Peter's for it.

Francisco let his arm hang loose overboard, staring into the water like a cat at an aquarium; his teeth chattered, and soon he dozed off. Peter wondered, Maybe he doesn't want to kill me. Maybe he doesn't know I want to kill him. How could he sleep otherwise?

Peter could not sleep. Even when snoring, he was half awake. Fearing death, he was exhausting himself and inviting it. Presently, Francisco woke up and stretched his arms. Peter didn't look him in the face, thinking that the seed of murder that was growing in his blood must have reached his eyes, lurking in them. They each had a glass of water, their only glass for the day; their rations were down to one gallon.

Around noon, the sky and the water turned gray and dark. The air was musty with water hanging between the sky and the ocean, yet the water wouldn't fall.

Francisco said, "It will rain."

"Why?"

"My leg hurts where I broke it years ago playing soccer. The leg knows."

The water suddenly fell from the air above them; it fell into the ocean in several massive avalanches. Peter and Francisco opened their mouths like baby hawks awaiting their mother to drop torn sparrows into their beaks. They tried to collect the water in a fragment of the plastic boat cover.

The flashing and lightening through the darkness seemed like a dance of death to Francisco. He was homesick for the land. The real homeland was down there buried in the grave of the oceanic water. When I am dead, maybe none of my bones will be buried in the soil, not even on the ocean floor. Sharks will tear me apart. Maybe one of my molars will touch the floor, heavy with gold.

Francisco touched the golden tooth, a memento from the earth, from rocks—the purest part of a rock, used for dirtiest greed, dividing people into the rich and poor. It comes from the ground but is not ground because the ground is never pure. Gold is a symbol of purified self because it has no traces of the soil or anything else; it is only itself—noble, and it inspires you to try to become noble, a pure self detached from everybody, selfish to the extreme, inhuman. A human being is a mixture of elements and cultures, and to strive to create anything purely individual, purely monocultural, is purely monstrous.

They collected several gallons of water.

After the storm the sky cleared, the ocean was pacific, and though Peter and Francisco had filled their stomachs with water, they were dizzy. Francisco looked at Peter's shoulder, several streaks of muscles, and thought of cutting the muscles and chewing them. He thought he was merely entertaining himself by the image, but the image took hold of him. Can I kill Peter? How? Maybe the oar could smash his skull. How can I think like this? Peter is my only friend. But, we are animals; life is above everything. Life means eating life. Life communally survives on love, individually on hatred. Only mothers can die for their children, mothers and Jesus Christ, who is, after all, the mother of Christianity, a Virgin Mary dying on the cross with shriveled breasts. Too many mouths had sucked milk from the breasts, and when the milk dried up, they continued to suck blood, until Mary Christ died. Haven't I always been a cannibal? As a child I sucked my mother's breasts, draining her flesh. I longed to taste the salt of her blood through the salt of milk, trying to replace the blood that used to come to me through the umbilical cord, to flow through me like alcohol through an alcohol addict. Maybe only those of us who remember mother's blood become alcoholics, trying not to forget but to remember. We started with the mother; our basic nature stems not from the assassination of the father but from the slow killing of the mother.

Francisco was startled at his thoughts, as if it wasn't he thinking, but someone in him. And from the thought that he should kill Peter or that Peter would kill him, Francisco could no longer sleep. Half-awake, he held his hand on the oar. Without saying a word, each knew what the other was thinking; their alertness incriminated them.

Nights unsettled them. Francisco constantly imagined himself taking up the oar and crushing Peter's skull. It would take too much time. Peter would notice. They sat on the opposite ends of the boat. It was the third week of their starvation. They saw all the flickers of the light: is it a knife blade flickering? They heard all the rustling of waves: is he getting up to kill me?

A dawn at the end of the three weeks of starvation announced the divine splendor of the sun. The sun was scarlet. They both looked at it in amazement and then at each other's faces, overcast with a red hue; their eyes were bloodshot. They watched each other through a screen of blood, a blood prism, a salty crystal, and all the rainbows of the world collected in one color, rusty red.

They looked at each other with pity too, regretting to see biology vanquish their spirits. Their spirits were still friends, right then in the calm, as they reconciled themselves with death and didn't care to listen to the voices in them. Even tears appeared in their eyes, at the same time. They no longer cared for life at all costs. Peter was ashamed of his knife. But to throw it away would be to fully acknowledge that he had imagined and seen the murder scenario. The scenario was hovering in the air, resembling a dome painted by Michelangelo: pink muscles of edible flesh, elongated, darkened, as if El Greco had redone the ceiling, which was closing in on the boat. Peter's ceiling was filled with Franciscos stretching and flexing their flesh in various postures; Franciscos, with many Peters; and some deltoid and trapezoid muscles floated detached, like doves and kites. But to acknowledge it required too much courage.

Friendship somehow resurged. In their muscular chapel, they had both concluded that they were animals and not humans struggling to live. That was an exaggeration; thought usually is. Their friendship now spited their arteries. The salty tears, the bit of the oceanic water that rose through their eyes, were salty from blood yet not bloody.

Their eyes protruded out of deeply creased skin, piously gazing at the sharp outlines of their muscles. Their veins ran along like branches of a leafless tree.

A tooth irritated Francisco, and he shook it between his forefinger and thumb. The tooth remained in his fingers. Blood gushed and he spat it. Peter kneeled and licked the foamy blood off the boards. Francisco sucked his own gums.

Peter's gums bled too, and Peter swallowed the blood thirstily.

And they continued to stare at each other, with pity, love, and hunger. Their own blood shook them and crossed out their white flags of peace with death. The red shade disappeared from the sun, but through their drooping eyelids, the light still assumed an orange hue, leaning towards the red. In the evening the sun was larger and redder than they had ever seen it. The gory circle pushed towards the ocean slowly and unstoppably. It stabbed the ocean, cutting its stomach open; and the true color of the ocean came out of the blue veins—red, echoing the sky and the sunken god of life and violence, the sun. The ocean swallowed the Old Man of the Sky without a sound.

The waves played with the bronze light as if lulling it to sleep. The light moved with each wave, evasive, unsubstantial, without the deed in the illusion of blood. It lured the eyes to give the deed to the light, to murder. The sky turned a gloomy indigo, as though it were a gigantic blood vessel and the earth a blood clot in it. The full moon with dried-up oceans slipped out, eclipsing. Its light cast down an unprocessed film which, sunk in the chemicals of the ocean, began to develop; pictures appeared slowly, with emerging contrasts.

Their eyeballs flickered in the dark, like four candles at a medieval plague carnival.

I should have killed him as soon as I woke up, thought Peter.

I should grab the oar, thought Francisco.

No choice, thought Peter. I can't wait and wait. If I fall asleep again, he'll kill me.

Peter began to move slowly, holding an empty glass in his hand, as if he would fill it with water to drink, and in his other hand behind his back, he gripped the ivory handle of his hunting knife. Francisco tightened his muscles. Why did Peter move so slowly if he wanted to drink? Peter moved slowly like a tiger who needs to hide his movement, but on the boat nothing could be hidden. Even the moon failed to eclipse. Francisco grabbed the oar, still heavy from the water, acknowledging the imminent struggle. Peter hesitated. Is Francisco strong enough to use the oar? I must act swiftly. What if he falls overboard and drowns? We'd both die.

Peter crept nearer. Francisco's muscles tensed more, and he jumped. The boat shook. He flew at Peter, swinging the oar. Peter ducked sideways. The oar missed his head and smashed his left shoulder; the collar bone cracked loudly. Peter fell on the boards, his knife flying out of his hand. The motion swayed Francisco and he fell over the bench. Peter was in a knockdown. He tried to stand up and collapsed again. Francisco lifted himself slowly and took up the oar. Peter's hand was reaching for the knife. Francisco was dizzy; the waves made it hard for him to keep his balance. Peter, the knife in his hand, his consciousness crimson, half stood and half leaped at Francisco, like a runner at the start of a race. Francisco started sideways. Peter missed and fell over Francisco's feet. Francisco kicked in his face and hesitated because he felt pity for the bleeding Peter. The moon was not eclipsed. It came out of a thick cloud, full.

Peter quickly stood up—actually, the struggle took place in slow exhausted motion—and plunged and collapsed at Francisco again. Francisco jumped aside, but too slowly. The knife hit his rib cage, slid below it and climbed into his liver. Peter pulled the knife out and stabbed again. Francisco lay against the rudder, blood spurting out of him in the rhythm of his heart. Peter stabbed again, aiming at the heart, and his knife got stuck in Francisco's rib, between the head of the rib and the sternum. Peter pulled it out and the bones crunched. Peter's shoulder was ridden with scorching pangs of pain. He spat a couple of teeth from his mouth. Francisco stared at him with fervid fixedness. Peter kneeled on his side and pressed his four fingertips (he didn't use the thumb) into Francisco's lukewarm skin on the neck for pulse; he pressed in the front of the transverse muscle running from the back of the skull to the collar bone—sternocleidomastoidal muscle—and wasn't sure whose feeble pulse he felt, his or Francisco's. I should finish killing him. Peter lifted the knife in his hand and held it high; the blade smudged with blood flickered in the vague moonlight. He waited like Abraham when sacrificing Isaac, but no angels came from the sky to stop his hand, and there were no goats around the altar to be sacrificed in Isaac's stead. There was no faith to be proven; this was not a test. Out of pain in the shoulder more than decision, Peter's arm and hand went down; the knife slid between the collarbone and the upper ridge of the trapezoid muscle as smoothly as the sun had sunk into the ocean. Francisco's body convulsed, blood gushed; Francisco's frozen blue eyeballs crisscrossed focusing somewhere behind Peter's neck. He opened his mouth, and to Peter it was not clear whether his throat gurgled in giving up his ghost or whether he said: rhrhood luckrh, the way a Dutchman might say Good luck. The light vanished out of Francisco's eyes.

Francisco's blood, no longer spurting in the rhythm of the heart, flowed slowly and feebly. Peter licked the blood off the skin below the rib cage and sucked the wound behind the collarbone. And after that, numb, no longer in pursuit of blood, his warm awareness oozed below the surface of the ocean through the limbs of octopuses, past orange and green fish glowing into the Paradise beneath good and evil; with ease spreading throughout his body to his sore eyelids. Through his fluttering eyelashes, instead of one silvery moon, he saw four merging in and out of one. Silver light flashed at him from the lulling waves, never from one and the same place, never offering itself to be scrutinized. He leaned against the bench and the sideboards; his head was gently swayed in the rhythm of the ocean. The actorless play of elusive light went on for him. The moon disappeared in a large cloud resembling a hippopotamus, and soon was visible in the stomach of the hippo as if under X-rays.

The murmur and splashing of the waters was a purr of the oceanic mother cat suckling her kitten. The sounds changed and passed away, the light shifted, but the darkness always stayed in the ocean, steady and true. The warmth from the inside balmed his stomach and the cool from the outside balmed his lungs and forehead as if his mother's hand had touched him at the end of a long fever.

For breakfast, Peter cut through Francisco's left calf, amazed at the thickness of the skin. Shoes could be made of it. If a tent could be made of the foreskins of the Philistines David had killed, you could make shoes out of the skin; if you peeled off the skin of the foot and put it back together, you'd have a perfect foot-glove, a moccasin. Peter laughed, thinking how his thoughts displayed good Yankee ingenuity. He carved out the medial head of the *gastrocnemius*, cut the stubborn Achilles's tendon, and burnt the flesh on the propane cooker.

In the afternoon Peter grew bored. Now he had nobody to be tense with, nobody to keep him alert and conscious, so he dozed, but gradually, insomnia set in. And rather than turn away from the corpse, he turned to it, as if begging Francisco to talk to him. The body lay supine with the eyes closed, giving an impression of an irisless sculpture, a Rodin bronze sculpture of a sleeping philosopher, the one Rodin would have made had he lived longer. Peter wondered, What can I do to kill the time?

Why not study anatomy?—the most basic of the humanistic as well as of the natural sciences. . . . He took up his knife, and with his thumbnail scratched the brown fragile sheets of blood from the blade. He began to peel off the skin of the thinned left thigh. He tried to separate the layer of skin from the subcutaneous fat, but there was so little fat that it was no thicker than the *fascia lata* and the *perimysium*, the sheets enveloping the muscles below. Between the hardened thin layer of fat and the *fascia*, he freed the long saphenous vein, purple and limp. Then he cut sideways between *adductor longus* and *sartorius*, until he reached the femoral artery and vein, two thirds of the way between the skin and the bone. He separated the muscles and reached for the femur. He cut lightly into the bone and peeled off the *periosteum*, the yellowish white sheet of the bone. The femur was splendidly white, almost like the ivory handle of his knife. Throughout the *practicum* he was fascinated, highly alert and cautious, with his stomach growling. He tried to recall the objectivity of an anatomy lesson, the thingness of the corpse. His knife was much duller than the scalpel, and the fresh corpse was startlingly red compared with the old brown formaldehyde cadavers he had worked with, so that the procedure was like an autopsy, as if the cause of death had to be determined.

He began to separate the triceps and the biceps of the right arm, letting the muscle sheet stay with the biceps. He pressed the brachial artery, which bounced right back, and traced the artery, as it arose through the muscles and ran closer to the bone *humerus*, gradually twisting from the medial side to the front of it; his finger got stuck against its branch, *profunda brachii*, coiling backward through the triceps. Next to the brachial artery, farther from the bone, Peter separated a thick white string, *nervus medialis*, and though he pulled it as hard as he could, it wouldn't break nor slide much from between the muscles. Behind the string close to the skin ran a thinner string, the ulnar nerve, the nerve that he remembered playing with as a kid, striking the edge of the breakfast table with the elbow, coffee cups with violets clanking, sunny-sides-up trembling with little waves, his mother shouting, Pete, for Heaven's sake!—while he concentrated on the electric tingle in his forearm. He had imagined swarms of ants had covered his forearm, millions of little legs stepping inside his skin, skating over his muscles.

Peter stuck his knife into Francisco's crunchy sternum and tore through the abdomen to the navel, to the pubic bone. He tried to pull the abdomen apart, but it was too tight, so he made a transverse cut, through the navel, resulting in an inverse cross. He cut through several layers of muscles, each with fibers in a different direction, removed the abdominal wall with the peritoneum, the abdominal sheet, and plunged his hands into the slippery intestines. He started at the pinkish, gray, brown, reddish, white colors, impure, muted; there was a shade of blue in the ascending colon on the right, the transverse colon beneath the liver was still soaked in blood from the liver, the sigmoid colon on the low left was bluish. Upwards, beneath the shrunken stomach, his fingers felt the tonguelike, spongy pancreas and the walls of the duodenum that enveloped the head of the pancreas, like a lover embracing his beloved. Peter, driven by the curiosity to reach into the secrets of secreting matter, cut into the duodenum, and found the opening of the pancreatic ducts in its wall, and cutting through the pancreas, with his knife he traced the common bile duct. He followed the pancreatic duct, bearing a national name, he couldn't recall which, Danish, Langerhans? Or was it a German name, Wirsung? English? Why should parts of the body and of the world bear English names? Mount Everest—a colon-izing name of the old colonizing power. Shouldn't the mountain have a Tibetan name? Why hasn't somebody named the asshole Gladstone or Schliemann? I suppose nobody could claim to have discovered the asshole. Wirsung, yes, that's it. German, after all. Peter felt the pancreas to the right, as it thinned. He tried to pull it out, but it was firmly attached to the peritoneum in the back; he cut through the back peritoneum next to the bumpy spine and fingered the inferior *vena cava* and the rubbery *aorta abdominalis*. At the thin end of the pancreas he touched the smooth surface of the kidneylike crimson spleen, squeezed it and cut it out, with blood dripping.

Peter tore out half a yard of the intestines and threw them overboard. Shouldn't I have used the intestines for sausages?

It was getting dark, and Peter interrupted his anatomy lesson; and for supper, he simmered the spleen on the propane cooker.

Next pink dawn he recoiled from his sleep; he had been resting his head on a piece of Francisco's abdominal wall, torn and thin. What to do with the body, after the anatomy lesson? To embalm or not to embalm? He remembered what he had read about how the Egyptians did it. They stuck a hook through the nostrils into the brain and scratched inside the skull so the brain could flow out, and what remained of it was dissolved in natrum. They opened the inside of the body, took out the organs, and oiled the inner walls and sewed them back. And there was another method; you don't remove the intestines; you inject cedar oil into them through the anus, and the body pickles in natrum. After seventy days, the flesh is gone, and the skin remains taut on the bones, ready to last for thousands of years. But this was all useless to Peter; he had no natrum and he needed the flesh to eat.

To preserve the flesh as long as possible, he cleaned out the bacteria-rich intestines completely, because from them the rotting would spread. And then he paused, gazing at Francisco's corpse—well, it no longer belonged to Francisco but to Peter; so, in a way, he looked at his corpse.

He lifted some seawater in the bit of plastic boat cover; he soaked his clothes in the water. The salt that remained after the water evaporated he rubbed over a whole assortment of muscles, neatly filed on the boards: the broad *trapezes*, the broader *latissimus dorsi*, the twisting streaks of *pectoralis* with the swollen *deltoideus* above, *flexor carpi ulnaris sinister, rectus abdominis*, the tongue, and the heart, which, with severed blood vessels sticking out of it, lay like a defeated (and defeeted) octopus. He sliced the heart, admiring how thick the wall of the left ventricle was.

He cut out the right lung, light and airy, wetly smooth, with little veins crisscrossing the surface; he remembered what Francisco had told him—the Incas used to tell fortunes by tracing the vein patterns in the lungs of sacrificial llamas.

In the evening Peter gorged, anxious that there might not be enough food for him; and after it, he fell asleep. The bell is tolling. The sun has not risen yet. Maybe it won't. The horizon is rosy, the streets brown, the sky azure. Many people in black trod the cobbles of the narrow streets. The streets have been a dead silence that the bells pierced, coldly touching people through their fresh white shirts behind their black suits. The sound blows cold air into the people's hearts, through the pores of their skins, drawing blood from their faces, ashen green under blue-black hairs. Peter walks towards the gathering. Two black horses, steam arising from their backs, pull a black hearse covered with stiff green garlands, with purple ribbons and golden letters. Peter walks in the rhythm of the tolling. Four men carry an orange casket out of a gray bullet-riddled house. The bells cease to toll and a buzzing echo remains, rising in pitch. Hair stands upright on Peter's skin at the foreboding of the screeching of the coffin over the boards of the hearse. All of a sudden, one of the four coffin-carriers slides over a soft green piece of horse dung and falls onto the cobbles. The casket falls after him, crashes on his foot, and cracks open on the cobbles. From a white sheet rolls out a corpse, stiff and naked. Good chunks of flesh are missing. One leg is bare, that is, the bone on it is bare. Bones of one arm are white, without a trace of flesh, and one half of the face is missing, with the zygomatic bone and the mandible protruding, and the hollow of the eye stares out from some spookily calm darkness. The screams of the crowd echo against the church as the corpse rolls downhill towards Peter. Peter recoils: the corpse is he himself, Peter.

He woke up catching his scream as it was vanishing in the murmur of the Ocean.

Six days after he had killed Francisco, Peter noticed a coast, a blue rugged haze. Seeing patches of green in the gray haze, he was reassured. He threw Francisco's bones overboard. Some bones floated, others sank. Peter pushed the skull into the water, but it emerged, grinning its fleshless mouth at him.

In the afternoon, Peter saw white high-rise hotels and a sandy beach covered with bronze and pink bodies, orange and blue parasols, yellow and red water floats. Soon his sailboat cut into the sandy gravel, screeching. Bathers ran aside from the path of the boat. They saw

Peter's apparition: hollow cheeks, hollow orbits of the eyes out of which two sad and brutal eyes glowed, long salty blond hair, burnt brown skin, ribs showing through a salt-eaten shirt. He looked like a holy man or a forlorn lunatic or an adventurer who has survived a trip into the heart of a volcano. Popsicle-sucking children shrieked and ran away, lotioned men and women shrank back.

Peter walked straight to an outdoor cafe with little white tables and small palms with red flowers and ordered *una cerveza*. That much Spanish he knew. A young olive-skinned waiter, his hairs greasily wet, combed in parallels, gave the beer to Peter, scrutinizing him through his long eyelashes. To Peter there was something familiar in the face. Peter paid, handing out one salty dollar, and asked: "Hotel?"

"Esto completo," answered the lad. He drew a map on the back of a page from a notepad, which said Oasis, directing Peter into the periphery of the town. Peter found a small hotel in a slanted cobbled street. He rented a room and slept for a day straight. Next afternoon he went to a barber's and had his hair cut and his beard shaved. As the barber razed through the foam, tickling his neck with the gentle touch of the blade, Peter was uncomfortable; it would be so easy for the blade to cut beneath the sternocleidomastoidal muscle into the carotid artery. Unlike Cain, Peter had no sign on his forehead to brand him as a murderer, yet he felt as though he had one; and his sign, unlike Cain's, wouldn't protect him. But the shaving went on peacefully; the old barber, his eyes half closed, whistled *Gracias a la vida;* fresh air smelling of pines floated through the room, balming and invigorating Peter, who kept his eyes closed. When the barber asked him to take a look, Peter was startled by seeing himself in the mirror. His face was much darker than it used to be. His eyes were smaller; they no longer had the optimistic and frank air about them.

Strolling in the streets, he was surprised at how much Spanish he understood; he had never studied it. He had many déjà-vu sensations. After two or three days, he understood the conversations fully. Whenever he shopped, his English consonants were softened; he attributed that to his three missing teeth, which made him lisp and activate his tongue more, to roll his r's. His body felt different from what he was used to. His movements were faster, his eyes shiftier. He looked in the mirror. His eyes were no longer blue, but greenish, tending towards hazel. His nose was thinner and a bit aquiline. It seemed to him that Francisco stared back at him. Francisco's liquid glare cooled him. No, I must be hallucinating. I am going out of my mind! Next morning, as soon as he woke up, he rushed to the mirror to convince himself that he had hallucinated the previous days. Out of the mirror leered a dark-eyed face.

Although he used to despise religion, Peter walked into the bullet-riddled church across the square from his inn and listened to a sermon amidst incense. There were on both sides pale Jesuses with thick red rivulets flowing from their thorn-pierced foreheads, and even thicker rivulets out of the holes in the ribs. He recalled the crunching sound of his knife in Francisco's ribs, and shuddered at the monotonous words of the priest: *Porque el que quisiere salvar su vida, la perdera; y el que perdiere su vida por causa de mi, la salvara.* (For he who wants to save his life will lose it, and he who loses his life for my sake, will gain it.) Peter walked out of the cold church. The sun smarted his eyes. The bells began to toll, smarting his ears. His whole body was tense and sore as if it were all made of gums through which wisdom teeth grew.

Several days later he was on a steel Greyhound. As the bus neared the U.S. border, there was a dark low cloud in the sky. At the border, Peter handed his salt-eaten passport to a border policeman. The heavy-set cop commented, "Damn weather, it makes my bones ache!" Then he lifted his gray eyes and said: "But this is not you! You are not Peter Cunningham."

"Yes, of courrse I am. What are you dalking about?" said Peter.

Several cops interrogated Peter. He asked to be allowed to call his mother in Cleveland, and while dialing, he couldn't recall her number. He called information, got his mother's number, and dialed it. His mother's voice said: "You've got the wrong number."

"Bot, Mohder, dhis is Pete . . ." The dial signal cut in.

He dialed again. Same thing. He dialed again. His father's voice shouted: "Can't you dumb Puerto Ricans dial right? Can't you at least read numbers?"

A cop said, "Enough of this circus. We could jail you or fine you, but since our jails are too full and you are a poor bum, we'll just let you go." The cop winked at him leniently. "You better steal a passport with a Hispanic name, or forge better. This one's on our records, and so is your picture, so, if you try again . . ." The officer spoke slowly as if Peter was too estupido to understand English.

A week later Peter entered the States in the hay of a truck along with three Mexicans. In Texas he looked for work in tomato fields. He began dreaming of going into the oil fields in Wyoming. He was confused, wondering what had gone wrong, and wished to start his self-analysis from his childhood, but though he had prided himself on vivid childhood memories, he could recall nothing concrete of Cleveland. Instead of images of suburban hedges with tricycles, aluminum trash-cans, football eggs, his mind produced images of llamas and women in black skirts under which children's heads lurk, little fingers picking noses.

After four weeks of work, on a day off, Peter drove with several Mexicans on a mufflerless pickup to Beeville. They bought beer at 7-Eleven, and as they were about to enter their beat-up pickup, two police cars pulled up, flooding them with strong beams of light . . . Peter—but we should better call him from now on Francisco. Here we will make a full stop because what would follow sería una repetición de lo que había ocurrido tiempo ha; la entrada ilegal de Francisco en los Estados Unidos, explotación en el trabajo, terror de la MIGRA y . . .

THE PEACOCK EMPEROR MOTH

MARCEL COHEN

Translated from the French by Cid Corman

The water came up to his waist. He plunged in, took twenty or
so strokes out and then turned around to look at the summer shore.
Thousands of voices sounded like notes held, like a double-bass
vaguely let go and against the heavy metallic stridence of scattered
flutes. The sea was warm and clear: he was able to see, in the trans-
parence, the shadow of his body lighten on the sandy bottom as he
drew away from it. And the thought came to him, so limpidly and
rudely, that he had nothing to set against it: his life seemed like his
effort as a swimmer motionlessly struggling, in imperceptible
movements, to keep his body from covering up his shadow.

Every evening, returning from his stroll in the woods, a man
goes out of his way to be present at this spectacle which attracts
him as much as it disconcerts him: the two daughters of the woods-
keeper at their lessons, seated on the steps of their stoop, books on
their laps; the window from the kitchen open, where the mother
bustles about in the encroaching dimness; a doll abandoned at the
foot of a tree; the keeper's bicycle set against a hedge of euonymus;
the man, finally, whom the scraping of some tool indicates in the
kitchen garden. The sun is at the height of the peaks. Some minutes
yet and the dog, it's certain, will be pulling on his leash barking.

The stroller knows he will find nowhere else so closely knit a net-work of appearances. However, nothing can yet, in his eyes, seem like the beginning of a proof. He feels at once richer and, at the same time, by that infirmity which would always be a reversal of the signs, a vanishing mirage.

An old sailor recounts in what terms, and with what indignant vehemence, he was made to recall the order in his youth to have tried to throw a lifebuoy to the cabin boy who had fallen into the sea in heavy weather when his ship was preparing to round Cape Horn:

—It's a cruelty truly worthy of a devil to prolong the hope of the man who is going to drown, in such parts, when no hope exists of bearing him any help. If it were possible, charity would rather have commanded throwing a rock at his head.

Pretending a great sensitivity to light, a young woman never re-moves her outsize sunglasses in which her admirers are annoyed to see only their own smiles. Measured without their knowing, con-fronted by their own caricature when they look for some encour-agement (but not despairing of overcoming the distance to which they believe themselves confined in sport), how would they not feel particularly gauche?

Yet the young woman can make out only confused forms fidget-ing about. Three-quarters blind from an accident, and using all her coquetry to let nothing of it appear, she feels, herself, exposed de-fenseless to their eyes.

A man, for an entire day in Paris, prey to the memory of a woman whom he thought forgotten. Her first name cried out by a child whose mother she might have been and he the father, then a figure of an astonishing resemblance, a print dress like she wore, her brand of perfume in a shop window, her fragrance in the street, her voice in the Metro.

Their last dispute sprang up again in turn, word for word and, lit-tle by little, the exact atmosphere provoking the split. The man sees nothing to add, nothing to retract: a truly ineluctable slide.

Yet, the twinge at heart which persists despite all, he clearly realizes, is just what brought them together once as if, in the concatentation of the disaster, and despite the avatars of their passion, the match alone remained intact amidst the conflagration.

Paquirri's coffin borne on men's backs, for three hours, through the streets of Seville by thousands of aficionados from all over Spain. The crowd in mourning clothes which, spontaneously, bears it to the Maestranza for one last *paseo,* is swallowed up under the monumental gate, recites a paternoster before the empty tiers, howls, in tears: "Torero! Torero!" then "Olé! Olé!" while the remains sways on their shoulders, while white handkerchiefs flutter and flowers are thrown.

One man, wearing a black tie, who would try to disentangle the memory of the moment of grace, allied to the purest mastery, which had so perfectly permitted him to identify himself with his hero, of the sublime *faena* that he still expected of him and of which, to be capable of imagining it, he knows himself forever deprived by every other torero.

Was it the heat? The storm interminably threatening? The drag of too straight a path between the fields where he had become involved out of pure indolence and so seemed to be going nowhere?

He had stooped to look at a little sweetbrier. At that moment there came back to him all the despondency of his childhood when he used to wander alone in the countryside on Thursday afternoons: attracted by the very small, he would notice the least slope so saturated with life, the balance there at once so fragile and so perfect it seemed to him there was no space on earth left for him to get in on. Trampling the high grass, the wake of crushed plants was unbearable to him, irritating to see birds and insects rising in waves at his approach. Depressed, wherever he went, by never being there except by intrusion, he felt himself stifled under the weight of his own presence.

STREET SIGNS

ENID SHOMER

My brother, Beryl, was eleven when he decided to change his name. The kids at school had taunted him about it for years, insisting it sounded like a girl's name or a kind of fruit. Raspberyl, blueberyl, blackberyl. My parents were reluctant to agree: he was the only namesake for my mother's Great Uncle Beryl, a man famous for overturning with his bare arms a wagonful of Cossacks who had called him a Jew-dog and ordered him off the road. The story went that when the Cossacks came looking for him in the village the next day, even the goyim lied to protect him. This all happened in the Ukraine, in the dim ages before we spoke English.

"Pick a name that begins with 'B,' all right?" my mother said. "Maybe Bruce?"

My brother said he liked the name "Brad."

"'Brad' is that little brass thing on envelopes. Like a paper clip."

He must have given it quite a bit of advance thought. "Then 'Bart,'" he said. "I want to be called 'Bart.'"

"Rhymes with fart," my father said.

He was not discouraged. "'Bob?' Just plain old 'Bob?'"

Finally they settled on Barry. It didn't sound too ordinary, my mother said, or too gentile. It sounded a little French, a little continental.

They went downtown to the courthouse the next day after school. My brother told me if I ever called him Beryl again he would pour calamine lotion in my eyes while I was asleep.

After that, only my brother's best friend, Asher Levandowski, was allowed to call him Beryl, and only in private. Beryl and Asher were both born in August, which accounted, Mother claimed, for their sticky temperaments, her way of saying they were pests. I hated them most of the time. They were boys. They were vulgar. They picked their noses and ate it. They said bad words when no adults were listening, then denied it on their lives. At the movies on Saturday afternoons they waited until there was kissing on the screen, then exploded their popcorn boxes. Worst of all, they played the pinball machines on Georgia Avenue, a known hangout for hoodlums.

Asher would have liked to change his name, too, but his parents were religious—recent refugees from Europe. Because the Levandowskis had paid dearly for their heritage, Mother said, they were determined to keep it intact. The Levandowskis made no concessions to the *meshugos*, the crazinesses of "Amerikeh." The result was that Asher behaved as if he were two different people. At home he was obedient, dutiful, and careful. He took piano lessons and was not allowed to read trash like comic books. Asher's house on Friday nights and Saturdays was a dreadfully quiet place even my brother avoided.

The other Asher was hellbent on adventure, despite the oversized galoshes, the leather cap with earflaps, the heavy wool mittens and, of course, the umbrella. Mrs. Levandowski believed that the umbrella was the first bulwark against catching colds. At first she fastened it to Asher's coat sleeve with a giant safety pin. Later, he carried the large black umbrella hooked over his forearm. It gave him a formal appearance, as if he were about to bow. Like Beryl, Asher wore thick eyeglasses which he broke about once a month. That may have added to their camaraderie. Also, Asher understood Yiddish. He had always known that the name Beryl meant a great, ferocious bear.

Now they are widening the road that leads to my brother's house. Alongside the hilly, winding blacktop, giant backhoes churn and shovels drool uprooted sod. These are the first road improvements since Barry and his wife moved out there twenty-five years ago. He wanted his kids to grow up with plenty of trees, birds, and fresh air, the occasional wild rabbit and raccoon. He didn't want them subject to the push and tumble of city life, by which he meant our old house on Garfield Place. I thought we had enough of the countryside in the old neighborhood. We had stinkbomb trees and mimosas and acorn oaks. We had room in the backyard for Mother to raise a few tomatoes. We had the workmanlike sound of the garbage trucks in the morning and the dreamy whir of the streetcleaning machine at night.

He moved farther out than he had to, but then that was always his way.

From the sidewalk outside Rudy's Pinball Palace, you could hear the machines—they sounded like a hundred cash registers going at once—and see their lights flashing. It was a hot day in late September when I bribed Barry and Asher with a dollar apiece to take me there. I had saved up three weeks' allowance and scoured the house for *gefineneh gelt*—the loose change that disappeared into sofas, chairs, and the washing machine.

The double entrance doors were open and three ceiling fans chopped away at the heat. I followed them into the deepening gloom, past boys of all ages intently pushing buttons and flipping levers.

They chose a game called Frisco Goldrush. Barry said he'd kill me or Asher if we touched the machine. He released the first ball, then began pushing and leaning on the machine with all his weight. That was just like him: he was always making rules for other people and breaking them himself. Asher didn't seem to mind. Mother said Barry was a born ringleader and that he had Asher going in circles.

Around us, buzzers and bells rang as less skillful players made their machines go tilt. His score climbed rapidly: 500, 900, 1200.

"His best is 42,000," Asher said.

"Shut up!" Barry hissed. "I can't concentrate."

But he was concentrating. The lights of the machine reflected off his glasses, giving him a powerful look, as if the colors were zooming out from his head, like Superman's X-ray vision.

"Shit!" he cried, as the silver ball dropped into an alley.

"Double shit," Asher said. "Piss."

There was almost nothing as satisfying as hearing them curse. I had no desire to do it myself. My mother's speech was filled with euphemisms like heck, darn, and shoot. Naturally, she disapproved of indelicate language, which for her also included speaking Yiddish in the presence of non-Jews, something she considered rude and old-fashioned. On the other hand, nothing pleased her more than to hear a gentile use the word "goy" or Sammy Davis, Jr. say "schvartza."

Some older boys draped themselves around our machine and lit cigarettes. They had thin, sharp noses and stiff, oiled pompadours. They were what we called rocks.

"Who's the slit?" one of them asked.

"His sister," Asher said.

They glared at me. "This is no place for girls," the same boy said. I moved to the next machine and dropped my dime in.

"Give me a drag," Barry said.

"Yeah," Asher said. "I want to hotbox it."

The older boys passed their cigarettes to them. Barry and Asher inhaled deeply and made the tips of the cigarettes glow bright red. The idea was to see how long an ember you could make.

Afterwards, they bought peppermint candies to sweeten their breath. I had been scared to go to Rudy's alone. When I returned home, it struck me that Barry and Asher might have been afraid, too. But together they acted like they could take over the whole world.

Do you think the teachers at school were diplomatic about my brother's name change? They kept remarking on it, or forgetting it momentarily, so that the two names were strung together into a horrible long new one—Berylbarry. This marked the beginning of my brother's difficulties at school.

In those days bad behavior wasn't called hyperactivity or social skills deficits. It was called simply "discipline" and occupied an intimidating square outlined in bold black on our report cards. That fall, his grades changed from SP for Satisfactory Progress to UP, Unsatisfactory Progress, with remarks in the discipline box like "talks too much," "constantly disrupts the classroom," and "challenges the teacher."

Things went from bad to worse. Finally, during Passover that year, he crumbled some matzohs he had brought to school as snacks, and dumped them inside Sheila Green's jumper. Sheila had to be sent home. Her mother told my mother her skin was red and irritated. Mother said yes, she was sure that it was, because no cracker in this world had edges as sharp as a broken matzoh. Barry was suspended from school for two days. I remember how agitated my parents were about this incident. Could it be the teachers had said something derogatory about the matzoh in the first place? Did they know it was a ritual food? And most important of all, what was Barry thinking, desecrating the matzoh like that? On the eighth day of Passover, Mother threw out the leftover matzohs, something she had never done before.

The next afternoon, Barry came home from Asher's house, went up to his small attic bedroom, and cried. Mother and I both heard him. He didn't cry the way I did—silently into a pillow until it was soggy and cold. His tears were always accompanied by temper tantrums. He beat on the wall with his fists and wailed.

"Barry!" Mother shouted up the stairs. "What's wrong?"

"None of your business." His voice was muffled by the closed door.

If Dad had been home, he wouldn't have dared to answer her like that. She looked crushed and then, gradually, angry.

"Come down here this instant!" she yelled.

No sound from his room. She mounted the stairs and pushed the door open. Then she dragged him by his shirt collar down the steps into the kitchen and poured him a glass of cold milk to calm him down.

"What is it, Beryleh?" she asked quietly.

"Barry."

"Barry, then."

"Mrs. Levandowski heard about the matzohs." He choked up a little.

"And?"

"She kicked me out of the house."

Mother was silent for a moment. She glared at me so that I wouldn't say anything. "She'll get over it," she said.

"No, she won't. She said I can't come back." Barry sipped at the milk.

Though there was always a lot of yelling and screaming in our family, there was very little of the kind of quiet terror I imagined Mrs. Levandowski to be capable of. In our house, no matter what anyone said, we all knew that person didn't really mean it. The glue that held us together could not be dissolved by a flare-up in temper, no matter how severe. It was a special kind of permissiveness—perhaps a Jewish permissiveness. We were made to feel guilty, but we never doubted that we could redeem ourselves. There were no absolutes, only a kind of ongoing tug-of-war, run by parents who almost never stuck by anything they said if we pressed them hard enough. I could not imagine my mother ordering a child from her house. It was far too rude and arbitrary. But Mrs. Levandowski was another case. She reminded me of my Russian Grandma Bella—a stubborn and strict woman who stuck to a gallstone diet long after her gall bladder was removed and whose favorite food was laxatives.

"Just like that?" my mother asked. "What else did Mrs. Levandowski say?"

My brother looked up from his glass of milk. "I already told you."

"I mean, I want to know her exact words." Mother was always asking for peoples' exact words, as if she could insert herself into another person's head if she had enough information.

Barry gazed out the window toward the alley that separated Asher's street from ours. I looked out expecting to see one of the neighborhood kids there, but it was empty. "She said she was ashamed for me. About the matzoh and all."

"Oh." Now mother was getting indignant. "Who is she to call names?"

"She didn't call me any names. She just said I couldn't come to the house."

"We'll see about that," Mother said.

"I don't want you talking to her for me." Barry stood up. "I'm not a baby, you know. And it's none of your business."

From there on, the argument grew familiar. I knew Mother would win, but that it would take a long time to bring him around. She explained that when he beat his head against the wall it was her business, that the whole neighborhood was her business if she said it was, even Mrs. Levandowski. But she promised to be tactful. She promised not to get angry at Mrs. Levandowski. Barry made her swear that she wouldn't say anything to make the situation worse.

Once I saw a film of a house-raising in an Amish community. The sides of the house were laid out and nailed together on the ground. Ruddy men wearing overalls, straw hats, and carpenters' aprons swarmed over the wood frame like bees over a hive. Nails poked cheerfully out of their mouths instead of words. In the distance, other farmhouses they had built squatted like salt cellars on a great laid table. A field of summer corn swayed behind them, its deep treads and waves repeating the grain of the wood, the hanks of their hair. You could hear a communal hum of pleasure when the sides went up. This happened near one of those towns in eastern Pennsylvania like Paradise or Intercourse where tourists are always stealing the road signs.

Barry moved into Wildwood Estates right before his first child was born. All the streets bear the names of woodland flowers and trees. At the corner of Azalea and Bluet lived a profoundly deaf child whose parents arranged to have a special yellow sign like the ones used for dangerous curves and deer-crossings installed at the entrance to the subdivision. It said Deaf CAUTION Child. At least that is the way I always read it, because the word "caution" was sandwiched between the other two. I remember thinking that like all signs, it would become invisible after a while. But I liked the idea of a public notice for a single child. It seemed both extravagant and absolutely essential. I could imagine a neighborhood full of such signs: Blind Caution Child, Lame Caution Child, Shy or Fat Caution Child, Doesn't Understand Where Road Leads Caution Child.

Whenever Barry gave directions to his house, he'd always say turn right one block after deaf child. Then he'd take pleasure in explaining what that was.

Mother telephoned Mrs. Levandowski the next day. Barry stood right next to her, listening. I was arranging my dolls under the kitchen table in their own little fallout shelter.

"Sadie?" Mother said. "Sadie Levandowski?"

I had been to Asher's house many times to play the piano. I knew Mrs. Levandowski would be standing in the kitchen like Mother, most likely stirring or kneading something. She kept a kosher kitchen which meant, basically, that nobody else could touch anything in it, not even Mr. Levandowski. There was no neutral zone for the uninitiated among all those cabinets, shelves, and drawers. I felt like a barbarian, stranded between the *milchadik* and the *fleshadik*. When I drank a glass of milk, I was afraid to set it down anywhere, even in the double sink. I always handed it back to her.

"*Danken Gott*, the whole family is fine," Mother said. "Yours?"

Of course when Mother said the whole family was fine, she was referring to about forty people—all our aunts and uncles and cousins and grandparents. Mrs. Levandowski had one cousin in Detroit, her husband and son. The rest of the family had been killed in the War.

"Sadie, how would you like to come over for a cup of coffee?" Mother's voice was warm and sincere. "Sure I have tea."

They decided on Saturday afternoon. Mrs. Levandowski preferred Saturday after *schul* because she'd already be dressed.

Barry was two years older than me. Two years in the life of a child is a crucial, heartbreaking span. It is the difference between counting on your fingers and long division, between being confined to a few streets and wandering freely through the neighborhood. People were always assuring me that two years would be nothing once we were grown. But at the time, it seemed that Barry would always be smarter, taller, and faster, that I would never catch up. Even when I tried to imagine the two of us in our dotage, Barry was a white-haired gentleman walking ten steps ahead, talking a mile a minute to the blank air in front of him, and I was an old lady scrambling to keep pace like our Grandma Bella, who couldn't get out of the way of her own great fallen bosoms.

I often sneaked into his room to see the Lionel train setup which occupied most of it. He always left little scraps of paper jammed into the tracks and wheels so that he could tell if I played with it while he was out. But I didn't need to turn it on. I'd stare at the miniature cows and sheep fastened to their painted green pasture until I felt myself settled peacefully in that tiny, immobile landscape. Then I'd comfort myself with the thought that along with more privileges, Barry also ran into more trouble. As a toddler, he had been kept on a leash. He had set the house on fire accidentally the year before during a paper drive. He was sicklier than I was. His eyes itched and watered and he suffered sneezing fits. The doctor said Barry was allergic to himself, but that he would outgrow it.

Several times in going through his desk, I'd encountered his Hebrew books. That was one advantage I had over him. Because I was a girl, I didn't have to go to Hebrew school. Barry, like Asher, spent three afternoons a week at *Agudas Achim* synagogue to prepare for his bar mitzvah. The synagogue was walking distance from our house, but is was orthodox. Did the other members know that we ate hardshell crabs by the bushel in summer and ordered Lobster Cantonese at the Shanghai restaurant?

The thick black Hebrew letters reminded me of the symbols in cartoons when the character is exasperated and runs out of words. Though I had heard Barry read Hebrew out loud, I was still amazed that such foreign sounds could come from his mouth. Even my parents could not understand most of it.

The next Saturday morning was spent in preparation for Mrs. Levandowski's visit. My mother insisted that we make our beds and clean our closets just in case Mrs. Levandowski wanted to take the ten-cent tour. I always hated it when we had company, for then she would stalk the house anxiously grumbling as she checked for dust, fingerprints, smears, and stray hairs.

It has always struck me as odd that children become intimate with their neighbors while their parents often never set foot in their houses. I had seen Mr. and Mrs. Levandowski in their pajamas on Sunday morning. I knew that Mrs. Levandowski wore a thick layer of Noxzema cream on her face at home, even if Asher brought company. I had seen her watch TV in the living room in the evening, white-faced, smelling like a Vick's cough drop, dead to shame about her appearance. I had even heard her burp once at the kitchen table. She had excused herself, but she wasn't embarrassed.

Mrs. Levandowski arrived at two p.m. She was dressed in a navy print dress with a large white collar that spread out from her cleavage like wings and flapped into her face when she leaned forward. Her accent was Polish, her speech, even in English, filled with the gentle clicking and mewing of that tongue. The blood-red lipstick she wore made her face look extremely pale. Barry and I said hello, then sat down on the loveseat opposite the sofa where the two women sat, each turned slightly on one haunch toward the other. Mrs. Levandowski withdrew a huge deadly hatpin from her hat, removed the hat, and patted her hair. "In Europe we had cafés where to talk," she said.

"Oh? You mean sidewalk cafés?"

"Sidewalk, yes. On the street. In Warsaw we had many. We walked there."

"I see," Mother said.

"We didn't drive. Who needed a car in Warsaw?"

"I hate to drive," Mother said. This wasn't exactly true. We used to have a blue stick-shift Ford that Mother was unable to master. But once we got the Chrysler with the automatic transmission, she was jumping into it every chance she got.

"My husband, Zaichik, he drives."

"Yes," Mother said.

The kettle was whistling. Mother got up to fix the tea and told us to keep Asher's mother company. The three of us sat silently until she returned. Mrs. Levandowski looked around at everything in the room, not furtively, but as if she were searching for something familiar. She picked up the plate of cookies my mother had set out, chose two and put them in her lap. Her hands were meaty and slow-moving. They were as big as a man's.

Mother returned with the tea service on a tray. "I have sugar cubes, if you like," she said, offering her the good crystal sugar bowl. My grandparents from Russia drank tea with sugar cubes in their mouths. Mrs. Levandowski took her tea unsweetened.

Suddenly, the two of them were speaking the secret language,

Yiddish. Mrs. Levandowski spoke much faster than she had in English. Mother stumbled a bit, groping for words. They talked for a long time, until their voices were a drone in the room. I looked at Barry fidgeting and was happy to see he couldn't understand them either. Then, all of a sudden, dead silence. Mother lit a cigarette and blew a plume of smoke to one side.

"The world," Mrs. Levandowski said, addressing me and Barry, "is not a happy place. Once maybe, but never again . . ." Her voice trailed off.

"Dos iz nisht Warsaw, Sadie. Dos iz America," Mother said.

Mrs. Levandowski glowered at her and spoke some more in Yiddish. I could pick out the words "matzoh" and "Pesach." She pointed to Barry and counted off four fingers on one hand, each accompanied by a name.

Mother continued to smoke, but with her free hand she was pressing her thumbnail along her jaw, a nervous habit I'd seen before. Then, her voice quaking and high-pitched, she said something long and pleading in Yiddish to Mrs. Levandowski.

"Nein." Mrs. Levandowski shook her head. Her teacup rattled in the saucer as she set it down. She pushed up her left sleeve until small blue numbers appeared on her forearm. "Don't be fooled," she said. She reached across the sofa, took Mother's arm, and gently turned it over to expose the wrist, with its tracery of veins and smooth, finely textured skin. "Your arm is the accident," she said, "not mine."

Mrs. Levandowski stood up to leave. "Asher understands," she said. She picked up her hat and walked to the door. Mother thanked her for coming. They shook hands, something I had never seen two women do before. They looked like heads of state. "Goodbye to you," Mrs. Levandowski said.

Mother watched through the living room window as Mrs. Levandowski trudged down the pavement. Then she burst into tears and went upstairs to her bedroom. "I knew you wouldn't be able to change her mind," Barry shouted up at her, a note of righteousness in his voice, as if Mrs. Levandowski had not disappointed him.

For some time after that, Barry and Asher continued to be friends, though only on the street. Barry was not allowed in Asher's house, and Asher avoided our house, not because his mother had forbidden him to enter it, but because, I think, it held too much for him to reconcile. Eventually, of course, he had to choose. Perhaps if he had been a few years older, he'd have chosen Barry. But he was young then. So young that the choice must have felt to him simply like a gradual turning in the direction of his mother's pale insistent face and dark lips, a slight inclination of his head so that her lament came clearer to his ears and became, finally, his lament.

When Barry saw that new neighborhoods and shopping centers were sprouting near his subdivision on land formerly given to tobacco and horse pasture, he thought about moving farther out. But of his three children, only one lives at home now, and she'll be going away to college in the fall. Instead, he and his wife bought a large cabin-cruiser where they spend every weekend in good weather. He says the sea is the last open road.

I was surprised to see the old Deaf CAUTION Child sign relocated to the side of the newly widened road to his house. I like to imagine that the roadworders preserved it out of reverence, for surely they could have guessed from its battered condition that the deaf child was long since grown. But perhaps they were simply daunted by the prospect of discovering whether, in all those houses, there was still someone who lived in a markedly different world, one which could not be changed and needed protecting.

Barry says he barely remembers Asher and he does not know what became of him or his parents. This is nothing unusual or sad for a human being. The memories of children do not so much record the past as bury it.

The full story about Mother's Great Uncle Beryl is this: when he overturned the Cossack wagon into the ditch he wasn't just showing off. He was in quite desperate circumstances. He was a drayman and made his living hauling things—barrels of salt herring, household goods, sacks of flour and barley. His buckboard was full that day. He couldn't have moved it out of the way if he had wanted to. The road was narrow and steep, with deep culverts on either side. Mother said he must have reached the breaking point, sitting up high on his rig, looking into that dark ditch where the Cossacks expected him to tumble without a fight. It was perhaps the tenth or the hundredth time he had been called a Jew-dog. That was a common insult in his world of shtetls and pogroms. What matters—what aroused such ferocity—is what he saw from his rig: the dark ditch waiting for him.

After he overturned the Cossacks, it was said that their horses were so frightened by the sight of a wheel that they had to be sold for meat and glue. In the countryside, word of his bravery spread, exciting admiration among gentiles and Jews alike. The family celebrated and toasted him that night with wine, even his aged mother, for whom I am named, and who, I am told, tossed off her shoes and danced.

FOUR POEMS

HELENA KAMINSKI

FACE

Eye is late.
Got stopped in the a. m.
Got roughed up.
Had its camera smashed.
Rumored shot.
Rumored released.

Ear taped downtown today
But it's due back.
Just press "jungle" rewind and play.

Lip lies back on its unmade bed.
Don't shrug at me.
Where are they?

Eye took much shit.
Often, reporting back,
Got cut off before getting to the
Crux of what it saw.

Ear, talented. Talented. Maybe bionic.
Dogs lined up for lessons.

The day eye played it its video
Of mouth yapping about "Life"
As a School for the Deaf,
Ear burst, and underwent
A slow, shocked bealing.

Neighbours say
Things went on
That can't go on
Within a skull.

Why the waste
God why?

Mouth won
Because eye watched
Ear watch mouth
Bulldoze them both.
A writer wrote,
"This is where war turned civil."

Did the bush, grey with road dust
Kneel in near-defeat?
Did the sky mutter
Its crisis?

Don't remember.

Was mouth good or pretty
Bad? Was it

Don't remember.

Mouth, like Fidel,
Spoke for five hours.

It's late.
It's very late.

Damn it.
Who's in charge?

Lip lies back
Along the face,
Dazed body at the beach
On its pale towel.

Where are they?
Where could—

Ask mouth.
Mouth is boss.

from THE LAB

Who We Are

We leave the smears out.
In the morning there is often a surprise.

We signal for the trays.
The live scraps soon arrive.

Cat mat sat rat that hat
What hideous talent.

At level 10, we had a shock
The shock wore off.

Disaster is for amateurs
We are the pros.

Far below our lab
Two doom-planes are about to bump.
Right now they scissor to a city.

Flynn is on top of it.
That beauty.

See Flynn and two trainees
Down in the muck up to their
Knees, looking for slur
In what the pilot may have read.
Tom found the proof it was
The pilot, no, it was the plane.
Good boy, said Flynn.

Star bar car oar jar far
It doesn't mean the pilot was on something slow.
It doesn't mean.

We leave that to
Our sister lab in Lebo.

To be doublesure
They do things twice.
Then run them backwards to be nice.
Them and their monkeys.

"We tested the crew.
They tested clean."

Lebo on the news
Answering questions.

You buy a kit
You put the parts
On where they
Fit, you crazy glue
Them and you sit the parts
Get hard and stick

That isn't us.

We try to teach our scientists a science that is slow.

RIDDLE

The table
Stands in great delay.

A knife, a gun or bed.

Things stacked by a loading dock—goodies
Good for the head.

A tide shines in a foot or so and back.
Waterweep, caught in oil.

The understudy playing
My monster is up.

If I break
She opens for me off-off

In a small thing
On the 12th.

Tears are involved
But not the why of why.

Drunk from the rust of taps
—the bastards leak it on demand—
She mangles lines:

Always look back.
I kept your word.

I tell her look
Forget, then start again.

Just past this
Two are one.

She smiles from surfaces
That lust for sense

I warn her, look—
This is a job.

The window back of her
The room in front

Whoever cloned her added things.

You can't just fire me.
I disagree.

She pouts.
I never did.

Feet apart, each chair
Knows it has arms and legs

Word on the street is
Wood can walk

In dying towns the dust is lush
Seed drops from a pigeon's ass

In through the window
Along the arm

Remnants of a comet speck.

In great dark, they began,
Giants—someone—it wasn't me—
Once said.

Each turned a hero's head, the bevelled
Wrist allowed the hand
To circle full-holed roundness

Caught, they kissed.
Lips, white as the face
Went red. When mouth
Tastes flesh, it eats.
And speaks.

Between the crust and us, the floor.
I trust the stupid boards.

The lake gasps,
Black as a lung.

No, this isn't porn.

ROCKFACE IN UTAH

I am the view.

My great shoulder
Waiting to cool in hot shade.

To see sky
you must climb, in a cramp, a heat,
That are death denied.

The white and blue walled in me wishes you nothing.

Bits of the bone of my kind
Lie in a tonnage of spite.

The envy of minor, minor stone!

The noise of the parch sucking at trickles!

Sleepless soil divining flab,
And pouncing to drink.

Drink what the sun pours!
As I drank, drink.

Why do you stare?

My birth,
The hole I grip,
Were given.

I stand where I suddenly stood.

The same as the day
I opened the lid of the heat.

THE WAR IN THE FOREST

JAMES B. HALL

For Andrew Lytle

That winter in a forest where for days no sun came through the fog, where snow drifted against the trunks of trees, where metal—a tire iron, the knife, a machine pistol—burned the skin from our hands, where the Germans held snow-camouflaged log bunkers, their tree-burst mortar shells and a man cut down by a hurled tree limb lay in the snow while we squatted, saw ice form in a dead man's nostril; at that time in the winter forests of Alsace, we held no prisoners.

Germans surrendered or were captured; Americans also surrendered or were captured. But for nearly a month we shot and the Germans shot all prisoners. Our understanding.

Our 17th was a combat team, a loose functional outfit with the usual misfits.

We had few topo maps, but we did have ammunition, the morphine sterrettes stolen from medic packs, brandy or cognac in our canteens, a few anonymous, white, new-issue parkas. That winter our platoons were under strength, somewhere in Alsace, sometime in December.

The German platoons opposite were even more under strength, always with an older sergeant, a good corporal, the others young, in fact, boys.

They had less ammunition, no fuel, worse boots. Their supply line was short, their maps and local knowledge good, for other German troops had held this terrain a very long time. All summer their engineers concealed *shu* mines, Bouncing Bettys, land mines, trip wires now covered with snow. Those engineers were gone; their replacements came here from the Eastern fronts, the survivors of winter in Russia.

Neither side had men for additional guard duty, MPs, battle police, or a stockade. Neither side had a man to march prisoners back. So we shot prisoners in this way:

—Sergeant, march them back. Our regular route.

—Yes, Sah, and a sergeant always yelled, *Heraus!*

Our *Wermacht* prisoners, helmets gone, cold, eyes exceptionally bulged in their sockets as though the skin were frozen white on their skulls, always formed a line. Their older sergeant knew what was up; the boys sneered, no doubt believed they had again survived.

Then five or six prisoners got prodded along, hands on top of their heads, disappeared all in a row into the forest.

Out of sight, then off the path, then deeper in the forest drifts, those of us who knew to listen heard short bursts of an automatic pistol, his grease gun. Later the sergeant reported in:

—Sah, they runned. So I got off some rounds.

—Sergeant, only thing to do. So forget it.

Those of us who understood "regular route" also understood the sergeant first made them lie down. That way he avoided six single shots—something a chaplain under oath might later recall.

As though craftsmen in the same line of work, the Germans did almost the same thing with us, their prisoners, for we found men all in a row we knew very well, face down in a snowdrift. They, too, were shot, but always with one bullet through the head as though a *Waffen SS* sergeant or office had not much ammunition. There was, however, one small difference . . .

These things when our fighter-bombers were grounded for weeks by silent, dense fog.

II

As a colonel in division headquarters or a later historian might view it, our war was stalemate and therefore became the Order of Battle, a Summary of Casualties, MIAs, Significant Excerpts From Interrogation.

To us, however, everything except the cold and the forest and the snow became personal, almost domestic. We knew the enemy and they knew us.

At that time I was a warrant officer (reconnaissance) attached, but not assigned, a specialist in terrain, maps, gun emplacements; by rank neither a commissioned officer nor an enlisted man, not accepted wholly by either.

At age twenty-three, outwardly, I was a loner: field-smart, resourceful, a neck-scarf of red silk. Emotionally, I was about sixteen; more than anything, I wanted to stay alive, and to belong for tomorrow, or another tomorrow, I expected in some way to be killed and no one at all, no one, would remember either that moment or my circumstance. I had stopped writing letters home to Ohio where I was born.

Emaciated, touchy, I wore tailored shirts, was a talker, always armed, was always secretly excited to hear the burst-of-five roll of automatic weapons firing unseen somewhere in that forest. At the same time I avoided men of rank, all chaplains, believed deeply I lived without illusions, at a distance admired The Cajun.

So I was out before noon with Sergeant Brookshire to find some higher ground. Brookshire was also attached to the 17th with Quad-50 machine guns; his gun crews were always shooting at hawks. He wanted a more advanced gun position, maybe to get some real shooting.

The sergeant stepped around a man-sized fir, much like a snow-covered Christmas tree.

In fact, I thought "Christmas tree" as Brookshire for one moment stopped mid-step, looked up—and his lower face blew away.

For one second his very new parka held him upright. The he was down, one boot kicking and kicking the snow.

I rolled back, crouched behind a larger tree. No other sound, and nothing moved.

Upwind, probably from the crotch of a tree, a man called. To this day I am certain I heard it, in English:

—*Red Scarf. I get you!*

At that time I wore a red silk scarf, bought for cigarettes in a French dress shop. I was known; had a name.

I wanted to move. Could not move, not my boot, not my finger. I buried my face to conceal my own white breath-cloud.

Finally, I ran crouching deeper into the trees, headed back. After two hundred yards, I stopped, huddled in the snow to breathe.

Alone, parka-white in the fog among the fir trees, I drank cognac from my canteen, saw my leg and then my wrist begin to shake, but I was not now afraid.

I stood fully upright, went on in to report, and—worse—to tell Brookshire's gun crews.

Oddly, I began to laugh and laugh and said it first to myself and then said it out loud to the forest, with great elation said my outfit name: "Lucky Jim! Lucky Jim! Luck-ee Fucken Jim!"

In part my name came from my rank, always in the middle; in part it was a show-off, a gambler's name for someone sharp who again had come back when a good man like Sergeant Brookshire "stayed out," for by custom we seldom said a man had been killed.

I was alive, I was elated, and nothing else mattered; yet I knew others now would avoid me for here everyone was superstitious. The third time was the charm, so my luck had run out . . . beware the marked man.

Of course I was not superstitious, but I tried not to remember Brookshire; deeply I felt he had made some kind of error, so he got what he deserved. Later, morbidly, I thought more and more about our opposites, imagined vividly a man with a gun and a sniper's scope in a tree, looking down . . .

There were *Schutzstaffeln* (SS), a battalion, the Death's Head Standard, once of Hitler's personal bodyguard, later *Waffen* (armed) SS. Their insignia was the *Totenkopf*, the Death's Head; even in the field a *Hauptsturmführer* wore his black uniform, the collar patch distinctive, his leather, black, belt with the SS insignias.

Above all, an old-line officer had the dagger in its black sheath, the blade embossed, *Meine Ehre Heist Treue*, that blade, under oath, never to be surrendered. Those things were sinister and therefore highly prized; these things men sometimes died to possess. And the Luger, of course.

Now only the outward form of an SS elite remained; their replacements were not volunteers or "pure" of blood. Yet they were dug in and their *Oberscharführers* were cunning, lethal.

And we did shoot prisoners in our different ways.

We shot German prisoners with short bursts, the face up. Any head shot was through the forehead, that way helped identify a man found when the snows were gone, our "regular route."

When the SS shot us, it was face down, a massive single round into the back of the skull. That way blew off the frontal skull, the whole face. When found, when rolled over, our shock was the greater. In addition, time and place permitting, they cut off our fingers—to take high-school class rings.

Boston Bob and two others found Brookshire where I said: by then he was a block of ice, his parka gone. With a large safety pin—the sniper, no doubt—had fastened Brookshire's testicles to what remained of his upper lip—a frozen, grotesque, bulged-hair "mustache"—their play.

Quickly the word passed: "Asshole in our parka. Bring him in." Brookshire's corporal would personally take him our regular route—but more slowly.

For entirely different reasons, however, in pairs or alone at dusk officers like The Cajun, or sometimes two sergeants, or occasionally an almost silent, withdrawn PFC, disappeared into the forest, went out on a personal recon, or more accurately a long hunt.

Those man were gone sometimes one day, or three, and once The Cajun came in after four days—and then only to "re-up" it was said.

They hunted, stalked, a *Scharführer*, a sergeant, a "Scharfy." With great daring and patience, perhaps for a day and a night they might hole up within the sound of German voices; or, they ranged a long distance to take an officer—perhaps with driver and vehicle—at night, near a culvert.

About noon on the second or third day—unless he stayed out a man on recon returned, might display a wallet with children's pictures, an Iron Cross, German cigarettes, a Luger, Death's Head insignia, a black belt, or American high-school class rings. These things he sold to our replacements, but kept any SS dagger in its black sheath for his wife, back in the States:

—Got me a ugly son-of-bitch of an Over Scharfy,
  a-taking his shit. Got his left eye
  at 260 yahds—some windage.

Men who very much liked a long recon became loners; eventually they stayed out, but not The Cajun. He had no other line of work.

By contrast my work even then was perhaps an older form, but still hanging on.

On random, late afternoons, an order might come down:

Out Recon, 18:00 hrs.

I had a feel for those days, and nearly always had been wearing aviator glasses, avoiding bright light.

Corporal Scoofie, a German-speaking Syrian, said once to be of the New York Mafia, "shaped" (as he said) with five others who preferred a recon to guard duty—irregulars.

In the supply tent we stood in a circle, our parkas not white, but of our own camouflage design. I checked each man; in turn they checked me: anything which might rattle, taped down; nothing at all to catch the light. Ammo; no rings.

At our outpost, each man whispered this day's Right Word, followed me to where a safe path ended, and only those who had used their stolen morphine were not afraid.

Now the temperature was minus zero, the snow exceedingly dry, and we became shadows moving then stopping and then moving again keeping always to tree lines until I found higher ground and the trees thinned. For a minute overhead I saw the moon shine like beaten lead—dully—through the low clouds, was gone.

After one mile or more this ridge fell away towards a clearing. At its farthest edge, I saw rows of very large trees, but I did not go there.

On this higher ground above the clearing, I found a log well covered with snow. As had been understood at the onset, we lay down in a half-circle, our boots almost touching, each man facing a different sector, no two doped-up men together.

Silent, almost covered with blown snow, all around and overhead we heard only the wind among tree branches for one hour, then two.

My squad understood and I understood we were this night probably a "defensive" entry in a field report. Had there been tank or truck engine noises upwind, even very far away, we would hear them. Cowardice had nothing to do with it. In some way, soon, I expected to die, but not for a report, not for some colonel's words on paper.

Finally, like snowmen stiffly walking, we went back more closely together, back very much along our same trail—not good recon, but not mined—went back to the outpost where we began.

Mutt

And a voice somewhere in dark, ahead, answered:

Jeff

In that way we came in, and once again in the supply tent no words were spoken.

The OD took my report and without changing expression cranked a field telephone:

Recon in; no contact.

For a long time I lay awake in my bedroll inside a shelter made of truck bows and what was once a small-wall tent, a lean-to covered with snow. Because I could not prevent it, I saw again every shadow of this night, saw everything that next time might go wrong; yet, also, I saw the smokestack trees of this forest were like the shadows of an Ohio steel mill and my recon life was like the boy once on an Ohio farm who did not like but still yearned each Thursday evening for the lights, the band music, of a nearby market town . . .

At the time I was imaginative, but did not know it. Past three o'clock in the morning, as always, finally, I slept.

III

Two afternoons later, a new line of prisoners came in from the forest, their hands up.

We gathered around. I scented the curious odor of prisoners even in winter: feces, body odors.

Four German enlisted men; one officer. Our outpost had heard them a quarter-mile away. Half-blinded by the snow, half-frozen, not dressed for this weather, they stumbled past our guard, not ten feet from his post. The guard merely called ahead on his field telephone:
—*Open the shit house door . . ."*

Scoofie of recon spoke German to the officer, a captain.

Fuckin quartermaster troops, Scoofie told us. Replacements. But assholes. Not okay physically.

I looked at the German captain: stooped, long neck, an Adam's apple. His blond hair was thinning; even in a field coat his chest was concave. His rimless, octagon eyeglasses misted heavily. This one had schoolmaster written all over him. This one had done limited service for years at a supply base. Then a someone declared him combat-ready for an SS outfit in the forest. But he never made it.

No one could find The Cajun, said to be in his bedroll beating his dog.

This was Lieutenant Claggerd, an ROTC officer from LSU, once a highway engineer. The Cajun always referred to this winter forest as a "bye-you."

A loner, The Cajun was carried by the 17th from the Engineers, so Lieutenant Claggerd seldom reported to anyone. He had his own lean-to where he slept and stored his ammo and weapons.

The Cajun did only long hunts—and slept. Always he carried live grenades fastened to his shoulder straps. He liked very much his line of work: kill Germans and bring back trophies to sell.

Finally Lieutenant Claggerd showed up, helmet pushed back on his head, legs slightly bowed, smiling his turtle, man-eater, smile. He wore neither a ring nor a wristwatch. On the front of his helmet was a faded daub of white paint: First Lieutenant.

The Cajun walked once again around this bunch. He was armed with an issue .45, his Luger, a grease gun (machine pistol), and many ammo clips; his grenades were turtle shells hanging to his chest.

He glanced aloft: still enough light:

—Sah-jint. Take 'em back. Regular route.

—Sah! And a long-hunt sergeant took over: *Heraus* your asses!

There was also another form of things. Our sergeants shot German enlisted men; an officer shot captured German officers. Something like having separate clubs and latrines.

Abruptly, The Cajun turned to me, put his hands on his ammo clips, spoke loudly enough:

—And *Mister*—slurred in front of the noncoms:

—You-all get Big Boy.

The lieutenant gestured towards their captain:

—Mister, I'll *see* you take him. Regular route.

Scoofie understood, spoke German to the captain and the captain took two steps, reported almost formally to me. Someone in film or a moralist might say that precise moment was crucial, but it was not so.

I saw only the tops of trees. I saw a supply tent, two or three small-wall tents on packed snow; I saw little groups of men watching prisoners, and the final light of this day sliding down through the trunks of trees.

Smartly, GI, I answered the lieutenant, The Cajun:

"Roger," pronounced "Ra-Ja,"

understood.

To the over-age-in-grade, stooped, captain:

—*Heraus!*—asshole.

A line sergeant herded his German enlisted men all in a row to the far side of the clearing.

My .45 automatic came easily into my hand. I hit the butt end with my left palm, slammed home the clip. My German saw that, knew there was no round in the firing chamber.

This one was clearly relieved; now he was in charge of another officer.

The German's eyeglasses had cleared. He was exhausted from his two days and a night lost in the forest, but now he could see.

I poked him once in the back with my .45, herded him towards another path to the south. As we entered the forest the tops of the trees disappeared, taken by a white, sliding mist.

The footprints of our path ended at the trunk of a tree.

The German stopped, turned to see if there were some mistake. He heard the *snick-snack* of my gun's slide loading its round. With sudden, immense clarity that metal sliding told him something.

His mouth opened. He trembled first in his legs, then in his upper body. Standing roughly at attention in the snow, the forest all around, he could not believe. And then he did believe:

—*Frau, Frau. Kinder . . .*

—*Gott.*

When he raised his eyes towards the tops of the fir trees, I put the muzzle of the gun beneath his chin. Pulled the trigger.

For a moment he seemed to stand taller, on tiptoe. His head jolted back. He fell then into the snow.

He writhed, kicked once. There was no back at all to his head, for now all of that was gone.

I turned, walked not quickly back along the path; the acrid smell of a .45 automatic recently fired seemed to walk with me, even after I put the gun in its leather holster hanging as always on my webbed belt.

Farther to the west, I heard faint, short bursts of a machine pistol: the sergeant, at the end of our regular route.

—Made a break for it, I told The Cajun.

—So I skinned him.

Lieutenant Claggerd pushed his helmet higher off his face, laughed at something. Ironically, humorously, only for the form of it, he said:

—Mister, I *ain't* pleased. But you had a do it.

—Now didunt juh?

That night I drank some of the cognac hidden in my bedroll. I was so exhausted my hand did not move when so ordered. Then I understood The Cajun's meaning: "*You had a do it . . .*"

Had I said "No," or hesitated, The Cajun would have shown me the way, and that way was deeper into the forest.

At a path's end, first The Cajun would have shot the German officer. And then shot me, for if a man won't shoot a German, and especially a German officer, then you can't afford to keep the sonofabitch around.

And in those ways our war in the forest went on.

Much later, after The Cajun hooked up with another combat outfit and stayed out but was carried MIA, I saw it even more deeply: The Cajun did not like patrols to come in no contact; worse, when a Brookshire eats it, you shoot a sniper or a sniper ties your balls in a red silk scarf under your nose because you don't go out there to check.

And maybe it was not a sniper, maybe it was a German sergeant, a Scharfy, on his own long hunt.

IV

Past noon next day I awoke, came out into a light rain.

The entire 17th Combat Team was gone: Scoofie, Boston Bob, The Cajun. Too long in the woods, shot up, pulled back, gone. Because I was only attached (not assigned) no one remembered to wake me.

That did not matter for I was now attached to Ironsides, 22d Combat Team. Now I would have to do everything all over again, except new troops sometimes shoot each other after dark, and new officers at first would order daylight recons into the forest every day. Moreover a green outfit would attract German probes, night patrols in strength. Now one side or the other would shoot me; I saw this with a terrible clarity, understood this was so.

Ironsides was full strength, clean; every man had everything he was supposed to have. They chattered, shouted, told this forest they were new and they were here.

I found their adjutant, a major, who wore shining insignia on his hat, his collar, his parka, and who also had an overly large wristwatch with oversized black numbers—French.

He smiled a Texas A&M, ROTC, fullback's smile:

—Good lick, MacShit. Your ass is mine.

Just then with great longing, I remembered the 17th, even for that single moment when without illusion, wholly, I belonged: when The Cajun laughed and said, "You had a do it."

Because I was dried out by cognac, was hospital thin, they said I was just standing there on the snow, then went limp, fell.

When I awoke, a medic was holding a mirror near my face, was reflecting his small flashlight into my throat.

I saw my own face: not shaved, gaunt, very old, skin stretched tight across a skull, the eyes protruding as though to see beyond the mirror and more deeply into the trees . . .

"You're OK," the medic sergeant said, "No strep. Drink plenty of liquids."

In a few days the fog lifted and the sun seemed warmer than it was, especially towards nightfall.

With the sun our fighter-bombers got off the ground, were silver and sunshine-metal flashing just above the tops of the trees. When I saw them going in, I felt suddenly elated, the grim joy of reprieve.

Only a few thousand yards away, muffled by the terrain and the woods and the snow now melting from every branch, I heard the first bombs, felt the earth beneath the snow shrug a little.

Almost overnight I became useless, an anachronism, for now the terrain ahead had new definition; our forward elements marked a target and with much newer radios called in the fighter-bombers.

Even so, the army can be intimate: the word passes, and some things everyone believes.

In a few days, with neither irony nor respect intended, the sergeants of Ironsides began to call me Lucky Jim.

I was someone aged but not old, a man still walking around, displaced, who each night slept in the canvas bows of a different truck: off the ground, ready to move out.

One day at noon, the forward elements of Ironsides entered and then moved easily through a clearing not mined at all.

Beyond, the terrain fell down and away to low hills, and then to a plain where there were fields, and barns, and houses, and no snow at all on crossed, black lines which were stone walls.

In this clearing, our fighter-bombers had caught a German field headquarters.

Their dead horses lay where they reared or were running away when they died and were now beginning to swell. Field kitchens and dead men and trucks still burning, paybooks and boxes of ammo lay among fallen trees, as though something flooded this clearing, had flashed once, left only blue smoke, debris.

Because so many knew about a sergeant found with his balls pinned to his mouth—and his parka gone—and understood a Cajun officer was once behind the MLR for days but was now Missing In Action, a communications sergeant who once was a grade-school principal took me to the edge of this clearing to a downed tree. He thought I might want a souvenir.

The sergeant showed me the dead German, this one wearing a slightly soiled, but still an American, white parka stretched tight everywhere, for he was beginning to swell.

The arm was raised, askew, elbow and hand raised as though hitchhiking. Someone from Ironsides, someone now a veteran, someone already on the plain already shooting inside barns and houses and over stone walls, had cut off one finger, to take a class ring or a wedding band—something of value.

Looking back on it, very well I knew almost exactly what I was doing, or so it seemed.

But later they said in fact I fired and fired my army-issue automatic again and again into the belly and the chest and the face of a man dead between a log and boxes of ammunition. And not a real soldier: only someone in a headquarters caught when a clearing was bombed.

They said I was trying to load another clip when a supply sergeant pinned my arms and I heard him call and call into the smoke:

—*Medics, medics, medics* . . .

The rear doors of a field ambulance opened, and after the needle's metal tip foraged into my skin, the doors of the ambulance closed and everything was dark.

After all those things, for a long time, I believed our war in the forest began and in all those ways at last ended.

But in fact, my war in the forest went on, for as it was at the onset, deeply I wished to belong but cannot belong even though I have tried to belong all the days of my life.

IOVIS OMNIA PLENA

An Excerpt

ANNE WALDMAN

I see you everywhere

> *di mana-mana*

& the light of our day
speaks through us

I study you,
    eyes
    ears
    nose
          hair

apa kabar?
baik baik

> I see you everwhere
> & walking

salamat jalan
What is our language?
the study of thinking
    & through the mind to the melody we will play

together
or apart
                    walking
a man walking
                              What's your name
                                    siapa namanya?
with whom do you walk?

                              I'm lost (*saya teresat*)
I practice the syllables of your history Bali
I see you everywhere
because I am lost
                    I see you everywhere
You speak
any questions (*Ada pertanyaan*)
There is no answer to love
     Tidak ada jawaban

melihat, menonton, membaca
                              (to see, to watch, to read)
          I am a "penulis puisi"
a penniless poetry

      I come into you from a great distance a penniless poetry

You are my pitch
my sound my song
                    (the holy 3)
rendah, suara, lagu

I sing you my beloved
because I am lost without you
                              Is it forbidden?
listrik mati
I am dead without you

How many times I think "I am dead without you"
     cari apa?
                    I look for my own eyes
& for the switch to bring them on again

I see you everywhere
                    di mana-mana
        be still be silent
                this is *nipu sipi*   (*nyepi*)
the whole world died, no fire, murder the fire
  I was lost when they murdered the fire
                    the whole world died
  This is the child's first lesson
Bahasa Indonesia
            it is a simple tongue
tongue of the child
                            lost everywhere without
my child-man-speech
            guide to the temple
you must go there with torch, he says
listrik mati
                dead in the cave
lost without you
    child-man-deity
    call upon you as guide

call to the *langit gringsing wayang*
            flaming heaven of the *wayang*
    call to my ancestors who live inside me everywhere
        & abandon me in my weakness
                not making the proper ceremonies

Call upon Giri Putri, Dewi Gangga, Dewi Danu

Call Mother Uma
Stave off Durga
                        all could die here
                        in me
                        murder the fire
I see you everywhere
                (*di mana-mana*)
            Beloved Indra, active and warlike
    you bring down the rain to cleanse this heart
                everything that existed once dies now
                    it dies as I call upon you

BataraSiwa, divine hermaphrodite
                    source of all life, Windu   that
            takest away the static of the world
                            blow upon us
                        bring down the rain to cleanse this fire
            (for I am burning, burning)
                    dear shape shifter, dear Iovis
                                        who are you?
this is the dark moon of the ninth month
the puppets dance to activate the mind
            toward what great comedies & miracles?

Siwa once upon a time created beings with no ethics, no sila,
no code of behaviour, who went naked lived wild in caves, had
no religion. They mated under trees in the light of day, abandoned
their sad children, ate offal, lived like beasts. Siwa
was so horrified he imagined a son to destroy these
humans. He was copulating with his wife, he was coming into
her, he was excited with his plan, his great revenge on the
monsters he himself had created and he told her, he told Uma his
intentions. (He was fucking himself here.) She was indignant
and withdrew from him quickly and in the struggle
Siwa's sperm fell on the ground. He panicked, he called
the gods together and pointing to the sperm said that should it
develop life there would be great difficulties for them.
The alarmed gods began to shoot arrows at the sperm. The
sperm grew a pair of shoulders when the first arrow struck
it, hands and feet popped out after the second, and as they
continued to shoot into it, the drop of sperm grew into
a fantastical giant who stood as high as a mountain,
demanding food with which to pacify his insatiable hunger.
Siwa named him Kala and every day sent him down to earth
where he could eat his fill of people.

                    thus the barbarians dwindled
                        (put out the fire)
but again
it comes back
again, again

again
but do you hear
it when it comes?
the fire, can you hear it?

in its signal its plea
to not escape burning, burning
not to escape the comedy of burning,
miracle of burning
nor not be witness
to me, newly charged with power
coming out of the dangerous cave
      (tenget, angker)
                  manifesting one's holiness
      (mawinten) to bring out
the dormant power

come out!
come out now!
you can come out now

Take my tongue and inscribe on it all
the magic syllables
            ANG UNG MANG
make my voice sweet with the inscriptions
of honey

Make my epic, my song of male *sakti* sing!

I'll be Rangda
I'd be Durga to pursue you, male,
   seeing you everywhere
              di mana-mana

once I was *sebel*
now I'm clean

    seeing you everywhere
            di mana-mana

cleansed by seeing you everywhere
put out this fire with *tirta*

(Kala Rahu swallows the moon)

again, it comes back again
during the eclipse of the moon
   (Beggar's Bush, February, we sit drinking
   brem-arak)

a full moon
  bulan purnama

eclipse of the full moon
put me enthrall

             blaming you, the child
          & you, the man
menjual apa?
        (what do you sell?)

   & what do you see in me

cari apa?
          (what do you look for?)
          (in me)

I think in order to live
& live by seeing you everywhere
         di mana-mana

to receive love
(*terima kasih*)

& seeing in me the one-staying-up-at-night
        (*bergadang semalam sentuh*)
the one-burning-at-night-receiving-love
I am a carrier of this great love
        di mana-mana

a language: what? speaks in tongues: what? knows
no bondage: what? lasts the night: what? slaves
a day: who? Tends the rice: who? sweeps the
steps: who? tends the temple: he does. waits
by day: who? goes into trance: who? puts on
the mask: he does. dances with sword: he does.
climbs the mountain: many do this. walks in a
figure 8 (*ngumbang*): many do this. breaks for
a while (*angsel*): many do this. interprets the
"right": he does. interprets the "left": she does.
listens with 2 sets of ears: he does. binds
his breasts: he does. wanders off: who?
supplicates the deities: they all do this.
another language: whose? what does he say?
the answer is always yes. *Senang makan nasi?*
(do you like rice?): yes.

       stand before me
       of which object, me

you are part &
parting of

I will see you
or you are
never seen
by me again

& I am again
just here
at it again
seeing you

green duty
calling me
again to
what song?

Nothing but you
new in the path
of my sun
Come back or call

Reminding
I mean, remind me!
A tough number
to learn

The one with "exit"
all over the face
astride your
speech or heart

in a rapport
with thought
impulse
action

I'm the total they add to, and you have to have arms
for the woman, you know. Slow down, my genes do not
carry the same messages. Rancour? No, messages
like the one on at night, with flashes glowing at
the boundaries of the nucleus. I see them, but they
also see you. You who constitute the Balinese
universe: upper, immediate, lower worlds.

　　　Dear Naga Banda,
　　　　　We cling to you, the priest giving life to

you (*pedanda boda*) the priest taking it away (*pedanda
siwa*). We cling to you, vehicle for the soul into heaven,
phallic channel to heaven. . . .

Hari apa hari ini?
what is the date today?
the date of my cremation, for I am burning, burning
    the snake awaits me in the channel to new life
                    di mana-mana
what stays? nothing
what continues: no thing
who asks? I do

(the husband dreams I am the serpent, and he must
crush me in my power, writhing like a wild thing
on the kitchen floor. Mercy!
I am merely a long rope bound in greencloth,
with a great mane of *lalang* grass, effigy of the
serpent, mere effigy woman becoming man becoming
woman becoming man again. Mercy!
I flail under the boot)

        the whole world dies again
          no fire, not allowed to light the lamp

fire in the body?
murder that fire

It's *shiva latri*, night of Shiva
with a full moon, a red dot in the heavens
now wake the fire!

I'll play the
wife of Shiva
& we go dancing
to an old sweet
ancestor tune
& when you fall
I'll bow down to
pick up the
pieces of you
eclipsed
by the night
of me, the dreamer

(nothing compares to you)

di mana-mana
and I sing of how nothing compares:

  (blinding green, eyes tear
   on the back of the bike
because it is early
& you are beautiful
weep for how early it is
how beautiful you are

   and the debts to pay
because it is thus:

how early it is, and beautiful

    debts to the teachers (*resi*)
     to the ancestors (*pitra*)
      to gods & self (*dewata*)

  how early
   in
    us

some days I resume color
for I walked too far

      are you there?
      are you there but silent?
      did the world die?

did you do the proper chants?
did you perform the proper ceremonies?
are you restless (*gelisah*)?

I am mere body-bone
I break & wither
I burn in the fire
I am clever that way
I weep
I disappear
what am I?

I go a lot of places
I study language for a penniless poesy
I reap what I sow
what am I?

I beg you this heart is broken
It eats itself

It is self wounding
what kind of heart is this?

I came here to study
I came here to dance
I beat the gong with a steady hand
I left something behind
what was it?

    (I need this burning in order to live)
the poet needs these three (in order to live)

vyutpatti, culture, or vast knowledge of the world

abyhasa, a skill with language developed from constant
practice & apprenticeship with a master

sakti, creative power
                      no posturing
         her teaching is you, man
           or you, man-woman who stands in for phenomena
   & you   siddhas
        flaming languages
     erudite
       or simple

            & whatever the energy is,
               seize it!

grabbing the power from the male deities
       she lives inside them

they haunt her
eclipse her
increment by increment

a kind of bondage
& then she transmutes their form
(eyes & skull)
         to her own
eyes in every pore of her body
cervix is the window on her world

    Dear Deity,

        Thank you for showing me around the island.
Now I am lost. In the best sense. Now I am *kerawuhan*
(possessed). I no longer own this body. I dance for the

gods (including you). I dance in front of the dolls, the
effigies, all the ones gone before me, all ancestors,
lovers, poets. I recognize your world. Holy shadows on
the screen, ho! Thank you for the drinks, the cigarettes
of clove, imagination, and for pointing to the code
the smallest increments of which I would honor & obey.
You lead with your heart. *Terima kasih*

Anne-Who-Burns

    Singo nodo gegere
      (The roar of a lion)
    Sang dewoto kabeh
      (And all the dogs took flight)
    Wojo kasilat
      (It had teeth exposed like fangs)
    Wiyung tutup kadi pereng
      (Lips as wide as valleys)
    Rejeng irung kadi sumur bandung
      (A nose deep as a well)

Eyes like twin suns
  (Netro kadi suryo kembar)
Kerananiro kadi layaran
  (Ears large like 2 sails)
Rambut kuwel agimbal
  (Hair ratted & matted)
So tall was he that he caused fright
  (Ogah uger luguriro kang girigiri)
He was so tall he covered half the sky
  (Luthuriro tanpo toro
   Tutup kemadiane akoso)

the green idol
on board the *bemo*
go beyond knowing this or that
little green idol
match lights up
this or that is not strange
points to volcano
I am here
with my little green idol
his flowering top
his glowing eyes
gone beyond this or that
the battleground inside him
is the playground of the green idol's heart

(see him everywhere   *di mana mana*)

In Bali there are small but very mean dogs that bark all
night. And their eyes glow when you shine a flashlight.
And there are motorcycles all over the place. And twelve
year olds drive them. And babies ride on the back and
they are crazy drivers.

The island is very green. There are things called
rice fields that are everywhere.

The market is smelly and there are flies everywhere.
We bought mangosteens and 2 out of 5 were good. Things
in the market are cheap.

> the puppets are asleep in the box
> we never talk about time
> the puppets become shadows
> you start to make them from the eyes
> then make the rest come alive
> this is the creation of the world
> the *dalang* is god
> the screen is the world
> the oil lamp is the sun
> we never talk about time

Yet in sketching
the lines "do you? do you?"
& "you do if it pleases?"
do you not
sketch
the knots
that mount
to greet you?

around a shield
or warrior-stick
life guides
the writer
to the
morsel

again
again
might drive in
something
outside
the focus

of someone

writing that details
texture
&   is real   too
by turns

looking for
the right time
in   (on)
the man's wrist

then something
(the white plastic watch band)
explodes the portrait
as well as
looking for it

(see you everywhere)
in time
if all's well
eclipse precepts
salamat malam
or taste or hear
deflecting options
which allow for
language
who speaks here?

          he does, and does he quarrel?

he does, and does he strive?

     he does

& does he dance?

he does, on many a corpse

he carries the tusk
he carries scars
he bends over his magic
he has magic to burn

          Victor is in his cups tonight!
          The moon goes black
          I ask for more

more blackness, more light
more firewater

he complies, but does he?

amenable to night & a foreign tune (blues?)

I turn
& your eyes are also on the sky
your eyes which are his, and are his too
all the "his" of eyes on the sky

are you the shadow next to me or
are you the shadow next to me

who are you?

his eyes?

(the moon goes out)

listrik mati

I give up everything to know you

kenapa? kenapa?

you tell me

& tell me again

she lives inside them, she lives inside him, she
lives in the corner of his eye, she writes as
woman-who-had-stretched-to-this-point, to the
point of an eye or corner of "his" eye she writes
as one abused, she writes as collaborator, she writes
now she writes later
She-as-describer is always a person
& every syllable is conscious
& the unconscious, too, structured like a language
language moving us up & down

Is it revealed to the man?

Is it revealed to the woman?
Is it only revealed to the man?

the imagined world is quite real, a tree with its roots
in heaven, tree rooted in highest heaven, one branch
goes into "god" itself, the branches are sentences, the
leaves are like words

    language a living system

rhythm, pace, sonic blast, parapraxes
    inherent in my nervous system
        a patterning to live for

      what does it mean to rot?

holding out against experience

          & my words not to sing
but entheogenic, entheogenic!
      liquid, sap, blood, semen will nourish my words

image   forth   naming
image   forth   naming
          dear Gabriel (Angel of Words)
            hear my plea
hear my plea to name the cause "ambivalent"

Candidasa at night:
I believe in the exquisite manners of the gentleman
& yet I look for a telephone in the dark
I am not crazy I don't abandon anyone
Everyone is partially true because everyone is already dead
Water beats against the stone walls
They only chide who wish me ill
No temples here the sea is alive
I walk a tighter, tightening rope
unless to believe "to cut through the veil of outward form,
    dissolve in air" is a human solution
6,000 rupiahs for the night

"When I was a child, I learned that the moon was the goddess
Dewi Ratih. Then Neil Armstrong landed on it. I still look

up at night and pray to Dewi Ratih."

  step through the *candi bentar*
enter your own life
You walk through the split in your life
you are half male, half female
you are never too late to meet yourself halfway
each step brings you closer to the split that forced you here
arriving in a red car, a white car
into the inner temple of your mind

          look. . . .
it's simple.

I'm no fool.

I cross every ocean, reach every foreign shore, leave my home
to acquire wisdom, you friend of my heart, you friend of my
secret passion. You need not ask, I join every adventurous
trip, I join you faithfully, taking care of those parts
you leave in my charge. This, because I honor you.
I haven't cut my hair, it looks all right even for conservatives,
since I wear no moustache anymore. In the West, it seems
to be better like this, but in Indonesia, a moustache is more
advantageous.

open
unoriginated
space
of *dharmakaya*
gives birth to *bija*
or seed syllable

Primordial
sound
becomes the basis
for all manifestation
of form

O M
(lietmotif of
"religious" life)

Mantras grow from experience &
from the collective knowledge

of many generations

HO HUM

(without fear/without hope)

                                        ONG!
di mana-mana

I fear you go from me language
when the world goes dead, goes silent
& I was burning burning
I fear you sleep too long

Peliatan: the night, the table, the books, the "spirits"
    & who are you?
                        (I fear I slept too long)
I see you everywhere
    the cues (*sasmita*) are transmitted musically visually verbally

    what signals us here?

what pulls us into motion, what navigates our forms?
what priest is behind all this, activating our tongues
what got left behind when we agreed to enter this day together?
what intersected with what?
what cycle are you on?
        the loop or the coil
                        tearing about the island to see, to see
to burn, to see

(even requests for drinks, cigarettes, or betelnut
 are made through the mouths of the *wayang* puppets)

who is alluding to whom on what screen or otherwise
field of play, field of Mars

what forfeits itself to co-exist

what does the boy say who sobs as he departs
("how was your trip?" (he shrugs) "okay")

                        (nuance vs. nonchalance)

inviting the voice to speak
it arises out of chaos
& I am burning burning
my wit (it burns)
my grand style (burning)
my books (burn them!)
special privileges (burning)
who's talking? (I burn)
shut the man down who crosses me here (burn him!)
    (Rent a motorbike for a week & ride it all over Bali)
        returning to the source of shut down! shut down!
            silence the chromosomes one small day

"I was talking about time"
"So?"
"I was talking about real time"
"Brahma dreamed it"
"Was he lying to save us?"
"Lying by dreaming?"
"Yes"
"Were you inspired"
"I was & said so"
"How 'mantra' of you"
"You joke with me"
"I spied myself inside blinding green"
"It was the last color to come into consciousness you know"
"I didn't"
"Didn't what?"
"Didn't know"
"Green is like that, coming later"
"Maybe we were too narrow to see it"
"Just blue & yellow, sea & sun"
"But here it enters your veins, your skin turns green"
"You become the green deity"
"I'll pray to you"
"It won't help"
"It was always there, we didn't see it"
"It was hiding under the desert"
"I couldn't look when I landed it was too vivid"
"Everyone spies it & is afraid"
"Afraid of what"

"Of losing it after they see it"
"It makes them happy"
"A kind of parlance, weary traveller"
"It still makes them happy after they lose it"
"Green makes them feel alive"
"I'm not exempt"
"I paid for this with good green money"
"Are you proud?"
"Like most men"

Dear Grandfather,
    It takes 23 hours to get to Bali and a little less going
back. For us, it took longer to get back. On the way there
we stopped in Salt Lake City, then Los Angeles, then in
Honolulu, then in Irian Jaya (near Papua New Guinea), then
you get to Bali. On the way back our plane broke down in
Irian Jaya (Biak). First they said the plane would be fixed
in one hour, then they said we'd have to stay 2 nights!
But luckily we only stayed one. They took our passports and
our tickets and we had to stay in a funky hotel called
Hotel Irian. In the lobby people were watching a Mohammed
Ali boxing match, or was it Leon Spinks? from 1976. We had eaten
on the plane (but I didn't eat). We couldn't make a call
out of Indonesia. We went to the market in the morning after
a very funky breakfast. We saw dancers at the airport who
wore grass skirts and painted faces and had guitars and drums
and spears. This was interesting. Finally they got us a plane
from Jakarta to take us to Honolulu, then to L.A. Then we
changed planes and came to Denver.
                    Love,
                        Ambrose

TWO PROSE POEMS

JAY MEEK

THE OLD PEOPLE

Each morning the old people went into the orchard with cloth sacks which they carried on their shoulders. But when they came out in the evening their sacks hung limp, like the expressions of people who do not know what they feel.

At the end of the day, there were heads of infants hanging in the bare trees, from leather thongs that had been strung through their ears and looped around the branches, and the eyes of the infants were closed as though they were sleeping under a deep protection. Then to the orchard came the bees that entered the small mouths and gathered against the cold, mindless of the beauty of ornaments.

VISITORS TO HIS COTTTAGE

When the woodsman returned from the forest, he sat down on the edge of his bed and rubbed his face with his hands, as though waking up. Then he saw his fingernails begin to glow, not enough to illuminate a secret place in the forest, but a glowing nevertheless, and the man rubbed his eyes again. This time when he looked at his hands he saw that in each of his fingernails there were faces developing, as if they were rising out of a solution, and he held his hands out before him. They were no one he knew. He put his hands in a basin of cold water, but the faces persisted. He thought perhaps they were relatives on his father's side, those he had never met, all of them dead now. He put his hands in his pockets. That night, he slept with gloves on, and in the morning when he awoke and removed them there were ten new faces on his fingernails. The next day, ten more and ten more after that. Perhaps they were also relatives, strangers who had become a momentary part of him. When he tried to keep awake that night, to see what faces would grow out of him, he heard a knock on his cottage door, and he opened it. Outside, there were ten people huddled together, grey and glowing, and when he stepped back in alarm, they entered and raised their hands and their hands were burning.

THREE POEMS

BERNADETTE MAYER

HEADDRESS

Philologically speaking I love you my word
Most in your syncretistic habilements
What happened to your voice darling?
You sound so weird tonight
I can't figure it that as I bend you toward myself
A different sound comes out of my mouth—
It is my mouth, isn't it? & yours this month?
How the fuck're we ever gonna pay the rent?
I aint not so sure about none a this
Excepting maybe our genuine perversity
At living with out irony sort of together
In the little rose rooms of our traditional genders
So onward Sweet William! Cheers!

EXPERIMENTATION IN RUBRICS

I red will not be good
I red will not do what I should
I red will at random rubricate

Your beautiful ass tonight
You are my specific sentence
You're my first letter
My any A or letter else of any color
No one can hear our sounds
My words outloud are gone the sky's
Lost its unknown animals now it's
Black as the pen is law as are
So many centuries will pass before
You come home to my house I pray
You will conduct me glossily
In sex & its love proscribed
By all four of our parents
Tonight today now later
Like a title for a chapter
Of an illumined book

MARIE MAKES FUN OF ME AT THE SHORE

Marie says
look tiny red spiders
are walking
across the pools
& just as I am writing down
tiny red
spiders are
walking across the pools
She says Mom I can just see it
in your poem it'll say
tiny red spiders are walking
across the pools

SEVEN HAPPY CATS

KAZUKO SHIRAISHI

Translated from the Japanese by John Solt

seven cats are happy
always together with poet and wife
from east to west
coming over from that side to this
they got shots from doctors
they got names, identity cards, passports and visas
they arrived safely, all right

no matter who lives next door
the seven cats are happy
always together with poet and wife

who is the poet's mother?
where is her grave?
why did they come to live on this side?

no one needs to know the reason
the tight-lipped poet says nothing
his kind wife is a fine cook

the seven cats were happy
ten years passed

three died last year of old age
three died last year
nothing could stop it

who is the poet's mother?
where is her grave?
that's why they came to live on this side

this is a great place
the tight-lipped poet speaks for the first time
"my wife really is a fine cook"

(Written to Günter Kunert)

THE MAN IN THE WALL

J. LAUGHLIN

I was waiting for the bus on Canal Street
near an old deserted brick warehouse   sud-

denly I noticed a movement in the bricks
on the surface of the wall   as I watched

the figure of a man appeared on the wall
at first just a faint gray shape that be-

came clearer until it was a whole man (but
the face not very clear) a gray man in a

rumpled gray suit   he wasn't dead because
he moved his arm as if he wanted to get my

attention   the passersby on the street
didn't seem to notice him   he was no one

I had ever seen before   did he want to
speak to me   had he been sent by someone

who knew me with a message   he lasted only
a few moments then faded back into the

bricks of the wall   there was no longer
a person there   what did he want to tell

me   did he mean to warn me   did he intend
to say   you too have appeared and will van-

ish   don't hope for more   there is no more
the bus came to the curb and I climbed aboard.

Based on a photograph by Virginia Schendler

NOTES ON CONTRIBUTORS

DAVID ANTIN's *Selected Poems: 1963–1973* was published this year by Sun & Moon Press. His two most recent books of talk-poems, *Talking at the Boundaries*, and *Tuning*, are published by New Directions. He is now at work on a new collection.

E. M. BEEKMAN is a frequent contributor to the New Directions Annual. He is the general editor of *The Library of the Indies*, a twelve-volume series of Dutch colonial literature in English translation, published by the University of Massachusetts Press. He teaches German and Comparative Literature at Amherst.

A widely traveled journalist, MARCEL COHEN has published numerous books of poetry in France. The translator, CID CORMAN, the founding editor of *Origin*, now lives in Japan. He is currently working on a five-volume book of poems called *OF*.

MARTHA COLLINS is the co-winner of the 1989 Alice Fay Di Castagnola Award, given by the Poetry Society of America. She has published two books of poetry, and received fellowships from the National Endowment for the Arts (1990), the Ingram Merrill Foundation, and the Bunting Institute at Radcliffe.

Creator of *Streetfare Journal*, a nationwide project of poetry posters for buses and subways, GEORGE EVANS is the author of two books of poems, *Nightvision*, and *Sudden Dreams*. He is also the editor of *Charles Olson and Cid Corman, The Complete Correspondence 1956–1964*.

JAMES B. HALL is a regular contributor to the ND Annual. He has published several collections of short stories, the most recent of which is *Stopping on the Edge to Wave*. He lives in Santa Cruz, CA.

A graduate student in comparative literature at Harvard University, HELENA KAMINSKI has published poems in *The Harvard Quarterly* and *The Paris Review*. In 1989, she co-edited and co-published the *Squaw Valley Community of Writers Anthology*.

Some of JAMES LAUGHLIN's recent books include *Random Stories, Random Essays, The Bird of Endless Time*, and *Pound as Wuz: Essays & Lectures on Ezra Pound*. VIRGINIA SCHENDLER is a portrait photographer known for her studies of artists and writers. "The Man in the Wall" is part of a series of street images photographed in lower Manhattan during the past two years.

BERNADETTE MAYER's recent publications include *The Formal Field of Kissing* and *Sonnets*. Forthcoming from New Directions in the spring of 1992 is *A Bernadette Mayer Reader*.

Poetry editor of the *North Dakota Quarterly*, JAY MEEK will publish his fifth book, *Windows*, a collection of prose poems, in 1992 with the Carnegie Mellon University Press. He has received awards from the NEA, the Guggenheim Foundation, and the Bush Foundation. He teaches at the University of North Dakota at Grand Forks.

Publisher and editor of Sun & Moon Press, DOUGLAS MESSERLI is the author of four books of poetry: *Dinner on the Lawn, Some Distance, River to Rivet: A Manifesto, Maxims from My Mother's Milk: Hymns to Him, a Dialog*. He is currently working on a dramatic trilogy, the first volume of which will be published in 1992.

EILEEN MYLES's most recent publication is *Not Me*, a collection of poems from Semiotext (e). Two collections of her stories, *Bread and Water* and *1969*, are published by Hanuman. She is currently touring "Leaving New York," a performance of her stories and poems.

Editor of *Scarlet*, ALICE NOTLEY has four books of poetry in print: *Alice Ordered Me To Be Made, At Night in the States, Margaret and Dusty*, and *Waltzing Matilda*.

JOSIP NOVAKOVICH's stories have appeared in such magazines as *Antaeus, The Paris Review,* and *Ploughshares.*

FIONA PITT-KETHLEY has published several collections of poetry in England, one of which, *Journeys to the Underworld,* is available in the U.S. through Random-Century. Her first novel was published this past spring, and she is currently working on an anthology of prose and poetry about sex.

MURRAY POMERANCE's stories have appeared in *Chelsea, The Boston Review, Confrontation, The Kenyon Review,* and *The Paris Review.*

PETER PORTER has published six books of poetry with Oxford University Press. He has also edited Crown's Great Poets Series. He lives in London.

ANTHONY ROBBINS's poems have appeared in *The American Poetry Review, Partisan Review, Southern Review, New Letters, Sulfur, Exquisite Corpse, Yellow Silk, Pulpsmith,* and *New Directions 52.* He lives in Baton Rouge, LA.

An American long resident in Paris, EDOUARD RODITI is an internationally known linguist, scholar, and art critic as well as the author and translator of a considerable number of works of fiction, poetry, criticism, and biography. His critical study *Oscar Wilde* and his short story collection *The Delights of Turkey* are both available from New Directions.

Stories by HENRY H. ROTH have appeared in *New Directions 54* and *New Directions 52.* His novel *The Cruz Chronicle* was published by Rutgers University Press in 1989. He teaches in the English Department of the City College of New York.

JOHN A. SCOTT has published nine, often interelated, books of poetry and prose since 1976 and received a number of major Australian writing awards. His novel, *Blair,* was published by New Directions in 1989. Formerly a television comedy writer, Mr. Scott now lectures in media and resides in Melbourne.

ENID SHOMER's latest book of poems, *This Close to the Earth,* will be published by the University of Arkansas Press in the fall of 1992. She has published poetry in numerous magazines and anthologies and received fellowships from the NEA and the Florida Arts Council.

Internationally known for her readings, the poet KAZUKO SHIRAISHI is a native of Japan. A collection of her poetry translated into English, *Seasons of Sacred Lust,* is published by New Directions.

CHARLES SIMIC has published fifteen books of poetry. His most recent collection, *The Book of Gods and Devils,* won him a Pulitzer Prize in 1990.

The Russian writer SERGEI TASK's poems and stories have been widely published in his native U.S.S.R. He has also published numerous translations from English into Russian—from *Nabokov's Letters* and Orwell's *Animal Farm* to novels by Stephen King. He is currently teaching in Putney, Vt. MARIAN SCHWARTZ has published translations of the work of several Russian writers, among them Marina Tsvetaeva and Nina Berberova.

Director of the Jack Kerouac School of Disembodied Poetics at the Naropa Institute, ANNE WALDMAN is the author of over thirteen books of poetry, the latest of which is *Helping the Dreamer: New and Selected Poems 1966–1988.*

CYNTHIA ZARIN is a staff writer for *The New Yorker.* Her first book of poems, *The Swordfish Tooth,* was published by Knopf in 1988.